"We can talk about our date tonight."

"Our what when?"

"Our date, silly. We'll call this Phase One. Being seen in public together. We've probably planted seeds in the whisper network by standing out here with you in your skivvies."

Lucas pulled his robe up to his neck. "Madam."

"Oh, don't be bashful, Cheese Hermit. Phase Two will be a brief engagement followed by Phase Three—our public yet amicable breakup by Valentine's Day."

"Okay, you've clearly got this all planned out. Why a Valentine's Day deadline?"

"It's a month before my due date," she replied. "I'll need to stay at your place after Mrs. Van Ressler kicks me out, but I need to be established in a place of my own before the baby comes. You don't want this kid to start calling you Daddy Cheese Hermit, do you?"

No, of course not. Not really?

And yet...

Dear Reader,

While the town of Crystal Hill is fictional, the mountains and valleys of Upstate New York are real and beautiful places to visit. My husband and I took a trip recently to the town of Rhinebeck, New York, and being a history nerd, I was adamant that we had to go to the Home of Franklin D. Roosevelt National Historic Site. The site is a tribute to a man whose words have resonated throughout history, most notably the quote "The only thing we have to fear is fear itself."

This book is about what can happen when we allow fear to take over our lives and our choices. Fear of repeating mistakes, fear of rejection, even the fear associated with getting what we want only to risk losing it.

It's also a story about the wonderful things we find when we open ourselves up to others. Admitting that you need someone takes more courage than almost anything else; so, in a way, love is the bravest thing that human beings do.

Also, there's cheese. A lot of cheese. As in your cholesterol levels might skyrocket just by reading this book, but I promise it's worth it.

Happy reading!

Laurie

THE VALENTINE PLAN

LAURIE BATZEL

Harlequin

HEARTWARMING

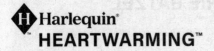

Harlequin®
HEARTWARMING™

Recycling programs for this product may not exist in your area.

ISBN-13: 978-1-335-05140-0

The Valentine Plan

Copyright © 2025 by Laurie Batzel

 Harlequin Enterprises ULC
22 Adelaide St. West, 41st Floor
Toronto, Ontario M5H 4E3, Canada
www.Harlequin.com

Printed in Lithuania

MIX
Paper | Supporting responsible forestry
FSC® C021394

Laurie Batzel lives in the Poconos with her husband, their four two-legged children and their two four-legged children, Stuart the Corgi and Midge the Marvelous Rescue Pup. Her first book, *With My Soul*, was published in 2019, and her essays can be found in several editions of *Chicken Soup for the Soul*, as well as online at *McSweeney's Internet Tendencies*, *Longreads* and Harvard University's *Tuesday Magazine*. When not writing romance that is equal parts swoons, sniffles and smiles, she can be found watching too much TV under too many blankets, testing the acceptable limits of caffeine consumption and perfecting her recipe for chocolate chip cookies. Learn more at authorlauriebatzel.com.

Also by Laurie Batzel

Harlequin Heartwarming

A Crystal Hill Romance

The Dairy Queen's Second Chance

Visit the Author Profile page at Harlequin.com.

This one's for my incredible husband, James.
To misquote one of our favorite movies, "Your life
makes [the best things in] my life possible." You
are the only person with whom I will share my
good aged Gouda, and that includes the adorable
bottomless pits that are our children.
So endlessly thankful for you, my love.

Acknowledgments

To my family: my husband, James, and my kids,
Charles, Cameron, Cody and Caroline. You are
all my inspiration, my heart and my home.

To my agent, Stacey Graham, and 3 Seas Literary:
thank you for going along on this journey with me.
Cheese Hunk made it across the finish line!

To the team at Harlequin Heartwarming, especially
Johanna Raisanen and Kathleen Scheibling, I am
so grateful for your enthusiastic support and
insightful direction.

To my DeSales crew and our Everlasting Thread:
thank you for cheering me on and supplying
all the cheesemaker jokes/GIFs!

To my parents, in-laws and extended family,
thank you for all your support and encouragement.

Finally, and always to CJ: thanks for today.

CHAPTER ONE

New Year's Eve

AN UNINFORMED OBSERVER popping into Lucas Carl's shop that afternoon might have come to one of two possible conclusions: either the magazine he flipped through as he sat behind the cash register was very exciting or his job was very boring.

Neither was true, and Lucas was a stickler for honesty.

First of all the magazine wasn't that thrilling. It wasn't even the newest issue of *Cheese Club Monthly*. It was from last fall and had been reread so many times that the cover featuring that year's Golden Rind winner was tattered and creased.

"Gutfeld's Dairy, really?" Lucas muttered to himself for only the fourth time that hour. "They don't even do their own processing, and their cave cheese selections are so laughable they make The Laughing Cow cheese look like Mildly Amused cheese."

He snorted loud enough at his own terrible joke that Ms. Hooker nearly dropped the container of yogurt she was inspecting. To be fair, everyone in Crystal Hill knew that Ms. Hooker startled if a leaf rustled too industriously within earshot. They tried to accommodate her as much as possible, which was one of the benefits of living in a small town where everyone knew everyone else's stories and quirks. For example, everyone knew that if they brought up the subject of string cheese around Lucas, they were asking for a fifteen-minute lecture on crimes against dairy.

Second of all, his job was the most interesting job in the world. Lucas ran Crystal Hill Dairy and Cheese Shop. The shop had been owned by his family since his grandmother moved to the hamlet sheltered by the Adirondack Mountains in the 1930s. They had started with a few Holsteins, delivering milk by the bottle doorstep to doorstep. Now Lucas's cousin, BeeBee, ran the growing farm that included the recent addition of several Italian water buffaloes, thanks in large part to her win in the New York State Queen of the Dairy pageant a year and a half ago. Lucas had started working in the shop downtown as soon as he was tall enough to reach the top shelf of the refrigerator, where the milk should always be stored. Milk stored in refrigerator doors prompted a visceral response similar to string cheese, which was also probably one of the reasons the town's matchmaking elder generation had long since given up on trying to find Lucas's perfect mate. This was just fine with him.

Like the glorious cheese he sold in his store, he stood alone.

"Cheese Man?" A small voice piped up from behind the display of gift-wrapped cheese wheels. "Can I have a sample, please?"

Lucas stood up straight and closed the magazine. This was worth shelving his snarky comments about Rudy Gutfeld's schmaltzy Oktoberfest cheese-stuffed pretzel stunt for later.

"Of course, Jeremy," he said, smiling. He walked to the small temperature-controlled display of specialty cheeses and lifted open the glass case. "I have a wonderful aged gouda with a nutty sweetness. Oh, and there's a new soft cheese I've been experimenting with using a blend of the cow and the water buffalo milk—"

"Do you have white cheese?" Jeremy asked, wiping his nose on the back of his sleeve. "Square white cheese?"

Lucas's shoulders dropped. He should have known better than to get excited. "He means white American cheese, right, Mrs. Binkus?"

The boy's mom nodded before placing a container of the dairy's special eggnog on the counter. "That's the one. How did you know?"

He pulled out a block of white American and plopped it on the slicer next to the case. "It's a gift," he replied, shaving off a generous slice of white, then handing it to Jeremy. "Also, Jeremy has been asking for a slice of white American since he was in a stroller. One of these days you're going to shock me and ask for something wild like Swiss, huh, Jeremy?"

Jeremy giggled at the absurdity of Lucas's suggestion. "You're funny, Cheese Man."

"Jeremy, you know Mr. Carl's name," Mrs. Binkus admonished.

Lucas held up a hand as he strolled back to his spot behind the counter and rang up the eggnog. "No, no," he said earnestly. "I like Cheese Man."

Mrs. Binkus chuckled and shook her head. "Happy New Year, Lucas," she said, taking the eggnog in one hand and Jeremy in the other.

"Now if only we could find you a Cheese Woman," a soft voice said from behind him.

As the doorbell jingled behind Jeremy, Lucas said, without looking up from the cash register, "I heard that, Ma."

"That was the intention," she replied. The shuffling sound of her orthotic shoes along the red tiled floor nearly muffled her words.

Lucas bent down and pulled out the stool from

under the counter for her to sit. His mom had been diagnosed with Parkinson's disease four years ago. She was still able to walk short distances without a walker, but he and his dad had installed a handrail along the corridor that led from the shop into the back of the building where his folks lived. He lived upstairs on the second floor. It worked out perfectly, not only so he could be there to help his parents, but also if inspiration for a new cheese creation struck him at three in the morning, all he had to do was walk down the stairs. Well, and throw on a hairnet and apron and wash his hands.

His mom shook her head at the stool. "No, thanks. I want to make it back to the living room without stopping. If I sit down, it will take me ages to get going again."

Lucas nodded and pushed the stool away. Initiating movement had gotten much harder for her over the last few months. The physical therapist had suggested putting brightly colored tape along the hall floor because the visual cues would help. His dad had, in typical fashion, gone overboard and covered every surface of the two-story building's floor in glow-in-the-dark painter's tape. "You hungry? Thirsty? I can put some thickener in the eggnog for you."

She reached the counter and held on with both hands. Her posture had become slightly stooped, so she couldn't look all the way up at him. Lucas was six-three, so he was used to most people's eyes stopping somewhere around the dark beard covering his chin. But seeing his tall, Viking warrior of a mom bowed by disease? He would never get used to that. "You're as bad as your father," she said. "I just came to make sure you didn't have plans for dinner tonight."

"And miss your New Year's Eve feast?" Lucas chuckled. "The only thing that would make me miss dinner would be an actual Cheese Woman, and by that, I mean a person sculpted entirely out of Manchego."

"Don't you mean 'womanchego'?" His father's voice boomed from down the hallway.

Unlike Ms. Hooker, Lucas wasn't startled by his father's sonic boom of a voice. Gus Carl wasn't as tall as Lucas, but more than made up for it with his gregarious personality, a feature that he shared with Lucas's older brother, Lawson. Meanwhile, the only thing Lucas had gotten from his dad was his love of good cheese and bad puns. In every other aspect, he was exactly like his mom. When you didn't talk all that often, people tended to listen more when you did.

Gus ambled behind Lucas and clapped him on the shoulder with one hand before turning to his wife. "You going for hikes without me,

Rose? Only married thirty-five years and you're already sick of me."

"Never." Lucas's mom looked at his dad like a starry-eyed teenager. "Just wanted to remind your son about dinner in case he got in the cheese zone again and lost track of time."

"One time," Lucas mumbled as he started to close out the cash register. "You work for twenty-four hours straight one time and they never let you hear the end of it. Besides, that was the day of the hot honey-infused burrata. I regret nothing."

Gus reached over Lucas's shoulder and picked up the magazine. "Lucas, why are you reading old issues of *Cheese Club Monthly*? We get enough business from the locals during the year and the tourists from the city in summer. Who cares about some silly accolade in a magazine?"

"It would just be nice to have our hard work acknowledged." Lucas shut the register drawer with a loud clang. "I mean, Gutfeld's?"

"The whole Bavarian theme is gimmicky, sure, but if that's what people like, who am I to judge?" Gus shrugged.

"Maybe you should try wearing lederhosen," Rose suggested to Lucas. "Even if it doesn't draw the magazine's attention, the ladies will notice."

Lucas rolled his eyes. "And you wonder why I spend all my time in my cheese cave." He crossed the room and flipped the sign on the door to

Closed, pausing to look out the four-paned window at the top. It had just started to snow, and the main drag, Jane Street, looked like something out of a Thomas Kinkade painting. The black iron streetlights flickered on, giving the swirling flakes a twinkling effect. People dashed to their cars with their chins tucked to their chests against the wind, couples and families nestling against one another for warmth. Despite the insulated wood-paneled walls and thick red curtains bracketing the picture window beside the door, a chill penetrated through his plaid flannel shirt and white apron. Shaking his head, Lucas pushed the padlock shut. So what if he didn't have someone cuddled under his arm? Any time spent in the futile pursuit of getting a woman to choose him was time away from his work. His previous attempts at romance had gotten him nowhere, but his cheese never let him down.

"By the way, your brother's coming for dinner tonight," Rose said over her shoulder as she pivoted in small, tremulous steps.

"I thought Lawson was in Vail this winter." Lucas frowned. "Wasn't semiprofessional snowboarding his latest lifelong calling?"

"Be nice," Gus admonished him. "We talked to him last night and he said he would be here. We have something important to discuss with you boys, so behave."

"Pop, I'm twenty-seven years old, and Lawson is almost thirty," Lucas pointed out. "You don't need to treat us like we're squabbling children. Besides, he's the one who can't keep track of time. At least when I'm MIA it's because I'm working, not because I'm chasing my latest obsession at a gong-ringers' convention."

Gus pointed one finger at Lucas before putting his hand under Rose's elbow and sliding the other around her waist. "He's family, and family supports each other. Still," he muttered under his breath as they started back down the hall, "that gong was a thousand bucks and now we're using it as a salad bowl."

Rose said something to him in her gentle voice that Lucas couldn't make out as their shadows merged in the retreating light.

Checking his watch, Lucas bit his lip and glanced longingly at his cheese lab. New Year's Eve dinner was usually on the later side, between seven and eight. That would give him at least an hour to tinker with some new flavor ideas or sketch out a new shelving arrangement to highlight the cheese better. It was something, even if it wasn't as flashy as lederhosen and an admittedly lovely pavilion overlooking the lake that *Cheese Club Monthly* had cited as "a trip to the Rhine minus the expensive flight to Germany."

If only he had the space to create something

like that. The dairy shop was small, and because they also sold milk and yogurt, products that required large refrigerators, there wasn't much room left over to get creative. The brick duplex was both the shop and their living space, with Lucas's apartment upstairs and his parents' living room, kitchen and bedrooms on the first floor behind the shop. Lucas's cheese lab, where he processed the milk from the dairy farm and transformed it into his cheese, took up the first floor of the other half of the duplex and they rented the second floor of that part for additional income to pay for his mother's medical care. In his head, he could see a room with several small tables, a carved bar in one corner and a stone raclette oven in the other. A sophisticated alcove that whisked you away to Old World Europe, where cheese was an entire course of the menu.

He sighed and pulled his apron over his head. It was only a dream and about as realistic as an actual Cheese Woman. There was no room to expand the way he would like, to grow the business beyond a small dairy where the only cheese people routinely requested was "white square." He couldn't control the situation any more than he could control the fact that women preferred charming guys like his brother.

Two hours later, Lucas looked up from the water bath where his mozzarella balls were soaking to the clock on the wall of his cheese lab and groaned. It was almost eight o'clock. He quickly transferred the pearly white balls to the tray, covered them with plastic wrap and carried them out to the refrigerator in the shop. Those would go to Mama Renata's Italian Ristorante tomorrow for the anticipated surge of holiday pizza delivery orders. Stripping off his hair covering and apron, Lucas balled them in his hands as he jogged down the hallway. The smell of fresh milk clung to him and he was relatively sure there were drops of it in his eyebrows, but at least he was somewhat on time. Lawson, if he even showed up, probably wouldn't make it until Pop was bringing out the champagne for the midnight toast.

The door to the part of the building where his parents lived was slightly ajar, leaving a sliver of light that caught the reflective tape on the hardwood floor. They typically kept it locked during the day when the shop was open. His dad had claimed that, aside from safety, it was to help him maintain a work-life balance, a way to leave his work behind him at the end of the day. Lucas thought this was the most ridiculous thing he had ever heard of: it made it sound like the job of making and selling quality dairy products, like cheese, was a chore, rather than a calling.

Still, like so many of his feelings and opinions, Lucas kept this to himself.

As he neared the door, his parents' laughter floated in the air, harmonizing like a trained chorus. He paused for a moment with his hand on the doorknob to listen to the sound, and as he did, a kind of wistful pang shot through him. It wasn't as if he hadn't had girlfriends or relationships, but the rhythm had always felt off, as if the woman had moved to a polka tune and Lucas…well, he supposed he marched to more of a military band drumbeat. Strong and steady, if perhaps somewhat monotonous.

He pushed the door open and raised his hand in greeting, but the hello stopped just short of his lips when he saw three heads turn around to greet him from the couch.

Lawson smiled broadly at him from between their parents, his sandy hair neatly cropped on the sides and gelled in a trendy style on top. "'Sup, Cheesebro? Nice of you to finally join us. Thought we were going to have to send in whatever is the dairy equivalent of a canary in a coal mine."

"Ha! A raven in the Roquefort." Gus guffawed and slapped his knee.

Lucas folded his arms over his chest and scowled. "That's ridiculous and unsanitary. Do you know how many diseases birds carry? No animals in my cheese shop. That's rule number one, in case you've forgotten."

Lawson stood and clapped his fists on his hips, shaking his head. "It was a joke. You really don't change, do you, Luke?"

"Lucas." It often seemed like everyone in this town had a nickname they went by. Lawson, the junior league ice hockey champ, was Law. All of his female cousins had variations on their names, and even his dad hadn't been called August in years. Lucas, on the other hand, remained steadfast in his refusal to accept anything other than his full name. "It says Lucas on my driver's license and if it's good enough for the state of New York, it's good enough for me."

"Oh, really?" Lawson let out a surprised huff of breath. "So there is something that's good enough for your ridiculous standards? Wait a second." He cupped a hand around one ear and leaned in the direction of one of the back windows next to the fireplace. "I think—yup, I just heard the pigs flying past. Better close a window or one of your cheeses might get infected with swine pox."

"All right, boys," their mom said. "That's enough now. Law, stop picking on your brother. Lucas, why don't you go into the kitchen and start setting the table?"

Lucas stalked behind the couch past his brother

and pushed open the door to the kitchen on the left side of the living room. He let out a low growl under his breath as he opened the drawer and grabbed a handful of forks. Usually, Law's inability to take anything or anyone seriously didn't bother him that much. But his brother had caught him off guard by actually showing up on time tonight—heck, even showing up at all. He had missed the last three New Year's Eve dinners because of his passion of the month. Drumming with a band on tour, fixing up classic cars and most recently, semiprofessional snowboarding. He changed careers more often than Lucas changed the display counter at the shop, and no matter what the vocation was, it always seemed to keep him away from his hometown and his family.

The door swung open as Lucas began to set the silverware around the plates already laid out on their round kitchen table. The family had always eaten in the small kitchen. It was dated, sure, with white appliances almost as old as Lucas himself, yellow tiles on the floor and sunflowers on the wallpaper that appeared wilted with age. He had offered more than once to fix up the kitchen for his parents, but they repeatedly told him not to bother. It wasn't like they were ever going to sell the place, so as long as they were happy, he was…well, as close to happy as Lucas got when dealing with something that didn't come out of a cow.

"Thank you, sweetheart," Rose said as she walked slowly by Gus, who was holding the door open for her. "What a lucky lady I am, to be surrounded by three handsome gentlemen."

Lucas looked down, pretending to study the pink rose pattern on his mother's good porcelain. He swallowed the hard lump that had risen to his throat. Only his amazing mother would say out loud how lucky she was while battling a progressive neurological disease. He watched her struggle with the simplest tasks most people took for granted, like standing up from a chair or putting on a jacket, yet she never complained. When he looked up, he caught his dad's eyes from across the room. The unshed tears reflected in the kitchen's flickering fluorescent lights betrayed Gus's own pain. He couldn't imagine what it was like for him, to watch the woman he loved suffer.

Lucas pulled out a chair and offered it to his mom. "Have a seat, Ma."

As she moved slowly toward the chair, Lawson dashed across the kitchen and opened the refrigerator door. The sound of rattling jars and containers was followed by him jumping out from behind the door, brandishing a bottle of champagne. "Let's get this party started. First glass of champagne goes to Mom, of course."

Lucas shot his brother a glare. "She can't have that. Thickened liquids only, or else it's a choking hazard."

His mom reached back and patted his hand resting on the back of her chair. "It's all right, Lucas. He didn't know."

A flush darkened Lawson's clean-shaven face. Even though he was technically three years older than Lucas, his shorter height and impeccably groomed hair made him look like the younger of the two. It also didn't help that he acted like a modern-day Peter Pan—forever jumping from adventure to adventure and never growing up.

"How about you, Pop?" Law looked across the room and nodded at their dad. "What would you say to a drink?"

"I'd say, what's a nice flute like you doing with a mug like mine?" Gus quipped, reaching for the bottle. "Thanks, son. You should come home more often. It's nice to have someone around who knows how to let loose every once in a while."

Lucas threw up his hands indignantly. "What about me?"

Law and Gus exchanged amused looks. Gus set the bottle on the counter and reached up on the shelf for two champagne glasses before turning back around and nodding at Lucas. "Tell me something, Lucas. What did you do last Friday night?"

Settling himself into the chair next to his mom's, Lucas ticked off a list on his fingers. "I labeled a new batch of parmesan Reggiano to age, then mixed a new flavor of yogurt to put into the kid-friendly section by the cash register." He leaned one elbow on the table and said proudly to his mom, "I got a little nutty and mixed some crushed pineapple into the strawberry." He leaned back in his chair and gave his dad and brother a smug look. Pineapple *and* strawberry. How was that for letting loose?

Law dropped his chin and shook his head, then held up both hands. "My bad. Didn't know you were such a party animal."

Gus snorted as he pulled the cork on the bottle and it let out a loud pop. Pouring the champagne into the glasses, he handed one to Law and held the other out to Lucas. "There's more to life than work, son. How about your resolution this year be something other than making the cover of that magazine I caught you obsessing over earlier?"

Law wrinkled his nose and made a disgusted face. "Seriously, Lucas. With our mother in the next room."

Lucas walked over to take the glass from his dad, "accidentally" stepping on his brother's toes as he passed. "Whoops," he said in a deadpan voice as Law limped back to the table. "It was *Cheese Club Monthly*, for the record, and I wasn't obsessing." He turned and muttered under his breath. "I'll get you next time, Gutfeld. You'll be yodeling a different tune when it's me on the cover."

As they settled down at the table, his mother held out her hands to each of her sons. "Let's say grace before we eat." As Lucas held her hand, her fingers curled and twitched in the pill-rolling motion that had been one of the first clues that something was wrong. He closed his eyes and breathed through the unspoken worry that sat more heavily on his heart each day.

As they finished with an Amen, Rose put her hands in her lap and gave Gus a meaningful look.

Gus cleared his throat and tapped the champagne glass with the tip of his spoon. "Boys, if we could have your full attention for a moment. Your mom and I have an announcement to make."

Law drained the last few drops of his glass and set it down with gusto. "I'm getting another little brother, aren't I?" He hooked a thumb at Lucas. "I know this one came out kind of a dud, but I'm glad you're giving it another go. I mean, look at how great your first attempt worked."

"How many days last year did you live in your van?" Lucas countered.

Law took Lucas's nearly full glass and poured it into his empty one.

"We're moving to South Carolina," Gus announced. "The warmer climate is better for your mom's mobility, and we have a friend who's giving us a great deal on his condo by the beach. We're leaving next week to sign the papers, then coming back later to pack up everything in here that's not nailed down."

Lucas blinked at his parents. "Seriously? But what about your treatment? Your doctors are in Manhattan." His mom had just completed a clinical trial that had seemed to be slowing the disease, even if it wasn't a cure. "Can you continue it down there?"

"I can," she said, patting his hand. "I have an appointment with a specialist as soon as we get there. Now eat, eat. Those lentils won't be any good cold."

Law reached forward and scooped a heaping serving of steaming lentil soup into his bowl. "I've got a buddy down in Charleston. He makes custom surfboards. I bet I could get him to give you guys a good discount."

Lucas leaned forward and stared at his brother. In what universe did he think either of his parents could use a custom surfboard? Deciding not to pick that ridiculous battle, he took the soup ladle and poured a large serving into his mom's bowl. "I can help get started on the packing while you're down there. Is the place furnished? I'm sure Bill would be happy to help me load the big stuff for you, if you'd like."

Law frowned, his spoon midway to his mouth. "Why wouldn't you ask me to help?"

"Because unlike you, Bill won't get distracted by a pretty girl and drop a sofa on me halfway through the process," Lucas said pointedly. Bill was engaged to their cousin BeeBee and so utterly smitten Lucas doubted he even recognized that other women existed.

Law shrugged. "What can I say? The ladies love my natural charisma. It's a curse." He popped the spoon in his mouth, then tipped his head to one side. Swallowing, he nodded at the door to the living room. "So who will live here when you guys leave?"

Lucas's spine straightened. For once, his brother had actually said something useful. This space would be a perfect way to expand the shop. A picture formed in his head of a room dedicated entirely to displaying and sampling his gourmet cheese. It would be a sophisticated grotto, a European-style oasis with rustic wooden accents. Built-in shelves for the wheels, a long, high table perfect for setting down a beautiful cheese board for the discerning tourists who came into town every summer seeking something beyond "square and white." Herb-infused oils in antique bottles. Black-and-white photos of the great cheese-making destinations all over the globe: Paris, Amsterdam, Tuscany. Forget about imitating the Rhine: Lucas's gourmet cheese-tasting experience would take his customers on a journey around the world in eighty flavors. If that didn't get him on the cover of *Cheese Club Monthly*, nothing would.

He caught Law's eye. Apparently, they were having the same thought because they both shouted "Dibs" simultaneously.

Lucas leaned one elbow on the table to look directly at his brother. "What on earth would you do with the space? You don't live here. You don't live anywhere for longer than a month before you find a new soulmate or a new life's calling."

"Well, maybe I'm looking to change that," Law said indignantly. "Maybe I want to stay in Crystal Hill for good. This space would be a perfect place for my woodshop."

"Woodshop?" Lucas scoffed. "Since when do you do woodworking? And burning pictures of a hunk of cheese with my face on it at a bonfire with your snowboarding buddies doesn't count." He narrowed his eyes. "It wasn't even the right shape for a wedge of Swiss, anyway."

"I'll have you know, I started doing carving demonstrations at the lodge in Colorado where I was the snowboarding instructor last year," Law countered, leaning on the table to mirror Lucas's posture and jab his spoon at him. "The gift shop started selling my stuff and I had people asking for my website. I've got over ten thousand followers on my Instagram and a shop on Etsy. I'm making good money, but I need a space for real equipment to do it full-time."

"Well, I need it to expand my business that's already in this location and actually helps the community." Lucas jabbed back with his spoon.

Rose put up both her hands. "That's enough. We will not have a repeat of the infamous fork throwing incident of 2003."

Lucas rubbed his forehead gingerly. "I still have tines marks on my scalp."

"Oh, so that's why you're rocking the same haircut as Shaggy from *Scooby-Doo*," Law remarked. "I thought you were entering your Yeti era."

"At least I'm a gainfully employed Yeti," Lucas shot back.

"Boys." Rose's voice rose louder than Lucas had heard it in years. "Put the spoons down, elbows off the table." She looked from right to left. "You two used to be best friends when you were little. Now every time you get together, it's World War Three, and worse, neither of you seem to have any interest in settling down and starting a family."

"Hey, I've been in more than my share of relationships," Law protested, even as he slid his elbow off the table and sat back in his chair.

For once, Lucas couldn't argue with what his brother said. Law had been in more than his fair share of relationships. He had helped himself to other people's share of that particular pie more than once.

"Yes," Gus added wryly. "And yet you've never brought any of these women home to meet us. Lucas, on the other hand, refuses to leave the shop long enough to meet a woman." He took a sip of his champagne and gestured at Rose. "Your mother and I aren't getting any younger. The only way we'll feel comfortable being so far away from you two is if we know you're happy and settled down with someone you love. To that end, we came up with a solution. A competition, since you refuse to do anything but fight each other anyway."

"What kind of competition?" Lucas asked warily.

"The first one of you to get engaged gets the space," Rose said, her voice back to its usual butter-soft decibel, but with an amused lilt to it. "We'll have the people in town report back to us on your progress, and whoever finds his true love and puts a ring on her finger first can take over our place."

Lucas sat back in his chair as his brother's sputtered protests faded into background noise. As much as he liked a good challenge—he had once made cheese with cafeteria milk and a hot plate in his college dorm room—this wasn't a challenge. This was literally mission impossible. Law was the town golden boy. The hockey star, the lead singer in every concert and star of every school play. Homecoming *and* prom king. If he wanted to get engaged, all he would have to do was stand in front of the gazebo and whistle. For Lucas, it was a different story. The last three women he had dated had made it very clear their preferences lay elsewhere…and for two of them, *elsewhere* was gesticulating wildly on the other side of the table from him.

"This is ridiculous." Law's voice came back into focus. "This isn't the 1800s. You can't expect us to agree to some arranged marriage contract. It's not fair."

"First of all, we're not arranging any marriages for you," Rose explained calmly. "You can pick who and when and where. All of that is completely up to you and Lucas. As for fairness, it makes sense when you think about it. Whoever gets married first will have greater need for the space, either to live in or to augment your finances so you can provide for your family. It's actually very pragmatic."

Gus reached across the small table and squeezed his wife's hand. "My darling. I love when you talk pragmatism."

Law groaned. "Ugh. Cool it, Morticia and Gomez. We get it. You're soulmates."

Lucas shook his head. "I don't understand why you're so against this. You have the obvious advantage here. Lisa Haberchek still asks about you every time she comes into the shop, and you two broke up twelve years ago. She's been married and divorced in that time. You can have any woman you want," he said, then added under his breath, "no matter who she's dating at the time."

Law stood up and picked up his plate, glaring down at Lucas. "For the last time, I did not steal your girlfriend."

"Girlfriends." Lucas put emphasis on the *s* at the end. "Plural." Mere days after Law had breezed back into town between whatever gig he was pulling at the time, Lucas's first girlfriend after college had ended things with him, admitting outright that she had feelings for Law. The other girlfriend didn't need to say anything because Lucas had seen the two of them out on a date.

"I'm not arguing about this again," Law said before turning and dropping his dishes in the sink. Whipping back around, he pointed a finger at Gus. "And I'm not participating in this marriage contest, either. I think both Lucas and I can agree that you've taken parental meddling to an unhealthy level."

Rose shrugged and winked at Gus. "What can I say? Your dad and I play to win."

Gus silently mouthed "I love you so much," causing both Lucas and Law to groan in harmony.

"Oh," Rose added. "To sweeten the deal, the first one of you to give me a grandbaby gets the lot next to the dairy farm."

Lucas lifted his spoon and took a thoughtful bite of stew. The three-acre lot behind the dairy farm now run by his cousin wasn't as enticing as the idea of an addition to his shop. Still, there was potential there, especially given its proximity to his milk supply. An ice-cream shop maybe. Given the choice, Lucas would take cheese over ice cream any day of the week, but he realized he was the minority. Plus, the added income meant he could afford new equipment for his cheese lab. At the end of the day, however, none of it mattered unless he could find a woman he loved who actually wanted to spend the rest of her life with a cheese-obsessed Yeti, as his brother so nicely called him.

Law sat back down at the table and stared their mom down. "The land? With the trailer?"

"Yup." Rose ticked off on her fingers. "Mama Renata has grandbabies. Mrs. Van Ressler has great-grandbabies. Your cousin Georgia, her daughter is in second grade. And the way Bee-Bee and Bill look at each other, she'll be pregnant by the time the honeymoon is over."

Lucas wrinkled his nose. "Gross, but accurate."

"That will mean both of my younger sisters will have had grandbabies before me," she said. "There comes a time in a woman's life where she feels liberated to say exactly what she wants without caring that it sounds insane. I want grandbabies, and I want them while I still have the strength to hold them."

Lucas and Law exchanged glances and sighed.

"Fine," Law said reluctantly. He held out his hand across the table and proffered it to Lucas. "I'm in. Are you?"

Lucas started to reach for it, then withdrew his hand. "Are you going to pull it away and say 'Psych, too slow'?"

Law squinted one eye, then grinned. "Well, not now I'm not. You really do exist just to steal my joy, don't you?"

Lucas grunted. "Just shake on it, will you?"

They gripped hands and shook once.

Rose smiled wider than Lucas had seen in a long time. The Parkinson's limited her expressions, so he knew the effort that smile had cost her. This was important to his mom, and that meant he would really give this a try, even if it seemed like the most doomed of all lost causes. There wasn't a single woman in this town that would pick him over Law.

"Now, let's go out to the back porch and greet the New Year," she said. "Did you boys remember to wear your red underwear?"

"Ma," Lucas said, pushing his chair back to stand and offering his hand to help his mother up. "You've gotten Law and me to agree to try to find wives and have babies. How about you let us pick out our own underwear?"

CHAPTER TWO

BRUCE WAYNE LOOKED at Chrysta Ball with adoration in his green eyes.

Of course, that was probably because of the cat treats she was feeding him out of her coat pocket.

"Who is the darkness?" she crooned to the black Scottish Fold kitten in the pouch she had strapped to her shoulder. "You are. You are the furry darkness. Yes, you are."

Bill Danzig twisted in the front seat of the car to look back at her with a quizzical stare. "You really named that fuzz ball Bruce Wayne?"

"Look at him!" She held the pouch aloft. "What else could I possibly have named him?"

"Don't let Bill give you a hard time," BeeBee Long called from the driver's seat. "He named his new set of chef's knives after the Brady Bunch."

"So much for pillow talk being confidential." Bill rolled his eyes, but he couldn't help giving an adoring smile to his fiancée before looking back at Chrysta. A pang shot through her at how much the couple genuinely loved and respected each other. Once upon a time, she had thought she had that, too.

"Did Mrs. Van Ressler say it was okay for you to have a cat at the B and B?" BeeBee asked, glancing in her rearview mirror as she changed lanes to merge onto the off ramp.

"Yes, she did," Chrysta replied, giving the Dark Knight a boop on his heart-shaped nose.

"Hmph," BeeBee grunted. "So there isn't a law against animals at inns with fewer than twelve rooms. I knew that didn't sound real."

"To be fair, there is a difference between a tiny cat and you offering your water buffalo as on-site therapy animals," Bill murmured gently as he stroked her denim-clad knee with his left hand.

"It was the first thing I asked after she said there was a room available along with the job. Thanks again for the recommendation," Chrysta said with a nod in Bill's direction. "This job is a literal lifesaver."

"Don't mention it," he said. "Us charter yacht swabs have to stick together. I couldn't believe when Julia texted me and told me you got fired from the *Alegria*. You were seriously one of the best interior deck crew I've ever seen. Your charcuterie 'welcome a' boards were the stuff of legends."

"It wouldn't have mattered if I made a recreation of Van Gogh's *The Starry Night* out of Gouda," Chrysta said bitterly. "I broke the number one rule. The captain didn't have a choice."

Top of her class at Florida State with a major in international hospitality. Four years of working at five-star hotels and on luxury charter yachts. She had known better than anyone the risk of getting romantically involved with a guest. But Alastair Ball hadn't been another super rich client on holiday in the Maldives. He had been a hurricane, pummeling her with his category-five charm. The way he had looked at her—as if she were some dazzling creature from another world—had been enough to make her throw everything she had worked so hard for overboard.

Eager to change the subject to literally anything else, she leaned over to look out the window on her right. She had dozed off shortly after Bill and BeeBee had picked her up from JFK Airport, having recently developed a penchant for power napping, and when she woke up, the scenery outside had changed from the cityscape to trees sparkling with frost and a backdrop of snow-blanketed mountains. Everything looked so peaceful and quiet. She smiled. This was exactly what she needed after the turmoil and chaos of her life over the last year and a half.

"It's so beautiful here." Her voice trembled on

the last word. Of course, her eyes were already filling up with tears. Unlike the spontaneous napping, this wasn't anything new. Chrysta had always been prone to what her mom had called "emotional overpouring." Every feeling spilled out of her like champagne fizzing over the rim of a flute. Happy, angry or smitten, she had never been able to hide or contain it.

"It really is," Bill replied, staring not out the window, but at a smudge of either dirt or chocolate on BeeBee's cheek. She was a dairy farmer and Bill was a chef, so the odds of it being either were around fifty-fifty.

"You'll love Crystal Hill," BeeBee said. "I mean, it has its quirks and, like every small town, everyone knows everything about everyone the second they set foot on Jane Street. But you won't find anywhere else in the world like it. Right, Cappy?" She winked at Bill.

"Crystal Hill has a way of drawing you in," he answered. "And the lake really is beautiful. It's one of the clearest in the region. The streams in the area were once so rich with quartz deposits, people said the waters actually sparkled like diamonds. But if you ask me, the real treasure is the people. They make you feel like you belong, whether or not you were born there."

"There must be something in the water if it could make the seafaring Chef Bill settle down in one place," Chrysta said, wiping her eyes with the sleeve of her red peacoat. "I'd better stick to bottled water, just to be safe."

Bill chuckled. "The women in this town out-number the men three to one. I think you're pretty safe."

"That's a relief," Chrysta said. The ink was barely dry on her divorce papers. "I'm here to put down roots and focus on growing my busi-ness. I'll have plenty on my plate as it is."

"Speaking of, did you want to stop at the dairy shop to check out the cheese selection there?" Bill asked. "If we introduce you to Lucas, he'll give you the friends and family discount."

"I should go to the inn first thing and in-troduce myself to Mrs. Van Ressler," Chrysta said. "I want to make a good first impression on my new boss. During our phone interview she sounded very…formidable."

BeeBee let out a loud snort. "*Formidable* is an understatement. The SS *President McKinley* was formidable. Mrs. Van Ressler is terrifying." She yelped as Bill squeezed her knee, then hast-ily added, "But I'm sure you'll do great. I mean, working on charter yachts, you've gotta be used to high-maintenance old ladies, right?"

High-maintenance old ladies Chrysta could manage. It was the tech millionaires with clefts in their chins and a way of saying exactly what she needed to hear that no safety drill in the world could have prevented. Hugging Bruce Wayne even closer, Chrysta silently reminded herself that mixing business with romance was like mixing peanut butter with bacon jam to make a PB and J.

Her stomach turned as the car descended a winding road lined with fir trees and jagged leafless maples reaching overhead. Yet another thing in her life that was suddenly out of her control. Chrysta had always prided herself on having an iron stomach. She had carried raw sushi trays to charter yacht clients in the middle of gale force winds without a moment of queasiness, and now all it took was a car ride through a mountain pass to force her into rolling down the window and sucking in the frigid air like her life depended on it. Fortunately, the road quickly evened out into a single lane passing by a row of houses with smoke pumping out of their chimneys and Christmas decorations still in the yards. A large blue sign welcomed them to Crystal Hill, and Chrysta's stomach downgraded from imminent threat of disaster to the low-level gnawing anxiety that had been her constant companion for the past six months.

They slowed and came to a stop at the first traffic light Chrysta had seen in miles. As much as she had loved the excitement and energy of

living in London, it had never felt like home.
City life had always left her feeling lonely, although in hindsight that feeling may have had
something to do with the person she lived with
at the time. Here, there was only a three-block
stretch of red brick buildings and a handful of
people ducking their heads against the swirling
wind, yet Chrysta already felt the invisible em-
brace Bill had talked about. The call of home.

BeeBee parked the car in front of a light blue
Victorian house. With its circular bay window
and peaked turrets piled with snow, it reminded
Chrysta of the castle on the front of the Candy-
land board game, all glistening pastel sugar and
fluffy ice cream. Her rumbling stomach reminded
her that it was dinnertime in England.

"Here we are." BeeBee draped her arm around
the back of the seat and twisted her neck to grin
at Chrysta. "Do you want me to come in and introduce you? Mrs. Van Ressler isn't my biggest
fan, but we get along much better since I stopped
coming in wearing my work boots."

"No. Thank you, though," Chrysta said. She un-
clicked her seat belt and gathered Bruce Wayne's
carrier in her arms as she slid across the seat toward the door. "I've already taken up most of
your day just picking me up from the airport and
driving me here."

"It was no trouble," Bill and BeeBee said at

the same time, and then they both yelled, "Jinx!" BeeBee beat Bill to the punch with a "Double Jinx. Ha! You owe me a soda. And not a generic cola from the Shopwell Market, either. I want one of the good Italian sodas at Mama Renata's."

Chrysta quickly exited the car before the pair got any cuter. With Bruce Wayne tucked safely in his pouch and her single suitcase rolling behind her—years of working on charter yachts had taught her how to pack efficiently—she was ready for a new adventure. A new life, all on her own.

Well, not entirely on her own.

She placed a hand over her stomach where for the past seven-and-a-half months, a steadily growing companion had kept her company.

She walked carefully up the walkway. Snow had been shoveled off to both sides, forming natural walls leading up to the front porch. Hoisting her staircase up the three steps, Chrysta took a deep breath before ringing the doorbell. The air was crisp with the wonderful smell of another snowfall on its way. London had had its charms, but winters were gray and icy rather than snow covered. Looking behind her shoulder at the lake ringed with a pristine blanket of white, she smiled contentedly to herself. This was a place to put down roots, a place where children could go sledding and ice-skating without lines of tourists at every turn. This was a home.

The door opened and a Black woman, still strikingly beautiful even in her eighties, opened the door. Her hair was perfectly styled in a high chignon and she had strong cheekbones made for cosmetics ads. She looked Chrysta up and down with her silvery eyebrows pointing down toward her nose in an expression of extreme skepticism.

"Are you Chrysta Ball?" she asked, as if it was some kind of test one had to pass to gain entrance to the castle.

"Yes, hi there," Chrysta said warmly, sticking her hand out in greeting. "Mrs. Van Ressler. I recognize your voice from our phone interview. It's so lovely to meet you in person."

Mrs. Van Ressler gazed down at Chrysta's hand and sniffed. "I don't shake hands. A single strain of streptococcus at my age would be a death sentence."

"Right." Chrysta withdrew her hand and shoved it in her pocket. "So sorry. I mentioned on the phone that I would have my cat with me. Is that still all right?" She twisted her hip to display the mesh front of her pouch.

Mrs. Van Ressler bent forward, peered into the flap, then straightened up and gave a brief nod. "Cats are the only animals I tolerate indoors. They generally keep to themselves without causing a fuss. Dogs on the other hand are strictly prohibited." She shuddered. "Their tails alone could destroy my entire bottom shelf of Murano glass. Absolutely no dogs."

"Copy that. No dogs." She gave a small salute and instantly regretted it. It was becoming increasingly clear that Mrs. Van Ressler was many things, but lighthearted was not one of them.

"Hmm," she responded before turning around and walking slowly back into the inn's open lobby.

Chrysta hesitated, unsure of whether or not she was meant to follow until Mrs. Van Ressler added sharply, "I do hope you intend to close the door behind you. I don't know what you're used to back in London, but we don't have a butler here and the cold can be just as deadly to a fragile constitution as any virus."

"Right, sorry again," Chrysta called after her, rushing to step over the threshold and quickly pushing the door shut. "So which way, should I...?"

She let her words trail off as Mrs. Van Ressler either didn't hear or ignored her and turned sharply to her left. Chrysta stamped the snow off her boots onto a braided rug at the entrance before hastening to follow. The building had a central staircase with beautifully carved wooden banisters. Heat coming from a crackling fireplace beckoned from the room to the right, but

Chrysta ignored its siren call. A pair of portraits in gilded frames flanked the doorway to the left through which Mrs. Van Ressler had disappeared. One was of an older gentleman with snow-white hair and more wrinkles than the Shar-Pei that would have been instantly turned away had it dared show its forbidden jowls at the door. The portrait on the left was of a younger Mrs. Van Ressler. Her hair then had been ebony and her eyes bright and ringed with thick lashes. The unsmiling countenance, however, was unchanged.

Chrysta made her way through the doorway and stopped abruptly as light from the bay window turned the room's contents into a blinding array of colorful sparkles. Every wall was filled with shelves of colorful glass. Red-tinted apples, bluebirds, figures lined with gold filigree shone everywhere she looked. It was beautiful, albeit a little intimidating. Chrysta let go of her suitcase and held on to Bruce Wayne's pouch with both hands.

Mrs. Van Ressler sat on a burgundy velvet chaise in front of the window where maroon-and-gold brocade drapes had been pulled back to display a perfect view of the downtown scenery still festively decorated with wreaths and garlands from the holidays.

Chrysta looked around the room for somewhere else to sit, as Mrs. Van Ressler's ram-rod straight posture didn't exactly invite close contact. Spotting a small wooden stool between the chaise and an end table laden with a bowl of glass oranges, she lowered herself very care-fully onto the seat and draped her long red coat over her legs.

Mrs. Van Ressler arched a single eyebrow. "So Ms. Ball—not Mrs., correct?"

"Not anymore." Chrysta swallowed hard. The bitterness of her marriage's end still caught her off guard even though it had been over for a long time. "You can call me Chrysta if you want. I'll probably change it back to my maiden name eventually. Not that Chrysta Cryschevsky is any better, but it doesn't inspire the same degree of clairvoyant-related mockery as Chrysta Ball, am I right?"

Mrs. Van Ressler's thin lips somehow disap-peared altogether into a thin line.

"Ms. Ball is fine," Chrysta added, her shoul-ders sinking forward under the weight of her new boss's obvious distaste for nervous rambling.

"The position you've been hired for is guest services manager," Mrs. Van Ressler said. "Not that I can't manage the property on my own. I've been doing that since my husband died twenty years ago. But last year we received several re-views on something called Yelp, stating that my customers found my manners stiff and overly formal. They said I was, quote 'not the warm and fuzzy type of proprietor one might expect from a family-friendly destination.'" She paused as if waiting for Chrysta to respond.

"Erm." Chrysta shot a glance at the crystal snake on the shelf across from her that would more likely be called "warm and fuzzy" before Mrs. Van Ressler ever would. "Well, you know, they say you should never read the comments."

"Regardless, I refuse to let my business suffer," Mrs. Van Ressler went on. "Are 'warm and fuzzy'—" she said the words as if they were the very worst way a person could be described "—qualities you feel you possess?"

Chrysta smiled. "I think so." She had worked in hospitality service on charter yachts for four years and never received a complaint about her customer service. It was getting too warm and fuzzy with a guest that had gotten her fired.

Fuzzy was, in fact, the perfect way to describe that entire period of her life. Blurred around the edges, like a dream so real you weren't sure it was a memory of things that were or a premonition of things to come. The second Alastair had come aboard the yacht, she had felt all her good common sense dulled by the heady sensation of someone making her feel special. Adored. Little had she realized he had seen her only as an object of beauty to be collected, placed on display and then discarded when, like a child, he had moved on to new and more exciting ventures.

"And you did say you have experience with families and children?" Mrs. Van Ressler tipped her nose down to scrutinize her ever more closely. "One of the recent complaints on this Yelp was that the inn did not cater enough specifically to providing activities for families with young children." She eyed Chrysta's belly. "Outside of your own, of course." She didn't probe for further details, which Chrysta found a relief. Most people were all too eager to ask or even touch her belly without permission, so Mrs. Van Ressler's lack of personal interest was a welcome change. Plus, she had informed her potential future boss of her pregnancy during the phone interview to make sure maternity leave wouldn't be an issue.

"Um, well, to be honest, most of my clients in the past have been adults." Generally, the luxury yacht business catered to wealthy adults who either left their children in the care of nannies or were child-free by choice…a choice her ex made crystal clear was his preference. "But I like kids very much and they usually gravitate toward me. Probably because we're about the same size," Chrysta quipped. It was one of the few advantages of being just over five feet.

Mrs. Van Ressler did not seem to find this an amusing anecdote. "Well, you will have the opportunity to prove that fact soon. I have a family coming to stay tomorrow with two young children. You did say you were free to start immediately?"

"Yes." Chrysta cleared her throat. "Um, speaking of the phone interview, you did say that there would be free board included with the position?"

"About that…" Mrs. Van Ressler frowned even more deeply, the lines in her forehead becoming troughs. "This is typically an offseason for our honeymoon guests, so the newlywed suite is available. However, between Beatrice's engagement party in February and a stargazing group coming for meteor shower and lunar eclipse viewings, I'm afraid the inn is far busier than usual for this time of year. You are welcome to stay here for the next two weeks, but beyond that it would be best if you found your own lodgings off-site. Does that present a problem?"

"See the thing is, I'm just getting a start-up off the ground." Chrysta fought back the dueling tides of panic and nausea rising inside her. "I'll be hosting cheese-and-charcuterie-board-building parties, and I had allocated my savings based on free room and board for three months, not two weeks."

"A cheese board–building party business?"

Mrs. Van Ressler articulated each word as if each had lost its individual meaning.

Chrysta inhaled deeply to prepare her rehearsed pitch, then slumped with a sigh. Mrs. Van Ressler was not the person to practice this on, and Chrysta was already dangerously close to tears again. Two weeks was better than nothing. She would simply have to come up with a new plan. There was no problem in life that couldn't be solved with a plan.

"Never mind," she said. "I'll make it work." She always did.

Mrs. Van Ressler stood. "It's settled then. I'll show you to your room."

Chrysta made her away through the glittering obstacle course, clutching Bruce Wayne closely to her just in case he decided to make a break for it. Retrieving her suitcase at the doorway, she followed Mrs. Van Ressler up the creaking stairway and down the corridor lined with green-and-pink floral wallpaper. They stopped at the last door at the end of the hallway.

Mrs. Van Ressler handed her a skeleton key.

"Do be careful in here," she warned Chrysta. "My collection is extremely valuable."

More glass? Chrysta groaned internally and braced herself for a shimmering minefield. But when she pressed the wooden door open, it wasn't a wall of glass that startled her into jumping; it was the dolls. An entire room of porcelain dolls staring at her.

"They are all couples," Mrs. Van Ressler said. "You'll recognize the Madame Blanc film collection, Scarlett O'Hara and Rhett Butler, Robin Hood and Maid Marian. My royal romance collection—Princess Grace, Princess Diana and the others—are on the wall behind the door." She gestured with one wizened hand to the pair atop the table next to the bed. "And those are original Tasha Tudors. Their names are Marguerite and Edmond."

This was even worse than glass. An entire room of happy couples, judging her with unblinking stares while she slept. She had no idea who Tasha Tudor was, but Chrysta really wished her new employer had engaged in creating something less horrifying, like an army of taxidermied raccoons. From inside the carrier, Bruce Wayne let out a discontented *mrreeow*.

"Um, you know what? I actually need to run down to the cheese shop and dairy before it gets too late," she stammered, backing away from the room filled with couples who, unlike her, had been able to make it work. "My friend Bill said that the proprietor would be able to help me with my cheese board party business."

Mrs. Van Ressler sighed. "Is this what you young people are calling a 'side hustle'?" She sighed wearily. "You know, it used to be people worked one job and then came home to their families at night. If you ask me, change isn't always the same thing as progress." She gave the Marie Antoinette doll on the floating shelf beside the door a sympathetic glance.

"Yes, well, cost of living and all that," Chrysta said. Leaving her suitcase in the room, she walked briskly down the staircase in the hope that the feeling of the dolls' eyes on her would diminish more quickly the faster she moved away from them.

Back on the sidewalk of Jane Street, she fanned her long coat over Bruce Wayne's carrier to protect him from the bracing chill in the air. It was cold enough that drawing breath deeply was almost painful, and she had to squint for a minute or two until her eyes adjusted to the glare of the sun against the canvas of fresh snow. But who cared about a little cold and snow when you found the place that instantly made you feel at home? A man with a well-trimmed mustache wearing a bow tie gave her a genial nod from the window of the jewelry store, and the smell of vanilla and caramelizing sugar hung beckoningly in the air outside the bakery. Even the marquee of the old-fashioned theater across the street appeared to welcome her by announcing that one of her favorite movies would be playing that night: Ang Lee's masterful production of *Sense and Sensibility.*

Chrysta lifted the collar of her coat up to protect the back of her neck and headed for the cheese shop. It was next to last on the street with an Italian restaurant serving as the other bookend from the inn two blocks away. That was clever planning, putting the dairy next to the restaurant. Bill had said his friend Lucas who ran the shop was an immensely talented cheese maker who dedicated himself to his craft and the running of the family's retail dairy. A guy like that was probably already married with two adorable kids of his own. Not that she was looking. The last thing she needed right now was to catch feelings for anyone in this town. She was here to make a home of her very own, with her own friends and her own business. Never again would she allow some man to take over her life and subsume it only to leave her to clean up his mess when he was finished playing with her.

Standing outside the shop, Chrysta inhaled deeply and muttered under her breath sternly. "Remember, you are a business owner. You are a professional. You do not have to flirt for free samples of cheddar jack."

She pushed the door open and a bell jingled above her head. The smell of fresh milk and dried herbs greeted her first. The shop was small and warm, with red tiled floors and rustic wooden shelves lined with wheels of cheese, boxes of crackers and condiment jars. Two large refrigerator cases full of milk and yogurt flanked the cash register in the center. Chrysta peered around a large display of cave cheeses stacked on top of a small table in the center, but there was no one there. Bending down, she closed her eyes and sniffed the earthy round of Parmigiano Reggiano. Oh, that was good.

"Can I help you?"

Her eyes popped open and travelled up…and up. The man standing in front of her was well over six feet tall with dark hair that fell over his forehead and a beard in desperate need of a trim. A wave of relief swept over her. If this guy had been even remotely her type, she would have married him for his cheese alone. But the man standing before her was about as far from the kind of man she usually found attractive as he could be. At five foot one, she preferred guys on the shorter side, and while this one had broad shoulders, he was somewhat lanky. Definitely not like the muscular weight lifters she found appealing. Plus, she had never been one for facial hair. Keeping things professional was going to be a piece of cake. Cheesecake, anyway.

"Hi." She straightened up and extended her

hand. "I'm Chrysta. My friend Bill Danzig rec-
ommended your shop."

Dragging a hand through his hair to pull it
off his forehead, a wide grin broke through the
raven-colored beard. It changed his whole face,
crinkling the bridge of his long nose and lighting his blue eyes with an engaging warmth. He
stepped toward her and took her hand, encasing
it in a firm, confident grip.

Chrysta's heart flopped over in her chest, and
before she could stop it, her other hand flew up
to smooth a stray tendril of hair behind her ear.

Oh, no.

She was in big trouble.

CHAPTER THREE

WHEN BILL HAD texted Lucas that his friend Chris might be stopping by to discuss supplying cheese for a new business, Lucas had pictured another yacht chef like Bill, a tall scruffy pirate in need of a haircut.

The woman in the long scarlet coat in front of him was the complete opposite of that. She was more elf than pirate, petite with a pointed nose and heart-shaped face dominated by enormous brown eyes. Her long blond hair was pulled back in a high ponytail. Lucas wondered if the hairstyle was intended to give the illusion of height, a thought that amused him although he wouldn't say it out loud. He wasn't in any position to critique hairstyles, especially given that this morning Lawson had pulled up a picture of one of those Scottish cows with long hair and held his phone next to Lucas for a side-by-side comparison.

As Lucas shook her hand, a warmth spread through him like stepping into a beam of condensed sunlight. It was probably a pinched nerve or something. The woman had a surprisingly strong grip for someone that small. He released her hand, extending his fingers in a stretch afterward and the warmth vanished. Strangely, he kind of missed it.

"Bill said one of his charter yacht friends would be stopping by," Lucas said. "Are you a chef, too?"

She shook her head, her high ponytail swinging with the motion. "No, although I'm a decent enough home cook. I was a chief stew on the last two yachts I worked on with Bill." Lucas's expression must have registered his confusion because she added, "I was on the interior staff. Housekeeping, guest service, recreation planning, that sort of thing." She had a hint of Southern melody in her voice. Uh-oh. Southern accents were his kryptonite.

"Ah," Lucas said before a rustling motion from the oversize bag slung over her shoulder caught his attention. "Um, I don't know if you'd noticed, but your purse is moving."

"Oh." She looked down and laughed. It was loud and deep enough that it startled Lucas more than the animated handbag. "This is Bruce Wayne."

She made a small cooing sound and a round head covered in ebony fur poked out of the top of the pouch. It had large yellow-green eyes and long whiskers like a cat, but instead of pointed ears, it had little folded nubs on each side. He knew people had some strange emotional support animals—BeeBee and her water buffalo sprang readily to mind—but surely she wouldn't have brought an actual bat in a bag into his store.

Lucas took a small step backward. "What—what is that?"

Her eyebrows drew together into a point over her nose. "He's a cat. A Scottish Fold. See how his ears go down?"

"You named your cat Bruce Wayne?"

"Yes," she answered as if it was perfectly obvious.

"And you brought him into my shop."

She cringed. "I'm sorry. Is that a problem? I've been in Europe for the past few years and they're much more tolerant about animals in public spaces." Heaving a beleaguered sigh, she turned her head to the door. "I guess I can take him back to the inn and then come back. It's such a long walk, though, and I'm afraid we won't have time to talk about my business proposition before you close for the day. He's very well-behaved, I promise," she said. As the words piled on top of each other, her cheeks and the tip of her nose flushed from light pink to a deep rose.

"Hmm." Lucas grunted, scrubbing one hand over the lower half of his face. It wasn't that he didn't like animals. But animals meant shedding and inevitable hair in his milk supply. He glanced at her eyes, wide and pleading, then back at the cat. It regarded him with a regal solemnity that commanded respect even from a definitive non-cat person like himself. The inn was three blocks away and it was very cold outside. Plus, she had business to discuss. If he put her off, she might be so offended she would take her business to Gutfeld. "If he'll stay in the bag, it's all right. Just this once." Lucas held up one finger.

She nodded and patted the cat's head. It sank immediately back into the recesses from whence it came, like the shadow of the Loch Ness Monster. "Thank you," she said. A closed-lip smile carved a deep dimple into one of her cheeks.

Lucas bit his lower lip. An accent and an adorable dimple? His last girlfriend had one that came out on her chin when she smiled a certain way. Of course, she hadn't been smiling the last time he saw her. The time she told him it was over between them. His chest tightened and he threw a look over his shoulder at the corridor behind the counter. Lawson was in the contested space. He had struck an agreement with their parents to stay in the master bedroom rather than the spare room next to Lucas's up-stairs provided he help them pack up and make some repairs to the kitchen and bathroom. Since Lucas had spent years sleeping with pillows over his head to drown out his brother's snoring when they had shared a wall before, he had agreed to the temporary compromise. Temporary in the-ory only because Lawson had probably already started texting old girlfriends here in town who any minute would line up in front of the shop in full bridal regalia. History had made it abun-dantly clear that every woman in Crystal Hill would take Lawson over Lucas in a heartbeat.

Unless…

Unless they didn't get a chance to meet Law-son before Lucas had a chance to woo them him-self.

He should probably start by not using the word woo ever again.

Clearing his throat, Lucas turned back to face the woman. "So, you said you had a business proposition for me?" He lowered his voice, which was already at a comparatively deep register and now sounded like he was attempting his own version of the Dark Knight's growl. Women liked that, right? He racked his brain in a search for things he heard his cousins or the other countless women in town refer to as appealing. Leaning. Jackie, his romance novel aficionado cousin, had mentioned a heroic kind of leaning. He propped one elbow on the counter and crossed one ankle over the other. The counter was lower than he had realized, however, and twinges of pain shot up one side of his back. Gritting his teeth, he blurted out the kind of pickup line that seemed to work like gangbusters for Lawson. "Well, if you're looking for a cheese hunk, you've come to the right place."

Oh, God.

Her eyes flickered down to his awkwardly crossed legs, his curved spine and the mouth he wished he could retroactively sew shut. "Um, what are you doing?"

Lucas promptly uncrossed his legs and stood up straight. Rubbing his back, he shook his head. "Nothing. Doesn't matter." He closed his eyes and took a deep breath. This was hopeless. "What kind of business are you running?"

She stood up as tall as possible and held her hands out in front of her before launching into what sounded like a well-rehearsed speech. "I'm glad you asked. You probably know that char-cuterie boards are having a bit of a moment right now. You see them everywhere on social media, at the specialty food markets. But when you're throwing a party and try to put one together yourself, it just never looks the same as it does in the pictures. Instead of an artful arrangement that will impress your friends, family or corporate higher-ups, you get a disorganized mess that no one touches and you end up throwing away perfectly good cheese." Her voice cracked on the last word and she pressed her lips together before putting a hand up. "I'm sorry. This isn't part of the spiel. I'm just very passionate about quality cheese."

Lucas's mouth fell open. Was it possible? Had the perfect woman literally just walked into his cheese shop? Okay, so not the perfect woman. He side-eyed the pouch and its feline contents warily. But closer to perfect than anyone he had met in a long time. He folded his arms and nodded, keeping one ear trained to the corridor to listen for footsteps. "Go on."

She gathered herself and propped her hands on her hips. "Yes. So, anyway, my business is an experience and a service. Our grandmothers threw Tupperware parties and our moms threw Pampered Chef parties. Our generation of women needs its own signature way to gather and celebrate life's special moments, like engagements, promotions or even just TGIF parties. My business is cheese board parties." She paused.

Lucas inclined his neck forward, anticipating.

She blinked. "You're supposed to say, 'What is a cheese board party?'"

"It seems pretty obvious from the context."

She frowned and it was adorably menacing.

Lucas gave a small shake of his head. "I'm sorry. What is a cheese board party?" he repeated with wooden exaggeration.

"I'm so glad you asked." She smiled, yet her eyes still narrowed in an obvious threat if further noncompliance occurred. "A cheese board party is a bonding experience for women and men to gather at one person's house where I will act as host and instructor. I'll demonstrate different ways to arrange cheese and charcuterie boards for different themes and occasions. At the end of the evening, everyone will come away not only having had a wonderful time together, but also now armed with the tools to create an Instagram-worthy cheese board of their own. Once word spreads, I'll get sponsors and eventually franchise the brand throughout the region."

Lucas waited a beat before whispering, "Is this the end?"

"Yes," she replied. "Just so you know, when I practiced this, in my head people clapped. You don't have to clap. But you can if you want."

Lucas brought his hands up to clap them together, then froze. The sound of the back door creaking open stopped his heart. If Lawson came out right now, she would fall for his charms, he would propose in a week and Lucas would have to live the rest of his life with the perfect cheese woman as his sister-in-law.

"Tell you what," he said, striding forward and taking her by the elbow. "Why don't you go back to the inn and give me some time to put together a selection of cheese for you to try." He spoke quickly as he wheeled her toward the door. "I've got a really nice blue cheese and some Camembert and—"

And there in the middle of the store, she suddenly let out a sob.

Lucas jumped back, his hands flying away from her. "What's happening?" His focus whipped frantically from the inexplicably distraught woman to the impending charm offensive that would materialize any second and ruin his already fleeting chance with her. "Why are you making those sounds?"

"It's everything," she moaned even louder, and tears streamed down her cheeks. "My marriage is over. I'm so jet-lagged I'm not even sure if you're real or a very tall hallucination. I thought I had a place to live long enough for me to get my business off the ground, but the room at the inn is only available for the next two weeks and I don't have enough money to put down a deposit on a new place and start my business at the same time. Worst of all—" she drew a ragged breath followed by a hiccup "—I can't eat any of my favorite cheeses." With that, she burst into a new explosion of tears so heartrending Lucas wanted to gather her into his arms and hug her, cat and all.

It was hard to hear anything over her wails, but a light thud that could have been a footstep drove Lucas into action. He put his arm around her shoulder and guided her into the storage room. "Come with me," he said, bending down to whisper in her ear. "I'll show you where I go when I feel upset."

She sniffed and nodded.

Lucas took her to the back of the storage pantry and opened a door. The cool air of his temperature-controlled cheese cave greeted them, and he helped her down the steps. The motion sensor light turned on, and as he held his hand out at the bottom of the stairs, she took in the view.

Immediately, her tears ceased. "Wow." Gazing out at the shelves full of cheese wheels and blocks, she walked down the last step before turning to face Lucas. "It's beautiful."

Somehow, he had known this would be the place to take her to make her feel better. It was his happy place, anyway.

"Here." He reached under the counter to his left where he kept his cheese log and pulled out a stool. "Sit."

She obliged with a grateful bob of her head. "Thank you." Closing her eyes, she inhaled. "Oh, that smell."

"Nothing better." Lucas stepped back and folded his arms, looking over his bounty like a proud father. "I've organized the shelves chronologically from top to bottom and type of cheese from left to right." He looked at her, not wanting to start up the waterworks again, but curious about her last statement. "You said you can't eat your favorite cheeses anymore. Why not?"

Probably that thief of joy: lactose intolerance. So many people thought that the diagnosis meant a total embargo on all dairy when the reality was much more nuanced. There were plenty of cheeses—especially the buffalo milk cheeses—that were low enough in lactic acid to not trigger a reaction.

She looked down and slowly unbuttoned her voluminous red coat. When she stood, the bulge of her abdomen was prominent and undeniable through the long black sweater dress that fell to just above her knees.

"Oh," Lucas said. He felt a little silly for not noticing it sooner, but between her cat in a bag and her mesmerizing eyes, his own gaze had been a little distracted. A nagging voice in his head that sounded suspiciously like his ex-girlfriend reminded him that he had never been good at noticing things that were important to most women.

"Yup."

"So you're—"

"Pregnant, yes." She gave a wan smile. "Thirty weeks this week. Thirty weeks since I've been able to drink wine or have sushi or—or Camembert." Her eyes welled up once more and the sobs interspersed now with hiccups renewed with even greater vigor.

Comforting women was even less in Lucas's wheelhouse than charming them. "There, there, uh, I'm sorry, I forgot your name. Christina?"

She let out another sobbed word that he leaned forward to catch. "Chrystabell? That's pretty."

"No." A laugh broke through the crying. "Chrysta. Ball. My name is Chrysta Ball."

"Seriously?"

"I know, right?" She shook her head ruefully. "The last name alone should have been warning enough not to marry the guy. Anytime he introduced me to one of his tech bro buddies, the jokes flowed like the expensive tequila he got from a movie star buddy who owns a line." She deepened her voice and adopted a Silicon Valley affectation. "Can you tell us the future, Crystal Ball? What's the S&P gonna do next week?"

"Your husband sounds like a jerk."

"That's why he's not my husband anymore,"

she said bitterly. "Well, that and the fact that he doesn't want to be a father." She leaned back on her stool, her hands flattened protectively over her belly.

Lucas grabbed another stool and pulled it out to sit next to her. There was no need to lurch over her when she was probably already feeling vulnerable and small enough as it was. "He actually said that?"

She nodded. "I mean, it was a surprise for me, too. I hadn't planned on having kids, at least not for several years if ever." Her eyes lowered to her belly and she rubbed it almost apologetically. "But once the shock wore off, I was so happy. I thought… I assumed," she corrected herself, "that he would feel the same way. Instead, he accused me of trying to trap him into some outdated version of a family from the 1950s. Told me that he didn't ever want to be tied down with obligations or expectations like that. He called himself an unchained spirit who needed freedom to roam and wander and have fun."

Lucas's hands balled into fists. There was only one time in his life when he had even thought about punching another guy, and the only thing that had stopped him was that the other guy was his brother. That wouldn't be a problem this time. "So where is the 'unchained spirit' now?"

"Who knows?" She shrugged. "He left the

morning after I told him. A week later, I was signing divorce papers and agreeing to a one-time payment to release him from any parental rights or obligations. His father's a big-time lawyer in Britain, so it was easier to just go along with what they wanted rather than try to drag anything out in the courts. It was enough money to pay for my prenatal care back here in the States and start up my business before the baby comes. The problem is I had assumed the living quarters Mrs. Van Ressler had included in the job offer weren't quite as temporary as they turned out to be. I can only stay with her for a week, two tops."

Lucas scratched his chin thoughtfully. "So you're worried you won't be able to find a place in time?"

"I'm worried I won't be able to afford a place in time," she said. "I'm very good with numbers. The settlement will pay for the start-up costs of my business as well as my out-of-pocket medical expenses until the insurance coverage from the inn starts. There's nothing leftover for a down payment." Her eyes started to gleam again. "I don't know what to do."

"Why not hold off on starting the business?" Lucas suggested. "Can't you just wait until after the baby is born?"

Her bag stirred and she bent over awkwardly

to pick it up and put it on her knees. Reaching in to give Batman a reassuring stroke, she gave him a rueful half smile. "Because if I wait until after my baby comes, I know I'll never start it. Lucas, when I fall in love, I fall hard. I lose myself to the point where I can't think or see straight. I'm the type of person who brings her cat to a cheese shop because she thinks he'll be too scared in a new place by himself. A cat," she repeated emphatically. "I don't have any idea what it's like to be a mom, but I do know that I need to teach my son or daughter how to support themselves without relying on someone else. If I have a business of my own, I'll never have to worry about that no matter what happens. I have to at least have the foundations laid now, before he or she comes and I'm completely lost in the new love haze."

Lucas leaned his elbows on his knees and clasped his hands together. He didn't know what it meant to be "lost in the new love haze." No woman had ever made him feel that way. He did, however, know what it was like to have a dream, a singular goal that drove his every action and thought. He wanted to help Chrysta with hers. Would it be possible to help her and further his own objectives at the same time?

"I have a room," he said slowly. "Above the shop. I'm living there now, but my parents who live in the space back there—" he jutted his head backward "—are moving out and I could stay there while you moved in to my old place." It was the most personal information Lucas had given out in one breath in ages and yet he knew he had left out two significant details: his brother and the competition that had suddenly taken an interesting turn in his favor.

Her face brightened. "You would do that for me?"

"The thing is," he continued, his words plodding out like footsteps in snow, "my parents, well, they really want me to get married. Desperately. They'll have people in town spying on me and reporting back to them about my relationship status. So if it appeared that I had met someone—" he gestured at Chrysta "—and fallen in love quickly and gotten engaged in a whirlwind, then it would make sense that you would be living here for free." His stomach tightened in a knot of discomfort at not telling the whole truth. But if he did, she might be offended, or worse, ask to meet his brother, who would then steal her away like he always did.

She narrowed one big dark eye at him. "So it would be like a fake engagement?"

He shook his head. "No. I don't believe in fake anything. Faking things is how we got that orange block monstrosity that rhymes with

Schmelmeeta. It would be a real offer to help you. If people get a certain impression, then who are we to stop them?"

"But what happens when we don't get married?" She frowned. "Unlike The Jerk, I don't plan on roaming aimlessly through my life. I want to put down roots here, for my child to have a real home in a town where people care about each other."

Lucas's heart bobbed happily for some reason at this. As much as he complained about the town's general lack of open-mindedness when it came to expanding their cheese horizons, he loved it here. The fact that she saw its value enough to make it her home too pleased him.

"Trust me." He shook his head. "No one will be surprised when we don't actually get married. My cousin BeeBee calls me the Cheese Hermit of the Northeast." He nodded his head at the shelves behind him. "I basically live in a cheese cave. It's hurtful, but accurate."

She snorted. "I knew I liked her." Chrysta held on to her bag with one hand and pushed off the stool with the other to rise unsteadily. "I appreciate the offer, Lucas, but I don't think it's a good idea."

"Why not?" He stood quickly and offered his hand for support, but she waved it away with her own. "You need a place to stay. I need my parents to call off their spy ring. You'd have your own space. We wouldn't even be on the same floor of the building." It would mean him sharing the back space with Law, but that would make it easier to keep his brother from meeting Chrysta until the town rumor mill started.

"Because you're going to be my supplier," she protested. "The last time I lost my professional focus, I lost my job. I can't go through that again."

"I promise, no feelings involved," Lucas said, holding up two fingers in a Boy Scout salute. "I'm already in a committed relationship with cheese. I'm sure you're very nice and all, but unless that bump is made of aged Gruyère, we don't have a problem."

She tipped her head to one side and smiled. "I don't know. I've eaten a lot of cheese over the years. There's a good chance that I'm at least 5 percent mozzarella."

An honest-to-goodness cheese woman. Lucas blew a rogue strand of hair off his eyebrow and shook his head to dismiss the hopeful voice. "Strictly professional. I promise not to fall in love with you."

"That's good because I definitely will not be falling in love with you," she said, then clapped her hand over her mouth and closed her eyes. "I'm sorry. That sounded terrible. I just meant—"

He held up his hand. "No offense taken. At all. I mean, what woman would want to live in a cheese cave?" Cocking an ear to the stairway to listen for footsteps, he nodded at the silence and held out a hand to help her up the stairs. Opening the door, the afternoon light hit his eyes with a blinding strike. Good grief, he was turning into a cheese troll.

She ascended the steps with her bag in one arm while holding on to the stair rail. Once they were back in the shop, Chrysta paused at the doorway and turned to look back at him. Silhouetted in a golden halo of sunshine, she reminded him of the picture of the Madonna his mom kept above the fireplace. Serene, comforting. She reminded him of home even though they had only just met.

"Just so you know," she said. "As long as I was allowed to decorate it with some homey touches, a cheese cave sounds like my dream house."

She walked out of the door just before Lucas clutched his heart.

CHAPTER FOUR

CHRYSTA WAS NO stranger to doing hard things.

After her father died when she was fourteen, it quickly became clear that he had been the one keeping track of the family finances, the bank statements, the mortgage payments. Her mother was simply lost. Not just lost in grief, but completely unaware of how to manage their day-to-day lives. It had been up to Chrysta to track down the passwords for their online accounts, to determine which bills were paid automatically through the credit cards and which ones came from the checking account, an account her mother hadn't even thought to put jointly in her name.

Her career in hospitality had been no less stressful. Long hours catering to the slightest whims of people with lots of money for whom instant gratification was simply a given. Caviar and avocado toast at two in the morning? Of course, sir. An impromptu country and western–themed birthday party on a yacht in the Black

Sea? Yippee-ki-yay, Captain. Winds are at fifteen knots and she just heard someone call to release the Kraken, but the client wants you to lead a yoga meditation on the bow? *Namaste* out here and I'll get the mats ready for you.

So when Mrs. Van Ressler called her away from the front desk and asked her to entertain two of the guests' children while the adults enjoyed happy hour wine and hors d'oeuvres, Chrysta happily accepted the assignment. Surely, she could find something to do with a six-year-old and an eight-year-old for an hour. It was snowing too hard for outside games, but they could play board games by the fire in the sitting room or draw pictures of the snowmen they would build later. Cradling her belly as she walked through the back door leading into the hallway, she smiled to herself. When this kid came out, every day would be just as fun as this. She had this parenting thing down already.

"All right," she said in her enthusiastic hospitality voice. "Who's ready to have some fun?"

The kids—a boy and a girl—threw their hands in the air and simultaneously yelled, "Me, me!"

The boy, the younger of the two, added, "I want to go sledding down the hill out there."

Chrysta's gaze followed to where he pointed out the window at the slope on the other side of the lake, which was frozen but just enough that a sled would definitely fall through the ice. "Um, it's snowing pretty hard right now and neither of you have the right clothes. Or sleds. And also sledding down a hill into that lake would probably lead to drowning and/or hypothermia, so maybe another time?"

The boy pouted and flopped onto the velvet chair behind him. "I thought you said we were going to have fun."

"Do you have any video games?" The girl asked with wide, excited eyes behind her glasses.

"Well, there's no TV in here, so I'm gonna guess no." Chrysta looked around the room as desperation started to dampen the overconfidence that had lifted her spirits only moments earlier. The room was small with a white plaster fireplace flanked by mahogany shelves. At least these shelves were filled with books rather than very expensive and very breakable antiques. A low rectangular coffee table sat in the center of the room, perfectly sized for board or card games. Spying a tall cupboard in the corner behind her, Chrysta held up one hand. "Hold on just a second."

Flinging open the cupboard door, Chrysta suppressed a whoop of relief when she spotted a stack of board games. She reached forward to grab them, grunting. At her last doctor's appointment almost three weeks ago, the OB had told her she was measuring small for twenty-eight weeks and wanted her to come in for another ultrasound next month just to be on the safe side. Chrysta had found this hard to believe as even elastic-waist pants were becoming an increasingly less comfortable wardrobe option, hence the switch to forgiving sweater dresses.

She set the boxes down on the coffee table and tapped the one on top. "We're going old-school fun this afternoon. Retro, as the kids say."

"I don't think anyone says that," the girl remarked with a side-eye better suited to eighteen than eight. "I've never heard of any of these games." She kneeled on the carpet and reviewed the stack of boxes skeptically.

"That can't be true." Chrysta blew a thick layer of dust off the top and peered at the title. "You must have played…um, okay, so I've never heard of Pay Day. But look, here's one called Wide World that's from…1957. Yikes," she muttered.

"You could read us a story," the boy said, pulling a book from the shelf to the right of the fireplace. "This one is about sports. See? It says ball on the front."

"It's actually Balzac, which is the author's name, and let's just put that one all the way up on the top shelf." Chrysta rushed over to grab the book out of his hands. For all she knew it was a first edition the kids might use as a coloring book. Or worse, read some of the poetry inside that was definitely not suitable for this age group.

"This one has a princess on the cover," the girl said, pointing to the next book her brother was examining. "But why doesn't the prince have a shirt on? Wouldn't he get cold?"

"Probably." Chrysta grabbed that one too, making a mental note to come back down to borrow it for her own bedtime story. "That seems silly. Do you guys like card games?" Except the only card games she knew were the ones they played on the yachts for casino nights. The parents probably wouldn't be too happy if the kids came running in to tell them about losing their allowance to a straight flush.

Good grief.

She was going to be the worst mother ever.

"Let's look at those board games one more time," Chrysta continued, putting her hands on the kids' shoulders and steering them away from the bookshelf that, despite containing many of her personal favorites, did not include a single volume of Dr. Seuss. "Who likes Parcheesi?"

As she crouched to peruse the bottom shelf of the cabinet, a familiar deep voice said, "Somebody say something about cheese?"

Chrysta's head jerked up at the sound and

promptly collided with the sharp corner of the cabinet door. She pushed onto her feet to see Lucas framed in the doorway. In one hand, he held a large white box with the words Crystal Hill Dairy and Cheese Shop written in bold black lettering on the side. The other hand rested on the shoulder of a little girl with strawberry blond curls poking out of a pink knit ski cap.

Rubbing the tender spot on her head, she winced. "What are you doing here?"

"I'm delivering the cheese for Mrs. Van Ressler's wine and cheese happy hour," he said, dangling the box by the string tied around it.

She nodded at the girl on his left, who smiled shyly at the other children. "I see you've brought your apprentice cheese hermit." Chrysta put her hands on her knees and bent down to smile at the girl. "Hi there. I'm Chrysta."

"I'm Caroline," the girl answered, her smile broadening to reveal front teeth with a small gap between them.

"Caroline is my cousin Georgia's daughter," Lucas said. "Georgia runs the bakery two doors down and she had to go on a supply run to the market. I told her I would take Caroline on my deliveries while she was gone."

"Well, Sweet Caroline, we were just trying to decide what game we wanted to play today,"

Chrysta said, gesturing to the children behind her. "Would you like to stay and play for a while?"

"Can I, Lucas?" Caroline looked up at the man who looked even taller than usual by virtue of comparison.

"Sure." Lucas nodded and she skipped across the room and sat between the brother and sister to thumb through the games. Keeping an eye on the girl, he leaned in to whisper in Chrysta's ear. "Thank you. Caroline is an only child and her dad passed away a few years ago. She gets lonely a lot."

Chrysta swallowed back the lump in her throat. Loneliness had been her companion after her own father had died and her mother had checked out. The constant proximity of her crewmates on the yacht had banished the feeling for a long time, but now that she was back on her own again, it was an acquaintance she hadn't been eager to renew. "Don't thank me too soon. The kid-friendly activities here at the Inn that Time Forgot are limited to bodice-ripper romance novels and board games from the Eisenhower administration." She sniffed the air as the smell of cheese wafted up from the box Lucas was holding. Pregnancy had heightened her already acute sense of smell to the point that she could probably serve as an alternate for German shepherds at airport security. "Holy Swiss, that smells good. What have you got in there? Wait, don't tell me." She took the box from Lucas's hand and held it up to her nose. "Cheddar. Gouda, aged at least two years by the smell. Parmigia—noo, hold on." She closed her eyes and inhaled deeply, her mouth watering. "Grana Padano. Another of my absolute favorites that I won't be able to have for nine weeks."

"Impressive," Lucas said. "Um, can I have the box back now?"

Chrysta opened her eyes, her nose still pressed to the box. "Fine. Here you go, party pooper," she said. But just as she offered the box back to him, she pulled it back to her chest. "Hang on. These are hard cheeses."

"Yessss," Lucas said, narrowing one skeptical eye at her. "My cheese, please?"

"Sliced cracker length, quarter-inch thick?"

"Okay, smelling is free, but looking's gonna cost you extra," Lucas quipped. "Also, creepy. How did you know?"

She rolled her eyes. "Do you know how many cheese boards I've made working in hospitality all these years?" Pushing the twine off the box, she lifted the lid and squealed. "Perfect. These will make the best Jenga blocks."

"No." Lucas shook his head and held out a hand with the palm turned up. "You are not using my beautiful cheeses for a children's game. That's sacrilege. That's blasphemy. That's—"

"Already happening," Chrysta said as she whirled on her heels to turn her back to Lucas. "Hey kids, who wants to play Cheese Jenga?"

A chorus of "yays" greeted her and she turned her head to give Lucas a smug grin. "Lighten up, Lucas. It's for a good cause." She jutted her chin at the hallway. "Besides, there are only two other guests besides this family and they're both vegan."

"How do you know that?"

"I asked them about dietary preferences when they checked in so I could recommend a restaurant," she said. "Details, my dear Cheese Hermit. Pay attention to the details about people and that's how you run a good business."

Lucas covered his mouth with one hand and scratched the side of his jaw. "Running my business doesn't include using cheese as anything other than food," he muttered. His eyes darted to Caroline as she chatted happily with the other children. "But if it will make the kids happy, do what you must. I want no part in your unholy shenanigans." He held up both hands and backed away. "I'll go tell Mrs. Van Ressler that I'll owe her a double portion next time."

Chrysta held the cheese up and indulged in one more sniff. "Oh, that's the stuff."

With some trial and error they discovered that the Grana Padano worked best for Jenga blocks. Chrysta's mouth watered every time it was her turn and the earthy smell of the cheese reached her extra sensitive nose. But she would not give in, no matter how badly she craved it. A good mother did what was best for her child. A good mother didn't allow herself to cave to momentary weakness or become consumed by what was lost. Chrysta was determined to be a good mother—no, scratch that—a *great* mother because she would have to be enough to make up for the fact that her baby wasn't going to have a father.

The kids were delighted by the game. It helped that even when someone lost and the tower of cheese collapsed, they could eat the remains and everyone was satisfied. From behind her, Chrysta could hear Lucas's heavy footfalls crossing the hallway, stopping and then turning around to walk the other way. When the feet lingered a little longer the second time, she pivoted herself around in her spot on the floor and lifted her chin to look up at him.

"Something you want to say, Hermit Man?"

His dark eyebrows furrowed above a slightly crooked but nicely shaped nose. He opened his mouth and then shook his head. "No. I refuse to condone this abuse of fine cheese."

Chrysta shrugged. "Suit yourself." Oh, it was her turn. Narrowing her eyes at the tower, she reached for a rectangle and paused when a strained grunt came from the man-shaped doorstop behind her. She turned her head slowly toward the source. "What?"

"I—nope, go on."

She reached for the piece once again, her eyes remaining fixed on his face as if daring him to participate in their unholy shenanigans.

Finally, he gave in and took a step inside the room to crouch next to her. "If you pick that piece, it's going to fall."

"No, it won't."

"I guarantee it will," he countered. "That's a load-bearing cheese."

"And from what establishment did you earn your degree in structural engineering?"

"You're going to lose."

"Listen, buddy. This isn't my first game of Cheese Jenga."

"This is everyone's first game of Cheese Jenga."

Out of the corner of her eye, she could see the children's heads going back and forth between them as they bantered.

Caroline leaned over and put her hand on Lucas's arm. "Can you play too, Uncle Lucas?"

Lucas tipped his chin down to give the little girl a stern stare. "This goes against everything I stand for."

"But you're sitting down," the little boy on the other side of the table pointed out helpfully.

Lucas shifted his gaze to the boy. "So it's like that, is it?"

The boy clapped a hand over his mouth and giggled with the uncanny ability children and cats possessed that allowed them to see people with the very best hearts.

Chrysta nudged Lucas in the side with her elbow. "Go on, Cheesemeister. Show us how it's done."

"Fine, Chrystabell." He echoed her gently teasing tone with the nickname, and the intensity behind his stare melted into a crackling warmth as he held her eyes and brushed the side of her arm with his hand when he reached for the tower.

Chrysta's heart thudded against her chest like it was applauding the forbidden emotion. Lucas was the supplier for her business. This was professional. Sure, he'd already seen her burst into tears, but that wasn't out of the ordinary. The way it felt as though the room had been quieted in a blanket of snow when he looked at her was, on the other hand, extraordinary. She could not have a repeat of what happened with Alastair.

This time it wasn't just *her* heart on the line. Her heart was beating for two now.

Lucas removed the block of cheese carefully. Placing it on top of the stack, he folded his arms and grinned smugly at Chrysta with an expression remarkably similar to the one Bruce Wayne wore when he spirited a gum wrapper out of her purse as a plaything. Of course, that expression—Lucas's, not her cat's—instantly changed to one of chagrin when the tower toppled onto the coffee table two seconds later.

He stood and looked down sadly as the children gobbled the remains of his defeat. "There's a saying about pride and falling and some such, isn't there?"

Chrysta placed a hand on the coffee table, preparing to stand. Even getting to her feet on her own was getting more difficult. And this was the easy part before the baby came. She swallowed back the rising fear, then turned her head as Lucas's outstretched hand appeared next to her.

Remembering the tingles that had flooded her with just a brush of that hand on her arm, she shook her head and placed her other hand on the table. "I can manage by myself, thanks."

As she concentrated all her energy on rising without releasing a grunt that would make Bee-Bee's water buffalo jealous, Lucas watched her with poorly contained amusement, then swiveled his head from side to side. "Hey, where's your furry sidekick?"

"Excuse me, Bruce Wayne is nobody's side-kick," she said as indignantly as was possible with her hands on her knees to catch her breath and a tiny fist using her bladder as a punching bag. "He's in the honeymoon suite."

"I try not to judge, but if you're the type of person who throws cat weddings—" he scrunched up the left side of his face "—I'm judging *hard*."

Chrysta straightened up and rolled her eyes. "It's where we're staying for at least another week or two unless someone books it. Although if you ask me, people who choose to spend their wedding night in a room filled with porcelain doll couples are just as out there as people who host events for their pets."

"You'll get no argument from me," Lucas said with a shudder. "I went in there once to help Mrs. Van Ressler with the radiator. It was…unsettling. That reminds me," he added, looking down at his shoes and rocking slightly back on his heels before glancing back up at Chrysta, "you never officially gave me an answer to my, um, offer the other day."

Chrysta looked over her shoulder. The kids had finished the cheese and opened the ancient board games, discarded the boards and pieces, and were using the dice in what looked very much like a tiny version of craps. Hmm. She'd let the parents sort that one out. Grabbing Lucas by the sleeve, she tugged him into the foyer.

"You mean, your bananapants proposal that we get fake engaged?" she whispered.

"Bananapants?" he repeated.

She crossed her arms and cocked an eyebrow at him. "Bananapants. As in so absurd an idea, you might as well be wearing pants made of actual bananas. It was a choice and I stand by it."

"First of all, that doesn't sound at all sanitary," he said. "Second of all, as I said before, it's not a fake engagement. It's a genuine offer to help each other out in our current predicaments."

A laugh bubbled up inside of her, echoing off the high ceiling. How in the world was he keeping a straight face? This was the most ridiculous thing she had ever heard. Surely it was all a big joke. Bill probably put him up to it in a misguided effort to cheer her up. "And what's your predicament again?"

"My parents want me to settle down and get married as soon as possible," he said matter-of-factly. "Since they're moving out of state, they have practically everyone in town spying on my every move to report back to them. If I appear to be in a serious relationship—or, even better, engaged—it will make them happy and allow me to get back to focusing on my work without constantly looking over my shoulder for hidden cameras." He bit his lip as if he was either holding something back or afraid he had said too much. If it was the former, she wouldn't be surprised, given her recent history with untrustworthy men. She hoped it was the latter. To be honest, Chrysta was startled by how much more she wanted to know about him. "What would you say at least to a pretend date somewhere in public to get the whisper network buzzing?"

"I would say is there anything I should know about your personal life their spies would uncover?" She probed, smiling up at him.

He flushed in response, then the door opened and a small woman with reddish-blond hair cut in a curly bob strode through. Removing her bright pink gloves, she smiled kindly at Lucas before shifting her gaze to Chrysta with unnerving interest.

"Well, hello there," she said in a voice that was almost comically sly. "Lucas, would you care to introduce me to your new friend who is holding your arm in a very familiar way?"

Chrysta suddenly realized that she was still clutching Lucas by the sleeve. Dropping her hand and taking a step back, she extended her right hand to the woman.

"Hi, I'm Chrysta," she said. "I'm not—we're not friends. Lucas and I are—"

"Mmm-hmm, not just friends, good to know," she murmured and her eyes darted to Chrysta's left hand, specifically the finger where her wedding ring had been right up until the moment Chrysta had tossed it into the Thames, narrowly avoiding a seagull. "Would you mind if I snapped a quick picture of you two with my phone? See, Mrs. Van Ressler was asking for pictures of people at the inn for her, uh, website and the light here is hitting you both so perfectly with excellent…aesthetic composition."

"I—sure, I guess?" Chrysta was too flummoxed to say anything else and before she knew it the woman had whipped out her phone and taken several pictures of the pair of them.

"Perfect," she said. "This will be perfect for the…the—"

"The website?" Chrysta offered.

"Yes, that's what I said." The woman flashed a wide grin. "I'm Georgia, by the way. Lucas and I are cousins. He was babysitting my daughter Caroline while I ran some errands for the bakery."

"She's in there playing with some new friends." He jutted a thumb over his shoulder at the sound of giggles coming from the sitting room.

"Thanks for taking her with you today." Georgia's green eyes softened. "It's so good to hear her laugh again."

Lucas shook his head and turned to face Chrysta. "Don't thank me. Chrysta invented a game that really brought Caroline out of her shell."

"Well then, you and I are going to be good friends," Georgia said to Chrysta. "Not that I have much time for friends. As a single mom, the only chance I get to socialize with other grown-ups is at PTA meetings."

"In that case—" Chrysta dug in the pocket of the red-and-black plaid cardigan she had pulled over her white blouse "—take a look at my card. I'm starting a business here in town that would be perfect for your next meeting. I'm hosting charcuterie board parties. You can have your PTA friends over to your house and I'll show everyone how to make the perfect board for any occasion. We could do a theme like Mom's Night Out with small wineglasses for condiments and maybe some wine-infused salami—"

"Paired with a nice wheel of aged Santa Marta," Lucas interrupted, then held up his hands. "Sorry. I didn't mean to say that out loud. Your show."

"No, the Santa Marta would be perfect." Chrysta grabbed his arm again. "We could even do Bento-box style, like kids' lunch packs, but for the moms to take home."

"That sounds amazing." Georgia took the card and nodded before slipping it in her purse. "We're always looking for ways to get more people to come to these meetings. I think this might be just the thing. We have one coming up next week. Would you be available that soon?"

"No problem," Chrysta replied. This was working out perfectly! Relief swept over her as she gave Lucas a smug grin. "See, I'll be able to afford a new place of my own in two weeks without your…offer."

Georgia's chin shot up. "A place around here? In two weeks?" She cringed as she started to put her gloves back on. "That's going to be a tough row to hoe. This is a really desirable school district. Rentals here are hard to come by and get snatched up quickly. I mean, you might get lucky." The sly tone crept back into her voice. "I'm sure Lucas won't mind showing you around to see if something opens up." She gave Lucas a dig with her elbow as she passed him on her way to the sitting room.

Lucas threw his arm out wordlessly in Georgia's direction in a blatant "See what I mean?" gesture.

Chrysta held up one finger and waggled it back in a silent but universal "no."

Miming taking pictures with an invisible camera then pointing to himself and wrapping an imaginary noose around his neck, Lucas ended with clasping his hands in front of his chest and whispering, "Please."

She laughed in spite of herself and threw up her hands in surrender. "Fine," she replied in a lowered voice as Georgia came back through the doorway with a smiling Caroline in tow. "One date. Just so we're seen in public by the paparazzi and so I can see whether or not you're actually as insane as I think you are."

"Thank you," he said, bending down so she could hear him. His face cracked into that same smile she had first noticed at the cheese shop, and once again, her heart flew up in her chest as if trying to get a closer look at it.

What kind of cheese hermit magic was this? Or maybe it was the hormones. That had to be it. Before this, she never would have given a guy like Lucas a second glance. Too serious and intense. He didn't have an entertaining bone in his body and she literally did entertainment for a living. After one date, they would probably drive each other so crazy, they would both agree that this whole fake engagement thing was a terrible idea and never speak of it again.

But as she watched Lucas crouch down and exchange a well-practiced secret handshake with Caroline that ended with what they called in her high school cheerleading days "spirit fingers," it occurred to her that there might be more to the cheese hermit than he showed on the outside.

CHAPTER FIVE

ONE OF THE things that set Crystal Hill apart from the other small hamlets dotting Upstate New York was its proclivity for holding town festivals and celebrations between officially recognized holidays. In the spring it was The Last Hurrah, a barbecue the week before Memorial Day. In the fall it was the Pastival, a celebration of Crystal Hill's past dating back to its colonial founding as a mining hub. In the winter the big celebration came after Christmas and New Year's in the form of the Torchlight Carnival. An entire block of Jane Street from the traffic light to the gazebo was blocked off for it.

The Torchlight Carnival happened to be Lucas's favorite. Food played a central role in each of these festivities, and the main attraction of the Carnival was always the raclette station. Over a specially made grill, an enormous block of raclette cheese would be melted at just the right temperature to drip like wax from a candle. The townspeople would come by with crusty bread, roasted potatoes and vegetables, and crisp pickles and scoop the cheese onto plates then sit around the gazebo under the merry blaze of wooden torches lining Jane Street. Big Joe's diner would pass around mugs of hot apple cider while the high school jazz band played standards from the Great American Songbook. Every year Lucas would watch the couples huddled together under thick flannel blankets and wonder if he would ever have someone to share the moment with.

This year he wouldn't have to wonder.

Lucas shook his head as he packed a second round of cheese into the cooler. This wasn't a real date, he reminded himself. Chrysta had agreed to meet him at the festival so that they could be seen in public together and plant the seeds of a rumor among his parents' eyes and ears in town. His mom had video-called him this morning, looking happier than he had seen her in a long time. It might have simply been the morning light behind the palmetto trees, but he could have sworn he saw a twinkle in her eye when she asked if he had met anyone recently. Dollars to doughnuts Georgia had texted her that picture of him and Chrysta the second she had left the inn the other day. There was a chance this could actually work.

Of course, for that to happen, he had to keep

Law occupied and away from Chrysta until Lucas sealed the deal and got her to agree to an engagement. From his cheese cave, he could hear Law's signature heavy footfall over his head as he clomped around the space they each hoped to claim. One good thing about Law (not that Lucas would ever say this out loud—his brother's head was big enough already) was that if you gave him a task in his wheelhouse he would run at it full tilt. So if Lucas, say, asked him to put up crown molding in the living room, that crown molding would get installed that day. And if that day happened to be the day Lucas needed his brother to remain inside and away from a certain young woman with velvety brown eyes and a smile with a tinge of wicked…that was just the cream rising to the top of the churn.

Hefting the cooler with both arms, Lucas tramped up the stairs and pushed the door open with his back. "Law," he called out in the direction of a saw buzzing. "I'm going out to the festival."

"What?" his brother yelled back.

"I'm going to the festival now," Lucas roared back louder over the drone of the tool.

"WHAT?"

"I'M—okay, this is getting ridiculous," Lucas grumbled, setting the cooler down on the counter next to the register and walking to the corridor. He opened the door to see Law with large red headphones over his ears, and a circular saw poised over a two-by-four. The whole room had been covered with protective blankets, which was a good thing since a thick layer of sawdust hung in the air. Despite the fact that it was well below freezing and the windows were cracked open, Law wore a white sleeveless shirt that displayed a number of tattoos Lucas hadn't seen before. Moving his head rhythmically, he didn't even seem to notice Lucas until he dropped the cooler on the ground with a thud. He would apologize to his cheese later.

"Oh, it's you," Law said, as he pulled his headphones down around his neck. "What's up? Tailgating at a cheese convention?" He nodded at the cooler.

Lucas rolled his eyes. "I'm manning the raclette station at the Torchlight Festival. I just wanted to see what kind of, um, progress you were making here."

"I just started laying out the notches for the chair rail molding," Law answered. "I thought that would add a more homey look than the crown molding. No need for a woodshop to be fancy."

Lucas held up a finger to object, then placed it over his lips. It was better if Law was overconfident. He wouldn't try as hard if he knew Lucas actually had a shot at winning. Also, the chair rail molding would actually work better for his sophisticated cheese-tasting room since customers would be seated at barstools around an island.

"I guess that will be all right," Lucas said. "So, does that mean you'll be here most of the night? You know, for security reasons. I don't like leaving my cheese unattended if I can help it."

This was a cover story that also happened to be true.

"I'll be here," Law said. "I invited Ada Brunner over."

Lucas's throat suddenly felt tight. Ada Brunner, the first girl to prefer Law to Lucas. In Law's defense, she had barely known Lucas existed. She and Law never officially dated, even though it had been obvious to anyone with eyes that she had a huge crush on him. She had gone to every hockey game, every show his band performed in and had been Homecoming Queen to his King. Law had enjoyed the attention, but then, as up until just now, had been unable to commit to any single person or place. Meanwhile, Lucas had hung in the background like a skinny puppy hoping for a leftover crumb of attention, a glance his way. Once, Ada had ruffled his hair in passing and he didn't wash it for a week.

"I thought you were going to be working on the molding all night," Lucas said. He picked up the cooler again and leaned against the door-frame.

"I am," Law said with a cocky grin. "She likes to watch me use the power tools." He punctuated the statement with a flex of his bicep, causing the tattoo of Tony the Tiger to look as if he was grimacing.

"That's sad on all the levels," Lucas replied. "But as long as you'll be here to watch the cheese."

"I'll protect it like the three babies Ada says we're going to have," Law taunted. "Which will guarantee me the lot next to the dairy farm. Three acres is plenty of room to build a warehouse for my custom furniture and decorative carvings."

"And presumably a house for the wife and children who got you that space, right?"

"You really do think ten steps ahead, don't you?"

"I think my head's going to explode." Lucas rubbed the bridge of his nose with one finger.

"Yeah, well, breathing in the smell of cheese all day will do that to you," Law retorted as he returned the headphones to his ears.

Coughing out the layer of sawdust that he had just inhaled, Lucas made a mental note to never use irony around his brother again.

The air outside the shop was crisp and had that slightly smoky scent heralding the arrival of another snow shower. Beneath his feet the rock salt covering the sidewalk crunched as he followed the line of torches to the gazebo.

"Hey, everybody," Mr. Stevenson, owner of the antiques and jewelry shop next to the dairy, called out. "Lucas is here with his cheese!"

A murmur of appreciation rippled out from among the tables up and down the blocked off portion of the street. Lucas raised the cooler in the form of a greeting. When you came bearing good cheese, who needed words?

The raclette oven was already set up and warming in front of the gazebo steps. After about two hours, Georgia would take his place with a pot of chocolate fondue, but right now, this was his time. He set the cooler down and unzipped it with the reverence of a priest preparing a baptismal font. This particular cheese was made specifically for the raclette. It was even called Raclette cheese. The flavor was mild, slightly nutty without the caramel notes of a Gouda and melted like a dream. Joe Kim had the grill going in front of his diner with roasting potatoes and sausages, the savory smell drifting over the breeze. Renata from the Italian restaurant at the end of the street sliced up crusty Italian bread and one by one people filled their plates and lined up to scoop the warm cheese onto their offerings.

"So you're here alone again?" Ms. Hooker said with her typical inquisitorial reporter's manner. She ran the town's small newspaper and everyone was used to her intolerance for small talk or colloquial pleasantries. Ironically enough, she was usually the last person in town to find anything out, but that didn't rule her out as one of his mother's minions.

"Actually, I—"

Georgia tipped her head to one side as she put a spoonful of cheese on a plate with two large slices of bread and handed it to Caroline. "What happened to your friend from the inn?"

"Well, she—"

"I liked her," Caroline piped up, the plate balanced precariously on the palms of her small hands. "You should marry her. She's already got a baby in her belly, so you could have a family right away."

Lucas squinted at the girl. Sure, she was only eight, but that made her an even more likely spy, since she could be bribed to do just about anything with a large candy bar and a trip to the comic book store in the neighboring town, Bingleyton. Her delivery *had* sounded awfully scripted.

"Don't let them henpeck you over there," Joe called out from behind his grill. "Nothing wrong with the bachelor life. You should join me and my buddies. We have a men's only group that does cold plunges in the lake every Sunday morning in the winter."

"So that's what that was." Ms. Hooker pushed her glasses up her nose and shook her head. "I thought it was some sort of nouveau pagan ritual meant to usher in the winter solstice."

"Nah," Joe replied. "It's just a good reason to get out of the house when it's cold, then warm up with a beer before ten in the morning. We just do it early in the morning because most of the fellas don't like to be seen without their shirts on."

"Tempting, but I'll pass," Lucas said. He shifted the cheese on the heat to melt the other side, then looked up and scanned the crowd for the familiar blond ponytail. The sun had already set, leaving the sky a soft pearly gray, and he peered through the waning light but saw no trace of her. The light at the inn was still on, though. Maybe Mrs. Van Ressler was making her stay late? Chrysta was new and therefore had no way of knowing that it was actually possible to say no to the admittedly intimidating proprietor.

Then again, maybe she had simply found better things to do with her night off than see him.

He swallowed that particularly bitter thought back before reaching out to tap Georgia on the shoulder. "I need to…take care of something real quick. Mind watching the raclette? It's almost gone anyway. You can start setting up your fondue whenever you're ready."

Georgia nodded and arched an eyebrow. "Sure thing. You go and take care of whoever you need to—I mean, whatever you need to, right?" She looked down at Caroline and the pair shared a wink.

Picking up the cooler and slinging the strap over his shoulder, Lucas ducked his head as he skirted the crowd gathered around the jazz band, which was currently playing "But Not for Me." Probably just a coincidental song choice yet, he still felt personally and lyrically attacked. When he got to the inn, he knocked on the door and at first, no one answered. Then from somewhere inside, he heard Chrysta's voice call out, "Be with you in a moment," followed by a sound that could only be described as a growl.

Without even thinking about Mrs. Van Ressler's firm rules regarding doorbell etiquette, he flung open the door and ran into the foyer, looking first right, then left. "Chrysta?"

"Down here."

He looked right again, into the sitting room, and there she was on the floor. Frustration and determination battled for dominance on her furrowed brow and both her legs were stretched out in front of her. Only one foot had a shoe on, however, and its mate lay several feet to her left.

She was wearing her bright scarlet coat and an adorable knit hat with black polka dots that reminded him of a ladybug.

He walked into the room and crouched on his haunches next to her. "What are you doing?"

"I was getting ready to meet you at the festival when I twisted my ankle trying to get my shoe on." She gestured helplessly to the black loafer on the floor. "I've been trying to get to my feet for the last ten minutes, but between my foot cramping up and my giant belly, it's easier said than done."

"Want me to rub your ankle and see if I can get it to loosen up?" Lucas offered, having known enough pregnant women in town to not say a word about her aforementioned belly or its relative size. But before he even lifted his hand, she screeched the word "DON'T" so loud it startled him into tumbling backward.

"I'm sorry." He held up both hands. "What did I do?"

Her panic-stricken expression melted as she closed her eyes and chuckled, shaking her head. "Nothing. I didn't mean to startle you. It's just that there's a pressure point on the lower leg that can trigger spontaneous labor. It's why you're told not to get foot massages in pregnancy. As rough as pregnancy is, I'm definitely not ready to have this baby yet."

Well, that was terrifying. "I had no idea. Geez, you'd think a self-destruct button would come with a clear label on it." As soon as the words left his mouth, Lucas sucked in a breath. He hadn't meant to say that out loud. Lucas knew full well that his sense of humor, like some of his favorite cheeses, was an acquired taste, and so he had learned long ago to keep his stupid puns and off-hand observations in his head. But something about Chrysta relaxed the taut reins he kept on his self-control. She was so open and free with her emotions. He would have to be extra careful if that kind of thing was contagious.

She stared at him with those giant brown eyes for a second, then tipped her head back and laughed out loud. Lucas joined in, mostly out of relief that she hadn't been completely offended.

"I'm sorry," he said again, regaining his breath as he returned to his kneeling position by her side. "That was a terrible joke. Us hermits sometimes forget how to behave in public."

She let out a small snort and wiped a tear from her eye. "It was terrible. So terrible it was actually hilarious. Or maybe I've been sitting close enough to the radiator to breathe in some noxious fumes. Either way, the giggle was much needed."

He held out his hand. "Can I help you up if I promise to be extra careful?"

She nodded and pushed behind her with her left hand, pulling herself up with her right hand in his. Once on her feet, she grimaced and rubbed her lower back. "Whew. This moving around for two thing is not all rainbows and unicorns. I was afraid I'd be stuck there all night." She looked up at him and bit her lower lip. "I'm so sorry we missed our chance to be seen in public together. We could still go if there's anyone there."

Lucas shook his head. "Don't worry about it. We'll have other chances. It's more important for you to rest." He nodded at the velvet chaise by the window. "Here, I'll help you over to the couch."

Using his arm as a support, she hobbled over to the chair and sank gratefully into it, then patted the space next to her.

Lucas sat down, making sure to give her space to stretch out if she needed to, and folded his hands in his lap.

Chrysta rolled her eyes. "At ease, Sergeant Cheese. I'm not made of glass." She leaned forward to peer across the hallway. "If I was, Mrs. Van Ressler would already have me stuck up on a curio shelf in there."

"She loves to remind everyone that she lived in Italy for a summer when she was young,"

Lucas remarked, relaxing his posture and leaning back into the cushioned armrest. "I heard she fell in love with a prince or an heir to a fortune or something and they almost ran away together, but he chickened out." He shrugged. "Then again, the rumor mill in a small town like this isn't always accurate."

"I wonder what they'll think about me," she said, placing one hand on her belly and giving it a small caress. "I really want to make a home for us here."

"I think," Lucas said carefully, "you seem like the type of person who other people want to be around. And the people here are very welcoming."

That seemed to put her at ease. She settled back into the corner of the couch and lifted the shoeless foot up to rest next to Lucas's thigh. It looked so small—not surprising given her height—and vulnerable. A strange, protective instinct flared up in him from somewhere deep inside, the urge to wrap that foot and the rest of her in a warm blanket and keep the cold from touching a single inch. Of course, he would probably end up overheating her and doing more damage. Clearly his instincts were not to be trusted. No wonder she had hesitated at his fake engagement offer. Nobody was going to hand a precious baby to a cheese hermit who lived in a cave.

"That's good to hear," she replied. "Pregnancy

is hard enough as it is. Obviously, I'm so grateful for the chance to be a mother. But no one ever tells you how strange it is to give up control over your own body this way. I have to second-guess everything I eat, look up any medication I even think about taking. I check the baby's movements every few hours and if they're being too still, I feel like my heart might stop until I feel them move again. I feel so helpless and scared all the time."

Lucas swallowed hard. Her words reminded him of his mother, trying so hard to maintain dominance over a body that wouldn't allow her to rest without tremors erupting. The simplest parts of life that so many people took for granted required ten times the effort for her to experience, walking down a hallway and standing up from a chair. He knew obviously that pregnancy and Parkinson's were two completely different physical conditions and buried the stab of pain that accompanied the thought. He would never be able to understand what Chrysta was going through. Any attempt to sympathize seemed so inadequate. So he turned to the only thing he knew he could do well. Standing up, he walked back to the hallway where he had left his cooler upon bursting in and brought it back to the couch.

"I thought earlier about what you said in the shop," he said, unzipping the liner and retrieving a small package wrapped in brown paper. "About not being able to eat your favorite cheeses and, well, that just won't do. So I did a little research and made a few batches of pregnancy-safe pasteurized Gran Padano and what I'm calling a 'baby blue' cheese. I cooked it and tested it for the bacteria that can cause harm. It's in the separate container that will keep it hot." He pulled the small thermos out of the bag. "I'm going to try the same thing with a Stilton, but it has to be eaten immediately because it melts easier than this variety."

Given her responses during previous interactions, he probably shouldn't have been surprised when her eyes took on a glossy sheen, then brimmed over with tears.

"I'm sorry," he said, instantly assuming he had done something wrong again. "I should have asked which cheese was your favorite first. It's brie, isn't it? I knew I should have gone with the baked brie." That was a rookie mistake and he was no rookie when it came to cheese.

"No, no." She wiped her eyes with her fingernails and he couldn't help noticing how they matched her coat perfectly, the same brilliant shade of red. She hadn't been kidding about details. "Don't apologize. These are happy tears. I can't believe you went out of your way for me like that."

The sides of Lucas's neck flushed as if someone had stuck one of the festival torches directly behind him. He made a noise under his breath that was somewhere between a grunt and a cough. "It's not a big deal. It's my job. Just... cheese."

"It's more than that." She sniffed, then offered him a smile that shone brighter than her eyes. "You listened to what I wanted instead of telling me what you thought I needed. I can count the number of men I've met who can do that on one hand and still have fingers to spare."

"Well, my dad always says that when it comes to him and my mom, he can either listen or wish he'd listened," Lucas quoted. "They've been married for thirty-five years and still act like a pair of teenagers around each other. Not a bad role model."

She reached forward and plucked one of the small white wedges out of the wrapper, popping it in her mouth and chewing thoughtfully before she swallowed with a satisfied sigh. Tipping her head to one side, Chrysta looked at him as if she could see right through him. "So why do you need a pretend fiancée to satisfy your parents? You're a nice guy, gainfully and deliciously employed, and somewhere under all that hair is a very attractive smile. What's with the charade?"

He closed the brown paper over the package, needing something to do with his hands. Lucas didn't like lying. No, that wasn't even entirely true enough for him. He *hated* lying. So he told the truth, or as much of it as he could. "My mom has Parkinson's disease. That's partly why they're moving to Charleston. The winters here are really hard on her and she hates to be stuck inside half the year because she's too afraid of falling on the ice. I—I just want her to be able to live where she wants without worrying about me being lonely."

This was not only the truth, it was painful to admit he had failed at giving Ma the only thing she had ever asked for. The worst part was he wanted those things for himself almost as badly. He wanted a wife. He wanted kids. But every time he'd come close, something, or someone, had gotten in the way.

Chrysta's mouth fell open for a moment. Then she pressed her lips together in a firm line and gave a thin imitation of her usual wide smile before speaking. "Ah. Okay. I get it." Her eyes flickered downward and she twisted one of her coat buttons between two fingers. "I… I know what it's like to feel like you have to protect your mom's feelings."

He wanted to ask more as she definitely seemed to be uncharacteristically holding back. But if he probed too much too soon, she might close herself off from him altogether. So instead he asked, "How was the cheese?"

She blinked and raised her eyes to him, as if opening the windows to her true self once more. "It was perfect. Thank you for that...and for coming to my aid tonight." Chrysta lifted her foot an inch off the sofa and wiggled her toes at him.

"I'm sure you would have gotten off the floor eventually," he joked. "I mean, not until the housekeeper came the next morning to vacuum, but you would have made it. I'm surprised Bruce Wayne didn't come to your rescue."

"Oh, he stays in the room most of the time," she said. "He keeps staring at one of the dolls like it's haunted or something."

Lucas didn't believe in ghosts. He did, however, share Bruce Wayne's opinion that Mrs. Van Ressler's collection of porcelain doll couples was anything but romantic. "Well, if you change your mind about my offer, I can at the very least promise you that none of my cheeses are possessed by evil spirits."

She laughed out loud at that one, drawing her knees up as she did and crossing her ankles. "Oh my goodness. Don't make me laugh like that or I'll have to set a world record for power hobbling to get to the bathroom." When her giggles subsided, she took a deep breath and regarded him with determined seriousness. "Here's the deal, Cheese Cave Man."

"I'm listening, Chrystabell."

"I'm willing to give your 'offer'—" she made quotation marks with her fingers "—a shot. But we're going to go one step at a time and I get to back out at any point it seems like it might backfire on me or my business. Agreed?"

"Talk me through the steps." Lucas sat up straight and folded his arms across his chest.

"Phase one—"

"I thought we were going in steps."

"Nobody likes a pedantic cheese hermit."

"Nobody likes a cheese hermit, period," he shot back. "That's what makes him a hermit."

She held up one finger and he made a motion of zipping his lips.

"Phase one is we're seen in public like we had planned on tonight," she said. "It will help get the rumor mill going for you, and you, in turn, can introduce me to people who might want to hold cheese board parties. I already have Georgia's booked, but I want to get at least four in before this baby comes."

"I can help with that," Lucas said. "And Step—Phase two, I assume, is you moving in with me? You'll need a place after Mrs. Van Ressler kicks you out."

She frowned. "I know. But I don't want to do

anything impulsive. What if we go out on a date and you find you can't stand me? Let's see how Stage One goes first."

Lucas mouthed "Stage?" silently, and she responded with a shake of her small fist that was intended to be threatening, but ended up making her look even more adorable than before. He couldn't stop the smile that spread across his face. He was beginning to really enjoy their impromptu pantomimes. He didn't say half the things he usually thought, anyway.

Through the window behind them, people started to pass as they walked back to their cars, hunkered together in pairs to keep out the cold. Chrysta's eyes followed his distracted gaze and for a few minutes, they simply sat there and watched the shadows rush by in the wavering light of the torches.

She turned her head back and looked at him. There was a serenity about her that made him long for the power to stop time, to stay in the perfect silence and warmth of that moment.

"Lucas, I love…" She paused and Lucas felt suddenly scared to even take a breath that might break the magic spell they had come under. "I love this town," she said, propping her elbow on the back of the couch and her hand under her chin for support. "I really hope I can make it work here. It's the perfect place for us."

"Us?" he ventured carefully.

"Me and the baby." She rolled her eyes at him for being silly enough to forget about the third person in the room.

"Oh, right." He shook his head and lifted his eyebrows. "Of course. Crystal Hill is a great place to raise a family. But running a business here can be tough."

She narrowed her eyes. "Why? Do you think I'm just some silly woman who hasn't done the market research? I know it's a niche business concept, but if I start small, using most of my budget for social media advertising and branding, I can scale it organically into something bigger. You're not the only expert in the cheese-based industry, you know." She folded her arms over her chest and looked away.

He did know that and it was one of many things he found so appealing about her. But he knew the people in this town better than she did, knew how resistant they were to anything different. He could help her if she trusted him. Given the way her lips were pursed into a tight rosebud, that didn't seem likely at the moment. It was even clearer now that he couldn't tell her about the battle between him and Law for the space. If she found out that he had withheld that information from the beginning, she wouldn't trust him or speak to him again.

"Never mind," he said. "I'm sure your parties are going to be a big hit."

"You bet they are," she said, yet there was a waver breaking up the defiance in her voice like static over a radio. "If I'm going to do this plan with you, we need to have a clear separation between personal and professional. Your roles will be real cheese supplier and fake boyfriend, got it?"

"Got it," he answered promptly. "Stick to the plan."

"Stick to the plan," she repeated. "One fake date somewhere you can show me off and I can make contacts. Easy peasy, Mr. Cheesy." Her smile still didn't reach her eyes, but at least she wasn't so mad she couldn't joke with him.

It was going to be hard to stick to the plan when she was so adorable he almost proposed right then and there. He needed to give himself some distance and cool himself down if this was going to work. Maybe the Polar Plunge wasn't the worst idea in the world.

CHAPTER SIX

CHRYSTA QUICKLY FOUND out something about her newly beloved hometown: you tended to run into the people you knew everywhere. She spotted Lucas ducking into his shop when she picked up her takeout from Mama Renata's last night and again on the sidewalk across from her as she shoveled the snow off the inn's walkway. She could have sworn she saw him hiding behind a clothing rack at the dry cleaner's while she was retrieving some shirts for a guest. If she didn't know any better, she might have thought he was trying to avoid her, which was the exact opposite of The Plan. Maybe he was having second thoughts about asking her to move in? She hoped not, because she only had one more week to find somewhere else to live and all her searches in town had come up empty. Once again, she found herself dependent on a man, and that hadn't exactly ended well the last time.

"It's not like I want to see him that badly," she said to Bruce Wayne as she laid a second dress on the bed in front of her. "He's a nice guy, that's all. And attractive. With a lifetime supply of cheese." She shook her head firmly. "No, Chrysta. Remember you're the one who made that big speech about sticking to the plan. We're focusing on the business here." Now, what would be the perfect dress to wear for her first hostessing gig? The burgundy knit sweater dress with the shawl collar, or the sleek black three-quarter sleeves with the red ribbon at the empire waist? Bruce Wayne made the decision for her by descending lightly from the "fairy-tale dolls" shelf and landing on the black dress.

"You're right, as usual." Chrysta picked him up before he had time to curl into a ball on the dress and leave a ring of fur on it. "The black is more professional. Good call, Catman."

Picking up the dress, she glanced over her shoulder. The unnerving feeling of several pairs of glass eyes on her while she changed never got easier. Sliding her feet into a pair of black boots with tufty fur at the top, she pulled her ponytail even tighter. She was a single mom. She could do hard things.

And she was going to have to get used to doing them on her own.

She made her way carefully down the stairs, then stopped midway down in surprise.

"BeeBee," she said to the tall woman standing in the foyer with a cooler in both arms. "It's nice to see you again."

BeeBee smiled, then leaned forward and peered into the parlor full of glass objects. "Is Mrs. Van Ressler here?"

"I think she's in the back, checking her porcelain souvenir plate collection," Chrysta replied, continuing down the stairs until she reached the landing. "She caught one of the guests' kids hovering by the china cabinet and now she's paranoid that one of them might be cracked."

"Yikes." BeeBee grimaced. "That reminds me of the last time she let me into the parlor. I barely breathed on one of the bluebirds and you would have thought that I had used it as a baseball."

"Was this when you were a kid?"

"Only if you consider a twenty-three-year-old a child," BeeBee said, then held up the cooler. "I come bearing cheese. Lucas sent me over with this for your party."

"Oh." Chrysta was surprised that her first reaction was a sinking disappointment. "Where's Lucas tonight?"

"Where else?" BeeBee rolled her eyes. "He's working in the shop. He muttered something about keeping an eye on the back room. Probably thinks there are cheese thieves lurking around. He's almost as bad as Mrs. Van Ressler."

"Did someone call me?" Mrs. Van Ressler's

voice emerged from the lobby and echoed through the parlor.

"It's just me," BeeBee called. "I'm bringing a delivery from Lucas's cheese shop."

"Did you take your boots off before entering the premises?"

BeeBee looked down at her boots, which, in addition to still being firmly on her feet, were dripping a mix of dirt and snow onto the welcome mat. "Yes."

Chrysta chuckled as she reached for the cooler. "Tell Lucas thank you. I'll stop by and pay him after the party." On top of the cooler was a card with her name on it. Setting the cooler down with a grunt, she picked up the card and flipped it over, but there was nothing written on the other side. The sinking disappointment tunneled deeper into a chasm. "Did, uh, did Lucas say anything else? About the delivery or, um, me or anything?"

Oh, no. She sounded like a schoolgirl with a crush on the quarterback. Chrysta told herself it was part of The Plan. To get the town spies buzzing, she needed to sound interested in the man. The fact that she had actually missed him since the last time she had seen him was not part of The Plan.

"Nope," BeeBee said promptly. "But that's Lucas for you. If you're not talking to him about the shop or his cheese, you're lucky to get much more than a few words grunted at you from behind his beard. It's a shame, too, because he's actually got a good sense of humor, even if it is a little cheesy." She snickered at her own pun, then pointed at the cooler. "So this party at Georgia's is like a cheese-tasting party?"

"It's more like a cheese-and-charcuterie-board-building party, but of course there is plenty extra to snack on as we go," Chrysta explained. "The whole point is using cheese board building as a creative medium while also providing a social experience for friends or coworkers. Georgia said that one of the moms is an education specialist for kids on the autism spectrum, so I'm going to show them how to make a butterfly-themed cheese board, since the butterfly is a symbol of pride and awareness of that community."

"Cool." BeeBee nodded along. "That sounds like fun. Are you going to do catering, too? I'm looking for someone to do the food at my engagement party and I don't want to ask Bill. He's already groomzilla as it is."

The second person to suggest this in two days? If Chrysta was the type of person who believed in signs, she would perhaps consider it. But there was no such thing as signs or destiny. In this world, you were on your own and you made your own luck through hard work and good planning.

She had veered away from her plans when she married Alastair and look where that had gotten her.

Chrysta shook her head. "Not unless someone wants an event fueled exclusively by cheese."

"Ha," BeeBee guffawed loudly. "I'm pretty sure that's Lucas's idea of a perfect meal. Most of the guests are my friends from the dairy pageant. Oh, I keep forgetting you're new here. About a year and a half ago, I won the New York State Queen of the Dairy pageant and used my prize money to buy a water buffalo stud. Afterward the other female dairy farmers and I set up a farming organization, so we've kept in touch. The girls love those little pastries that look like tiny cakes, so as long as there's dessert and dairy, we're good. Anyways, I'd better scoot before Mrs. Van Ressler comes around the corner and sees me wearing my boots inside. I'm still on probation from the time I leaned on the wall and left brown smudges on her wallpaper."

"I can't believe she got that upset over a little mud," Chrysta said.

BeeBee flushed and bit her lower lip. "Yeah… it was mostly mud. Good luck on your party tonight. Bye!"

She disappeared just as Mrs. Van Ressler rounded the corner and narrowed her eyes at the open door. "Leaving the door wide-open behind her," she said, making an actual tsking noise between her teeth. "If you couldn't tell that girl lives in a barn from the smell, you certainly would from her manners." She glanced down at the cooler on the floor. "This has your name on it."

"I was just going to move it." Chrysta bent down and picked it up off the floor. "I'm hosting my first cheese board–building party tonight at Georgia's."

"Hmph," Mrs. Van Ressler muttered. "Suit yourself. I never did care much for those."

"Cheese boards?" Chrysta was shocked. How could anyone not like a good cheese board?

"Parties," Mrs. Van Ressler replied before pivoting sharply on her heel, her cane clicking on the floor as she walked back to the lobby.

Digesting this new, but not surprising, piece of information about her employer, Chrysta hefted the box a little higher so it wasn't pressing on her belly and turned to set it down. She stopped at the closet behind the stairs to retrieve her coat and gloves, then sighed. Another bathroom break was definitely in order, and that required going all the way back up the stairs. As much as she didn't want to take Lucas up on his offer to live in his place, there was no denying this building was not made for a pregnant woman in her third trimester.

Twenty minutes later, bladder emptied and winter layers donned, she was on her way. While a right turn on Jane Street would take her to the bakery, Chrysta turned left at the corner and headed down Montgomery Street, a tree-lined residential avenue populated with Victorian homes that looked like wedding cakes with snow piled on their corner turrets. The sun setting behind her cast a magical glow on the neighborhood, making the frost-encrusted branches of the trees sparkle incandescently. Chrysta smiled with pleasure at her new hometown.

Georgia's home was a small white Cape Cod with a black roof. A lighted Moravian star hung in front of the door and Chrysta carefully stamped every bit of snow off her boots onto the welcome mat before ringing the doorbell.

From inside, a voice called out, "Oh my gosh, it's not five thirty already, is it, Caroline?"

After the sound of something crashing to the floor followed by the yowl of a very large cat or a small mountain lion, the door swung open. Caroline, Georgia's daughter who, with her curly red-gold hair and fair, round face looked like a miniature version of her mother, stood in front of it.

"Hi, Caroline." Chrysta smiled at the girl. "Do you remember me from the inn?"

"Of course," she said, returning Chrysta's

expression with a gap-toothed grin of her own. "You're the Cheese Games Lady. That was so much fun. I tried playing it at home, but all we had was string cheese, so it ended up being more like Lincoln Logs." The loud sound of pots banging against metal clashed in the background. "Do you want to come in?"

"Um, yes, but are you sure your mom is ready for me?" Chrysta peeked anxiously over the little girl's head, but could only see as far as the coatrack. "I came a little early to get set up. I can just leave my things here and take a walk around the neighborhood, if you'd like."

Georgia trotted down the center hallway, a towel wrapped around her head and one shoe on her foot. She reached over Caroline's head to push the screen open. "No, no, you don't have to do that," she said, a little breathlessly, yet still with the warmth that emanated from her as naturally as opening an oven door in her bakery. "I wouldn't make a pregnant woman take a lap around the block just because I'm running behind as usual. It might send you into labor and you'd end up delivering the baby on my messy kitchen floor."

Chrysta laughed. "I've still got nine weeks to go, so I don't think I have to worry about that."

Georgia beckoned with one hand, still holding the screen with the other. "Come on in, hon. Caroline, take Miss Chrysta's cooler for her."

Caroline reached up eagerly and took the cooler, staggering backward a little with the weight. "Whoa, there must be a lot of cheese in here."

"There's plastic cheese boards, fruit and decorations too." Chrysta closed the door behind her and shrugged her coat off. "But yes, I ordered a lot of cheese. Lucas checked off everything on my list."

"I'll bet he did." Georgia chuckled before clearing her throat. "I mean, that's great. The ladies from the PTA are so excited for this. We try to make our meetings fun, since for most of us that's like our big outing for the month. Usually, we try to get babysitters so we can really let our hair down, but I think a few of the ladies are bringing their kids tonight, too."

"Oh, okay," Chrysta said, hanging up her coat, then turning around to follow Georgia down the hall and into a small, brightly lit kitchen. She tried not to let the bubbles of anxiety boil over into panic. Why hadn't she thought about bringing activities for kids? How oblivious was she to assume that everyone had childcare? In a few months, she would be in the same boat. She squared her shoulders. This would be good practice for the requisite multitasking. She could do this. "No problem. The kids can sit quietly and color or something while I do the board-building demonstration."

Georgia crooked an eyebrow. "Suuuure. Anyway, so this is my kitchen." She spread her arms out to the side, then winced. "Sorry about the mess in the sink. I was trying to get the dishes done and my cat, Harley, decided to jump inside the dishwasher before I could load it. We had lasagna last night and she goes crazy for anything with a red sauce, hence my broken Pyrex."

Chrysta followed Georgia's glare to something rubbing itself against her feet. An enormous gray-and-white-striped cat with tufted ears and a gorgeous plumed tail meowed defiantly up at them. Chrysta had been around enough cats to decipher a "sorry not sorry" when she heard one. She chuckled and looked back up at Georgia. "It's all right. I have a cat, too. Mine is named Bruce Wayne. Is Harley short for Harley Quinn, because if so, you and I might be kindred spirits."

"It's actually short for Harley-Davidson," Georgia said, leaning back against the counter with her elbows. "My late husband loved motorcycles. Harley was his cat."

"I'm so sorry," Chrysta replied, and Georgia shook her head, her towel starting to unravel.

"No need," she said. "It's been a rough couple

of years, but we've managed to find a new normal between the three of us." Glancing across the kitchen to the table where Caroline had set down the cooler and was now peeking beneath the lid, she swallowed and quirked up one side of her mouth in a half smile. "Sometimes life doesn't go according to plan, right?"

"Right," Chrysta agreed outwardly, while screaming with horror internally. "Well, why don't you finish getting ready and I'll get everything set up here? We're expecting six ladies, is that correct?"

"Yes, and I think two are bringing their kids," Georgia said as she crossed the kitchen and rounded a corner to the steps behind the pantry.

As the sound of Georgia's footsteps diminished, Chrysta inhaled deeply and wrinkled her nose at Caroline. "You think the other kids coming tonight will sit quietly and color while the moms make cheese boards and drink wine?"

Caroline pressed her little lips into a grim line and shook her head. "Jeremy Binkus doesn't sit quietly to do anything," she said. Surveying the contents of the cooler, she hopped off the chair and shrugged. "And the only kind of cheese he eats is the square, white kind. Most of the other kids in my class are the same. It drives Uncle Lucas crazy."

"I'll bet." Chrysta snorted.

Poor Lucas. He probably didn't get much of a chance to spread his gourmand wings running a small-town dairy. No wonder he had doubted her business. So used to people ordering the basic dairy essentials for their day-to-day lives, it probably didn't even occur to him that they would be open to new, cheese-based entertainment. Well, she would prove that not only was her business model thoroughly planned out, but that it would work like a charm. Although…it was going to be a challenge fitting all the cheese, accoutrements and boards on Georgia's small oval kitchen table. She looked around for options. There was an island, but it was small and littered with Caroline's schoolwork, a smattering of hair ties and a basket of fruit. Maybe she could do her demonstration from the island and the moms could squeeze around the table? The living room was right behind a small partition next to the table. If the kids stayed in the living room to play, the moms could keep one eye on them and still have a good time. This was fine.

One hour later, everything was not fine.

The moms had arrived minutes after Georgia had come down the stairs and right as Chrysta had set out the last plastic cheese board on the table. In the center, she had arranged the fruit, cheese and dried herbs in separate bowls, and six rolls of white mozzarella (the butterfly's "body") sat on a plate in the center. Everything had started so well, the moms exchanging squeals of excitement over the premade board Chrysta had on display as a template. Two of them came with bottles of wine that would go nicely with the assortment of cheese, and Georgia's tray of small chocolate-hazelnut cream tarts would finish the evening perfectly. But before Chrysta could get the party started, two boys about Caroline's age burst from their moms' firm grips and chased each other around the island, knocking over the perfectly arranged monarch butterfly Chrysta had made from the cheese, dried apricots and black grapes.

"I'm so sorry," the tall woman with dark hair pulled into a messy bun had said before darting after one of the boys. "Jeremy, no running inside. We talked about this!"

"It's fine—oh, no, Georgia, the cat!" Chrysta exclaimed as Harley leaped over the gate pinning him on the staircase, and pounced onto the tray with unabashed glee.

Georgia had shooed Harley away, and while the butterfly appeared to have been smashed by the windshield of a speeding car, it was still serviceable as a demonstration-only model. With the chaos settled and the boys, Caroline and a three-year-old girl toddling after them tucked into the living room with Play-Doh and LEGO,

Chrysta had resumed her demonstration, picking up the pace a little more from the speed at which she rehearsed.

"So, ladies, we've all seen those cheese boards on Pinterest and thought, 'I could never do that,'" she said, pointing at the mangled butterfly with a grimace. "You know what I mean. Or we've thought, 'Hey, that looks easy enough,' only to find ourselves wandering the gourmet cheese aisle of the grocery store, googling the difference between a gruyere and a gouda. Tonight, I'm going to teach you the 'A-B-Cheese' of building a charcuterie board that will wow your party guests or just give you something fun to do with your friends on a Friday night."

"Mom, Jeremy dared me to eat Play-Doh," one of the boys said, pointing at the blond boy wearing a mischievous expression.

"I did not," the other boy said indignantly. "I said I would pay him a quarter if he ate it. That's not a dare, that's business."

"Ethan, we don't eat Play-Doh," one of the moms said, popping one of the Manchego balls into her mouth. "This is really good. What's this called again?"

"Manchego," Chrysta said. "It's really good paired with the dried apricots there. Now, for the wings you can do any of the fruits. You just want the ratio of sweet to savory to be—"

"Where did the LEGO Elsa's head go?" Caroline asked. "I just had it a minute ago."

"Uh-oh." One of the moms who didn't look much older than Chrysta jumped up. "Khaleesi, open your mouth, honey. Spit out the nice princess's head."

Chrysta felt her eyes bulge. She did not have royal cannibalism on her bingo card for the evening. She peered nervously over the partition into the living room where the mom had pried open the toddler's mouth. "Does she need to go to the hospital?"

The mom looked over her shoulder and shook her head. "Nah. It's gone already. She's still using the training potty. I'll get the LEGO back to you in thirty-six to forty-eight hours."

"Are you sure?" Chrysta looked at the other moms. "Shouldn't we try to Heimlich it out or something?"

The women around the table laughed as the toddler's mom rejoined them and took a sip of her wine. "Nah. That's tiny. Anything smaller than a nickel, the pediatrician said don't bother calling as long as it shows up in the diaper within a few days."

Georgia nodded. "I remember when Caroline went through the 'eating everything' phase. I had to put the cat food on a high shelf because she kept getting into the bag like they were Cheerios."

Chrysta rubbed her forehead wearily. "Wow."

"Here, hon, why don't you sit down for a minute?" Mrs. Binkus pulled out her chair and patted it.

Chrysta dropped into the chair gratefully and scanned the faces of the women at the table as they chatted quietly and arranged cheese and fruit on their boards as if a child ingesting a toy was just another day in paradise. She needed to get back to the demonstration, but suddenly the lights in the room felt brighter than the sun on a Caribbean cruise. "You moms are amazing, you know that?"

Khaleesi's mom smiled and nodded at Chrysta's belly. "Us moms. You're gonna be right here with us soon enough."

Georgia reached across and patted Chrysta on the arm. "See what I meant about making it up as you go? Now—" she held up her board "—what do you think about using the thyme sprigs for antennae?" She winked encouragingly at Chrysta.

Inhaling deeply, Chrysta mouthed "Thank you" and stood again. "I love that. See, the great thing about cheese boards is that you can really get creative and make them your own."

By the time the evening had finished, Chrysta was pretty sure she had sweated through her dress (the black had definitely been the right choice), yet the evening had gone well enough that all the moms had taken cards and one of them booked a party for a friend's birthday in two weeks. In addition to the tarts, Georgia had made chocolate chip cookies and brownies for the kids.

Chrysta held up her hand before the kids fell on the desserts. "Hold on. Cheese party rules. Before we have dessert, we each need to try a piece of cheese, meat or fruit that we've never tried before."

Jeremy narrowed his eyes at her. "Do we really have to?"

Chrysta put her hands on her hips. "Whoever eats the stinkiest cheese gets a cookie *and* a brownie," she announced before raising her eyebrows at the boys. "I triple dare you to try the blue cheese and then breathe stinky dragon breath at each other. Ready, set, go."

The boys' eyes lit up with delight at the challenge. Chrysta found herself wishing Lucas were there to watch Jeremy and Ethan eat aged blue cheese, then take turns huffing and puffing at one another with squeals of delight.

As the moms gathered their kids and wrapped their boards in plastic to take home, Georgia came up to the sink where Chrysta was washing her hands.

"That went really well," she said, handing her a checkered dish towel.

Chrysta wiped her hands dry and cast a skeptical side eye at her. "You sure about that?"

Mrs. Binkus came up behind them with her board in one hand and Jeremy, attempting to flap his dragon wings, wriggling in the other. "Chrysta, this was so much fun. And delicious, too."

"Yeah," Jeremy said. "Can we have cheese and dessert for dinner every night?" He roared like a dragon and his mom shuffled him out the door, reminding him to use his indoor roar until they got outside.

"You know, that's not such a bad idea," Georgia said. "If you ever want to join forces to cater small, private events, I think cheese boards and dessert would be a great combination."

Earlier, Chrysta would have bristled instantly at the idea of swerving even an inch from her plan. After tonight, however, it seemed clear that learning to pivot with the circumstances was going to be a necessary skill for her.

"I'll think about it," she said. "BeeBee already asked me about something just like that. I don't see why we couldn't combine catering and the cheese board party experience."

"Great," Georgia replied. They both turned and surveyed the demolished bowls of cheese and lipstick-stained wineglasses on the table, then sighed. "It's too bad your Bruce Wayne isn't the real Batman. It would take a superhero to clean this mess."

Chrysta walked over to the table and began to gather the bowls on top of one another. She shook her head. "Guess us moms—wow, that still seems too strange to say—have to be our own superheroes."

Georgia brought a box of gallon plastic Ziploc bags to the table and started putting the remaining cheese inside. "I know it feels overwhelming right now, but you're going to be just fine. You've already got great instincts." She held up a wedge of blue cheese with a visible bite taken out of it. "Getting Jeremy Binkus to eat blue cheese? Lucas has been tilting at that windmill for years."

The corners of Chrysta's lips turned up. "I learned a long time ago people will go for just about anything if you turn it into a game. My mama always says, 'Life is short. You might as well make it fun.'"

And her mom lived that mantra as if it were a Biblical commandment. As the wife to an Air Force colonel turned high-ranking official at NASA's Huntsville base, hosting parties for her husband's coworkers and wives was part of the job. Every Friday night, their living room turned into a society affair with silver trays of unpronounceable canapés, music playing softly in the background and spontaneous bursts of laughter following her mom like the scent of her Chanel perfume. On weekends, there was bingo, bridge club meetings and pyramid schemes from selling cosmetics to cookware in which Mama always ended up buying more than she sold. Still, if there was one useful legacy her mother had passed down, it had been "make it fun."

Of course, all games ended eventually. The world picked its winners and losers based on your accomplishments and your ability to make tough choices. Chrysta had learned that the hard way as she put her mom's good silver trays up for sale at antique markets so they could pay off their credit card each month. Fun was something she did for other people. Taking care of herself and her child was going to be hard work, and she was going to have to do it on her own.

"Were we supposed to use this?" Georgia dug a package out of the cooler that Chrysta hadn't seen. "It looks like it says Chrystabell, although it's hard to tell. Lucas's handwriting is worse than my doctor's."

Chrysta dropped the bowl in her hand on the floor. Instantly, Harley materialized to help with the clean-up efforts. "I—I don't know. That must have been something extra he threw in."

Georgia handed the package to her across the table and Chrysta unwrapped the brown paper.

Inside was a block of semisoft cheese. It was studded with dried red peppers and rosemary, spelling out the words "I'm sorry."

A small gasp escaped Chrysta's lips. So that's why he had been avoiding her. He thought she was mad at him. A man apologizing for something that wasn't his fault was rare enough. A man who said it with cheese?

You didn't find that every day.

CHAPTER SEVEN

WHILE IT WAS typical for Lucas to be up before sunrise for work, this was the first time he was out at dawn in a robe with five other guys to wade into Crystal Hill Lake in below freezing temperatures.

"I'm beginning to question every life decision I've ever made that has led me to this moment," Lucas grumbled under his breath to Joe. His toes were losing more feeling by the minute.

"Oh, don't be a baby," said Joe.

Lucas found this rather ironic, given that the fluffy white towel Joe had wrapped securely around his nether regions resembled nothing more than the cloth diapers Georgia had used on Caroline when she was a baby. He didn't say this out loud, of course. The fact that his usual internal thought bubble was basically a gray storm cloud was probably due to early stages of hypothermia.

"It's a perfect day for a plunge," announced Ed Stevenson.

"It's January," Lucas pointed out. "The lake is freezing over on the tree-lined side."

"That's what makes you feel alive," Joe announced. "Come on, guys. In we go."

Lucas groaned as he dropped his robe. The frigid air hitting his bare chest like a slap was just salt in the wound. As soon as they walked into the water, however, the air was the least of his problems. He had expected cold, but this was pain. Lucas couldn't stop himself from letting out a small shout as he continued to walk forward with the other men until the water was at hip level.

"Wh-wh-what d-do we d-d-do now?" Lucas said between chattering teeth. He marched his feet up and down hoping that movement might keep his body from turning into a solid block of ice.

"Sometimes we hum, sometimes we stay silent," Silas, Ed's husband, said calmly. Despite the bluish tinge growing on his skin, he seemed peaceful, almost Zen-like. He wasn't even shivering. Lucas suspected either sorcery or, more likely, Ed's homemade apple brandy was the cause.

"When it's this cold, I think it helps to talk," Joe said, waving his arms up and down like he was trying to land a plane. "Distracts you from the cold."

"What d-do we talk ab-bout?" Any distraction from the very real concern that he wouldn't be able to use his hands to make that day's quota of burrata for Mama Renata's would be helpful at this point.

"Anything," Ed replied. "This is a safe space to mention anything that's been bothering you or just on your mind lately."

Safe for everything, but my remaining digits, was Lucas's first thought. What came out of his mouth was wholly different and completely unplanned. "How do you get a woman to trust you?"

His Uncle Jack, BeeBee's dad, stopped hopping in circles and asked, "You mean the new woman who works at the inn?"

"How—how did you know?" Had Lucas been that obvious?

"BeeBee and Bill were over for dinner the other night and mentioned you two might hit it off," Uncle Jack said.

"Traitors," Lucas said, bringing his hand up to his beard to check for icicles. "Just in general. Hypothetically. If there was a woman I liked and she had been through a rough time with guys, how can I let her know that I'm not going to treat her the way the other jerks have?"

"You have to be vulnerable," Joe said, moving closer to Lucas and putting a hand on his shoulder. "Reveal your true self to her. Your thoughts, your feelings. Your heart."

Lucas furrowed his eyebrows. He was standing in the center of town in his bathing suit. That was vulnerable and revealing enough for one lifetime, thank you very much.

Ed and Silas exchanged glances. "We aren't exactly experts on women," Silas said with a smirk, "but Joe's right. If you don't trust her with your truth, how can she trust you with hers?"

"Hmm," Lucas murmured under his breath. "But what if you already tried letting her know what you think about something and it didn't work?"

"It depends," Uncle Ed said. "What was the subject in question?"

"Well, hypothermically—hypothetically..." Lucas corrected himself. The cold was now travelling up his spine and numbing his brain. "Her business."

The other four men shook their heads at him like a convocation of bobbleheads.

"*Never* offer business advice," Joe said. "Never offer unsolicited advice, period. That's what cost me my relationship with my meat supplier."

"Even I know you're not supposed to do that," Ed said. "Especially around here. The women run this town and they do a darned good job of it, too. They don't need us to tell them what to do. They need support. Encouragement."

"A guy who knows how they like their coffee and brings it to them without them asking for it," Uncle Jack said and all the other men made sounds of affirmation—that, or they had started doing the humming thing Joe had mentioned earlier.

"I—" Lucas started, then stopped. A familiar flash of red caught the corner of his eye. It was Chrysta's scarlet coat, leaving the inn and walking…oh, no. No, no, no. Straight toward the cheese shop where Lawson was currently in the process of moving furniture from the back space up to the attic. She would run into him for sure, they would commiserate over what a jerk Lucas was and before you knew it, he would be giving the toast at their wedding. "I've got to go."

As he scrambled stiffly back to the shore, he heard Joe say to the others, "Building off of what Lucas said, do you think I should try again with Zorina? After we broke up, she said she was going to lace my ground beef shipments with Elmer's glue, but that was just in the heat of a lover's spat, right?"

Lucas added his silent objection to the chorus of hearty "nos" that echoed in response as he grabbed his flannel robe, shoved his feet in his boots and crossed the street in front of the inn before trotting past the bakery to catch up with Chrysta.

"Chrysta!" He cupped the frozen sausages that used to be his fingers around his mouth and called out. "Hey, Chrysta. It's Lucas."

She turned around in front of Georgia's bakery. Her expressive face shifted through a series of reactions, beginning with a smile that transitioned rapidly into a look of shocked confusion furrowing into genuine concern. After Lucas crossed the street, he bent over as a side stitch attacked.

"Lucas, are you okay?" She touched his shoulder. "Why are you in a robe? And why are your fingers blue?"

He stood up straight once more, wincing. "I'm fine," he said. "The robe and the freezer-burned fingers are a long story."

He looked over his shoulder to see the rest of the men emerging from the lake. Swiveling his head back to Chrysta, who had followed his gaze and he assumed more or less figured out the scenario, Lucas wrapped his arms around himself and tried to think warm thoughts.

"I was actually just on my way to see you," she said. She bit her lower lip and the pop of her dimples told him she was desperately trying not to giggle. "By the way, you might want to tie your robe a little more securely. If the wind kicks up, I'll be seeing a lot more of you."

Lucas shook his head and wrapped his robe around him like an Egyptian mummy trying to return to eternal slumber. Given his level of humiliation at the moment, resting in peace didn't sound too bad right about now. "Thanks for the warning. By the way, how did your party go last night?"

"Actually—are you sure you don't want to go back to your shop and, you know, put on some clothes?"

"I'm fine." Given the choice between freezing solid and having Law win Chrysta, he would take refrigerator door number one every time. "The fresh air is invigorating."

"If you say so," she said, crossing her arms and looking firmly unconvinced. "Anyway, the party, well, there were some bumps in the road. I mean, it went well and I got another booking out of it. But, um…" She looked down at the ground and kicked at a large chunk of rock salt. "It was tougher than I had expected." She glanced up at him reluctantly from under her long fringe of dark eyelashes, as if expecting him to rub his triumph in her face or something. "You were right."

Instead, he brought his hands up to his lips and blew on his fingers to warm them.

"Did you hear what I said?" she repeated, sounding almost a little annoyed. "You were right."

He shrugged. "It was your first event. There were bound to be some hiccups. But I didn't mean to undermine your confidence. I should never have stuck my big nose in where it didn't belong."

"Your nose is just the right size," she said. She leaned back against the bakery's yellow siding and sighed, folding her arms over her belly. "I got defensive because when I was married to Alastair, I basically let him take over my whole life. I got so swept up in the feeling of being in love that I didn't even realize I'd done it. My only friends were the girlfriends and wives of his investors. I couldn't even get a job because I never knew when he'd want to take a private jet to Tokyo on a Wednesday. Once, I mentioned my idea—the cheese board party business—to him and he told me it sounded like a waste of time. Why would I do something that only made a few thousand dollars when I could just host parties for him and his business associates where they made multimillion dollar deals by the end of cocktail hour?"

The good thing was that Lucas no longer felt cold. That feeling had been replaced by a burning rage and the very uncharacteristic desire to punch someone. "I'm so sorry—on behalf of all men—that guys like Alastair exist."

"Yes, I got your cheese-gram," she said.

Lucas laughed. "Some men speak the language of flowers. I speak the language of fermented dairy."

"Well, message received and consumed, so thank you." She added her own throaty chuckle to his laughter. "I'm trying to learn my lesson and not let my feelings get in the way of my better judgment. I should welcome advice from successful local business owners like Georgia and you."

"Tell that to *Cheese Club Monthly* magazine," Lucas muttered under his breath, then cringed. "I didn't mean to say that out loud. Never mind." It was like his inhibitions played limbo every time she made him laugh. What was this magic power of hers? Had to be the black cat.

Yeah, I can't even get a woman like you to pretend to be my fiancée, let alone actually marry me. There was no witchcraft powerful enough to get Lucas to say that out loud. But the stab of longing that accompanied the thought was powerful enough to leave him breathless.

"So what do you think your business needs?" Lucas crossed his arms and half shrugged, half shivered. The cold was seeping through his robe in painful waves. Didn't matter. They were not going back to his shop, no matter how many pairs of warm pants he had back at his place.

"The biggest thing is that I really need a hosting space of my own," she declared. "Not only because Georgia's kitchen was really tight with all of us packed in, but I'm realizing how important it is for moms to have a place to go where they can relax and unwind without feeling like they have to clean up or keep an eye on their kids. Somewhere contained and homey, but still elegant enough that it makes them feel like they're getting a minivacation out of the experience."

A strange, prickly feeling had the hair on Lucas's arms standing up, and it wasn't the cold.

"Oh, and Georgia and I will be doing some light catering," she added. "Cheese boards, cold appetizers and desserts, so I need a place with a real kitchen where I can prep for events." She wrinkled her nose adorably. "I know, I know. Finding a place like that with actual living space for me and the baby? Might as well ask for a lifetime supply of free gourmet cheese while I'm shooting for the moon."

Lucas cleared his throat and rubbed his hands over his arms, commanding the goose bumps to stand down. "I promise I'll help with whatever you need."

She smiled. "We can talk about that more on our date tonight."

"Our what, when?"

"Our date, silly." She leaned forward and whispered, "Our date in a very public place somewhere, preferably in view of the Crystal Hill Spy Ring."

He quirked one eyebrow up at her. "I thought you didn't believe that was real."

"Oh, I'm leaning into it now," she said. "I actually think I might be suited for espionage. We'll call this Phase One. Being seen in public together. We've probably planted seeds in the whisper network by standing out here with you in your skivvies."

Lucas pulled his robe up to his neck. "Madam."

She made a "psssht" noise between her lips. "Oh don't be bashful, Cheese Hermit. I've lived on charter yachts with men. I have zero shame. Phase Two will be a brief engagement followed by Phase Three—our public yet amicable breakup by Valentine's Day."

"You weren't kidding about the brief part."

"As brief as the plaid shorty shorts you've got on under that robe," she teased. "I like the red, by the way. It's my favorite color."

"I'm starting to feel violated now," Lucas said. "Okay, you've clearly got this all planned out. Why a Valentine's Day deadline?"

"It's a month before my due date," she replied. "I'll need to stay at your place after Mrs. Van Ressler kicks me out, but I need to be established in a place of my own before the baby comes. You don't want this kid to start calling you Daddy Cheese Hermit, do you?"

No, of course not. Not really.

And yet…

Once again, he couldn't find the words to say what he was feeling.

Of course, when he was back at the shop and in the comfort of his cheese lab, the perfect answers flowed like a waterfall. Most of them involving the names he wanted to call Chrysta's ex for making her doubt her brilliance, her fortitude, her creativity. Here she was, several months pregnant, trying to make a home for herself and her child and starting a new business. Lucas shook his head before pulling his protective cap over his mop of hair. She was so brave. He could never do something like that. As more than one ex-girlfriend had pointed out, he was a creature of habit who did the same thing every day, in the same town, working at the same shop his family had operated for decades. But watching Chrysta reinvent her life from scratch armed with nothing more than a business plan and a cat with weird ears made him wonder what it would be like to have that kind of courage.

After throwing on his apron and shoe coverings, Lucas went to pull open the curtains that divided his cheese lab from the shop. A note taped to the divide between the worn red fabric stopped him and he squinted to read it in the dim light of the unopened store.

Luke—

"It's Lucas and he knows it," Lucas growled under his breath. "I'm going to start calling him Dawson instead of Lawson. Give him a taste of his own medicine." He cringed as soon as the words were out of his mouth. Weaponized nicknaming. Maybe he had lived in this town a little too long.

I'm going to a wood supplier in Bath for the oak I need to make the new fireplace mantel and built-ins to display MY carvings when I win this ridiculous challenge. After that, I'm going out on a date. To clarify, I'm taking a woman out for dinner and a movie, not the shriveled fruit you like to stuff with stinky cheese and call a dessert.

"Ma said my feta-stuffed dates were one of the best things she'd ever eaten," Lucas said with a *humph*. He crumpled the note and tossed it in the garbage can. "I'll show him who can plan a good date. Chrysta and I will be doing something a lot more fun than boring dinner and a movie." Lifting his bucket of cheddar curds from the truckle form where they had been pressed into a wheel shape, he covered them with a sheet of muslin soaked in lard and set it under the mechanized press once more. As it pushed the flavorful cloth deep into the cheese, he leaned his hand on the counter. "What would be fun? Other than doing this, of course. That's setting the bar pretty high."

There was one thing Lucas enjoyed almost as much as making cheese. He hadn't done it in ages, and naturally, Lawson was ten times better at it than him. Still, it was definitely something that would get them noticed by the gossips and in turn, Ma's Ring of Spies.

CHAPTER EIGHT

When Lucas showed up at the door of the inn that night with something hidden behind his back, Chrysta would have bet money on it being cheese-related. An indoor picnic at his cheese shop maybe? But that seemed unlikely. Lucas had yet to actually invite her into his shop. Since she had first barged in and promptly burst into tears, he had delivered his cheese directly to her and seemed extremely skittish when she offered to meet there. She had tried not to take offense. A crying woman was most men's worst nightmare. Still, a girlfriend-slash-soon-to-be-fiancée should be welcome at her man's place of work, even if the relationship was a ruse. Chrysta couldn't help wondering why Lucas insisted on keeping her out of such a very important place, especially when it was an interest they both clearly shared. Could he be hiding something from her besides cheese?

"Ice skates?" Chrysta exclaimed in surprise. "We're skating?"

Lucas bobbed his head in a nod. "Yup. It's one of my favorite things to do, outside of making cheese. I haven't done it in a really long time, but I think it's kind of like riding a bike." His brow suddenly wrinkled under his gray knit ski cap. "Oh, no. You're from the South. They don't get much snow in Alabama, do they? I should have thought this through better. You've probably never skated before."

"Actually, I have," Chrysta replied, taking her coat off the rack by the door and pulling it over the sleeves of her white knit sweater dress. "There was an indoor rink in Huntsville. I used to have my birthday parties there." She shook her head, smiling at the memory. "My mom used to make this big production of it, with a different international theme every year. One year it was Germany and she got a portable soft pretzel stand with all these different kinds of cheese dips and an actual accordion player skating on the rink with us while he played." Looking back now, she didn't even want to think about how much money her mom spent on those parties every year. But that was Mama. Never a thought about budget or planning out finances in advance. Just spend and enjoy the moment and let someone else deal with the consequences.

"Phew." Lucas grinned, then handed her the skates. "I got a peek at your shoes the other night when you twisted your ankle, so I knew what size to get."

"Sneaky cheese hermit." Chrysta tossed him a mischievous wink. "You're just full of surprises, aren't you?"

"Not usually," he admitted with a sheepish duck of his head. "In fact, I've been told on more than one occasion that I could stand to be more spontaneous instead of doing the same thing every day."

"Well," Chrysta said, closing the door behind her as they walked out into the evening air, "personally, I hate surprises. What's so wrong with having a plan and a routine as long as you're doing something you enjoy? If you ask me, spontaneity is highly overrated."

They got in his truck and drove through the neighborhood where Georgia lived, past two schools and a beautiful stone library, before pulling up at a large open pavilion. Twinkle lights had been strung from poles around the small outdoor ice rink and a long line of people waited outside a small wooden hut selling mugs of hot chocolate next to the rack where piles of shoes had been traded for ice skates. The sight sent a thrilling shiver through Chrysta. This wonderful, cozy place was where she would get to raise her child, where every winter they could go ice-skating together, then drink hot chocolate and watch the stars multiply overhead.

Chrysta winced and put her hand on her belly as she walked around the truck.

Lucas rounded the bed and was at her side in two large steps. "Are you all right?"

"I'm fine." She rubbed the side of her belly. "Someone's starting to run out of room. I love ice-skating, but it's one of the many things I love that I probably shouldn't do right now."

When he smiled, a twinkle lit up his blue eyes like the stars appearing one by one above them. "I had thought that might be an issue." He disappeared behind the hot chocolate stand and returned holding one of the large blue frames little kids used to hold on to when they were first learning to skate. In the middle was a seat almost like a wheelchair for the ice rink. She couldn't help returning his wide smile with one of her own.

"I don't know," she teased as he held the gate open for her to step inside the pavilion. "Are you sure you're a good enough skater to push me around without falling yourself?"

It was hard to tell beneath the beard, but it looked as though his lips twitched in an effort to hold back a laugh. "I guess we'll find out."

And find out she did. Lucas got his skates on and went onto the ice first. "I want to make sure it's safe for you," he said making a circle of the surface before suddenly launching himself into a fairly impressive double spin. Gliding back to her on one leg with the other stretched behind him in a pose far too graceful for a man that tall, he hopped the curb and grabbed the training chair to place it in front of the bench.

Chrysta took off her glove and hit him playfully on the shoulder with it. "You tricky hermit, you. Where did a cheese maker learn to skate like that?"

"Eh. I picked up a few things here and there. I'm not nearly as good as my bro—I mean, my bro that I used to watch on TV, Nathan Chen."

"I love watching the figure skating when the Olympics are on!" Chrysta said. "I give commentary on it the whole time, too. Like, 'Oh, she's going to get points off that triple Axel for two-footing the landing.' Drove my ex crazy with it last winter. He thought it was annoying."

Lucas helped her into the seat, then looked down at her with an earnest expression on his face. "I think it's adorable."

What kind of game was he playing? He was her business supplier, the epitome of forbidden fruit, and yet each tiny morsel he revealed about himself was more appealing than the last. Good-looking, got along with her crazy yachting friends, appreciated fine cheeses, loved ice-skating as much as she did. Sure, he was taller than she'd normally go for, but the way he always seemed to sit or kneel to be closer to her level made him even more endearing. He was the perfect guy in the most imperfect situation, not to mention the exquisitely bad timing. If it wasn't for the fact that he always seemed to keep some distance between them, she'd almost think he was trying to make her fall in love with him for real.

Worst of all, she was coming dangerously close to letting him. She gripped the rails of the chair as they glided onto the ice, feeling out of control in every way possible. It was terrifying.

"I promise I won't let you fall," he whispered into her ear, sending shivers down the back of her neck.

Great. On top of reading her mind, he smelled amazing. As he stepped backward onto the ice and waited for her to get her balance on the slippery surface, she couldn't stop herself from asking. "Were you working at the Italian restaurant today?"

He raised an eyebrow. "No. Why?"

"You smell like garlic." Inhaling deeply, she added, "I'm also getting basil and oregano. Red chili peppers—Calabrian chili peppers. And cheddar?" She twisted around and looked up at him in surprise. "Not mozzarella?"

"If there was a 'Guess that Cheese' game show,

your nose would win first prize," he said, chuckling. "I was working on a bruschetta-themed cheddar with a little kick to it. Sorry, is the smell too strong? I can move behind you so I'm not downwind."

"Don't you dare." She blinked up at him, the cold stinging her eyes. "You smell perfect."

The blue in his gaze deepened to nearly the same navy as the sky above them. She could feel all the things he wanted to say, all the things he felt in those eyes, and if they were anything like the feelings swirling inside her right now, she wished for him to shout them out. He opened his mouth—and then his eyes widened with what looked like alarm. Hunching over, he skated in front of her to pull her backward like a tugboat away from the hot chocolate stand.

Chrysta knew she was expanding as her pregnancy went along. Still the idea that someone as large as Lucas could hide behind her was borderline insulting.

"What on earth are you doing?"

His eyes darted furtively around her, then back up to her face without lifting his head. "Would you believe this is a new skating move? All the kids are doing it these days."

"Try again."

"I'm rehearsing to play Quasimodo in Disney on Ice?"

"Three strikes and you're dunzo, Cheese Man."

They made it to the farthest bench partially obscured by a pine tree. After helping her sit first, Lucas sat next to her. He rubbed his hands together as if to warm them even though he was wearing good thick knit gloves. "I saw...my ex-girlfriend back there."

"Oh." Chrysta understood the impulse to run from an ex better than most. Along with empathy, there was a strange rush of something a little more bitter. Something that felt almost like jealousy. Which was weird because this wasn't a real relationship. The fact that Lucas was so out of sorts he was rubbing his hand through his hair, causing it to look even more wild and unkempt than usual, shouldn't have provoked the primal urge to kiss him until he couldn't even have picked his ex out of a lineup. "Were—were you two together long?"

"About eleven months." He shrugged. "It doesn't sound like a long time when I say it out loud. Still, it was the longest relationship I've had." Glancing back over, his shoulders dropped in relief. "It's okay. They're gone now."

"They?"

"She and, um, her date. Do you want to go back out there?"

"No." Chrysta shook her head. "It's getting pretty late. I think I'm ready to head back to the inn now, if that's all right." The magic spell from earlier had been broken. Apparently, ghosts from their pasts were something else they had in common.

He knelt on one knee and started untying her skates. Chrysta pursed her lips, trying not to smile at how careful he was to avoid her ankle.

"How long ago did you two break up?"

"Well," Lucas said, pausing as he moved to the other shoe to look thoughtfully up at her, "it was about two years ago. Sarah broke up with me, technically." He pushed up on his knees to stand. "I'll go over and get our shoes from the shelf." Stepping back onto the ice, he glided gracefully across and stepped over the edge of the rink to the shoe rack. It was amazing how broad his back and shoulders were, something she didn't normally appreciate because he often stood slightly hunched, with his hands in his pockets. It was probably to her benefit that he had no idea how handsome he really was. All it would take was a decent haircut and some tailored clothes and the women in this town would be swarming him.

As they left the ice rink and walked down the street toward the inn, Chrysta slid a glance up at him. "So did your ex say why she broke up with you?"

Lucas looked down at her with one eyebrow raised. "Looking for a deal-breaker?"

"No," Chrysta said honestly. "I'm just curious."

He inhaled deeply, then let out his breath, the cold turning it into a plume of frosted smoke. "According to her, I barely acted like I had a girlfriend. I forgot our six-month anniversary." He ticked off the items on his fingers as he continued. "I didn't notice when she changed her hairstyle. I didn't take her to New York City for Valentine's Day although she apparently hinted at it for months. In short, I was a terrible boyfriend who cared more about peddling wheels of cheese to people in town than her feelings. She didn't say those words, exactly, but that was the gist."

Chrysta skipped ahead of him a few steps and put her hand on his chest. They stood in the haloed light of a streetlamp, the snowflakes illuminated like puffs of fairy dust around them. "Lucas," she said, choosing deliberately to use his name rather than her usual teasing nicknames. "I want you to listen to me. You were not a terrible boyfriend. All of those things—" she waved her other hand in small circles before placing that one on his chest as well "—they're small details. Maybe they matter to some people, but that has more to do with her not knowing what kind of person you really are. You're a

big-picture guy. You're devoted to your shop because it's important to your family. You're passionate about cheese not because you're some
clueless hermit, but because it's how you give
back to your community. I've only known you
two weeks and I can see it. So what if you don't
take notice of small things like dates or hairstyles? You're the kind of person whose passions
have a bigger purpose. Anyone who doesn't get
that doesn't deserve you."

They were standing so close that when the
baby threw an elbow against her belly, Lucas's
eyes widened. "Was that—did the baby just
move?"

Chrysta looked down and nodded. It never got
old, that feeling of never being truly alone. She
loved each and every movement, even when it
felt like her body couldn't possibly stretch anymore to accommodate it. "You can feel if you
want."

He looked at her from under those bushy furrowed eyebrows, then firmed his lips in concentration. So gently, he put one hand on the
side of her belly where the elbow had just poked
out. The baby shifted and rolled, until Chrysta
could feel that its back was pressed up against
Lucas's hand. Suddenly the expression on Lucas's face opened, like sunlight through a window. "That's…amazing." His eyes reluctantly

moved up from his hand to her face. "I guess some small things are worth paying attention to, huh?"

The tenderness in his gaze caught Chrysta's breath in her throat. She found herself leaning toward him almost as if by instinct and he bent his head toward her. The warmth of his breath against the cold air around them jarred her back into her senses. She couldn't do this. Not again. This time there was so much more at risk than just her heart. "Lucas, we…shouldn't. This is just supposed to be pretend, remember? Stick to the plan."

He swallowed hard, his hand falling away from her and swiping over his beard. "Right. The Valentine's Plan." Giving her a wavering grin, he crooked his elbow and offered it to her. "I know that plans are important to you."

"I know that there's only so much I can control in life," she said firmly, as if trying to convince herself of the truth of the statement. "But with a plan, even if something unexpected happens, I know what to do. It keeps me from rushing into something and making a mistake."

He nodded as they reached the inn's walkway. "I get that. Don't worry, Chrystabell. We'll stick to your plan. We can stay in Phase One as long as you'd like."

"You listened when I was talking about the

phases earlier?" She blinked, unsure why tears were suddenly pricking behind her eyes. It didn't make sense. She teased him about taking everything too seriously and yet when he took her rambling on about their fake dating plan to heart, it felt like he was the only person who really saw her for who she was. Like he respected her as more than just the girl who throws the silly cheese parties. That was enough to make her forget everything she had just sternly warned herself not to do and reach up for those strong, protective shoulders and—

"Oh, good, you're back," Mrs. Van Ressler's voice found them over the squeaking of the front door as she opened it. "I was looking for you, Ms. Ball."

"I have the night off, remember?" Chrysta hopped guiltily away from Lucas like a teenager caught out after curfew. "Is there something you need me to help you with?"

"No, I just wanted to let you know we've picked up a few bookings and the honeymoon suite will be occupied starting Sunday," she said. "So I'll need you to find a new place to live by tomorrow."

Chrysta looked over her shoulder at Lucas, who bit his lip like he was trying not to grin.

Smug cheese hermit.

CHAPTER NINE

"I STILL DON'T understand why you're moving me to the trailer," Law protested as he threw a handful of faded T-shirts with various rock band logos in his duffel bag.

As usual, Lucas tried to stick as closely to the truth as possible. "Because Bill's friend needs a place to crash, and you know what they say about three being a crowd," he said, standing in the doorway with his arms crossed, flicking a quick glance at his watch. He had told Chrysta to come over with her things at one and he would meet her out front, but just in case she was early and decided to follow the sounds of their voices, he wanted to be ready to run interference. "Your woodworking is noisy, you know that. It's only temporary."

Law zipped his bag and flung it over his shoulder, giving Lucas the same grin as when they were kids and he wheedled an extra cookie out of their mom. "Well, temporary for now. If things continue to go well with Ada, who knows?

I might be taking permanent ownership of the land out there, too, by next New Year's."

"Ada?" Lucas scrubbed his hand through his hair. "But I thought…the other night, weren't you with—" Lucas stopped himself. He couldn't let Law know he had seen him with Sarah and her friends at the ice rink on Friday. He wasn't in the mood to hear more of Law's excuses about why the two of them had started hanging out immediately after Sarah had told Lucas she wished he could be more like his brother. He just wanted Law out of the shop before Chrysta got there and realized there was another, better version of him walking around. "Never mind. Do you need any help with that?"

"No, I'm good." Law tossed his hair off his forehead with a shake of his head. "You know, this whole thing really is insane."

Lucas rubbed his chin with his hand and made a huffing noise that was not exactly disagreeing.

"We could—" Law paused thoughtfully, then continued with a mischievous flash in his eyes. "We could make a stand against it. Together, that is. Like we did when we were kids and Dad tried to make us wear those ridiculous traditional Italian costumes for family picture day?"

Lucas couldn't stop himself from laughing out loud at the memory. "The poofy white shirts with the bright green vests? The tight striped pants and the little hats? We looked like the Italian version of the Keebler elves."

Law chuckled. "Until we came down the stairs wearing only the hat and vests and our Spider-man underwear." He shook his head. "Dad tried so hard to be mad, but he couldn't stop laughing. I still can't believe he let us get away with it." The corners of his mouth fell slightly. "You know, we used to be a pretty good team."

"A team?" Lucas scoffed. "More like a tiny army of two with you as the general. You knew full well I would have done whatever you told me to do, even if it meant I would get in trouble."

"Yeah, well..." Law looked away, fiddling with the frayed threads on the duffel bag strap. "Guess that's not the case anymore."

Because you turned out to be Benedict Arnold, taking my secrets and using them to steal my girl when I wasn't looking, Lucas thought. He cracked his neck to relieve the tension building as his shoulders crept up around his ears. They weren't kids anymore. Why did he let Law get to him like that? "Of course, you could just agree to let me have the space to expand the shop. You're not actually planning to stay in Crystal Hill for good, are you?"

Even though it would suit Lucas's purposes for Law to agree that he never stayed in one place longer than a season, a part of him was relieved when Law's chin shot up indignantly.

"Actually, I am," he said defensively. "And when I choose the lucky lady I want to spend my life with, you'll just have to deal with me setting up my woodworking business behind your little cheese shop here. It might take some getting used to since there will actually be crowds and lines out the door for my place, but hey, maybe a few stragglers will wander back to pick up a carton of yogurt or something for the road."

Lucas crossed his arms, the nostalgic closeness evaporating by the second. "I get plenty of business, thank you. And when I win, you'll see my face on the copy of *Cheese Club Monthly* at a kiosk in whatever airport you fly out of because you refuse to commit to anything longer than a minute."

Law muttered something under his breath as he pushed past Lucas and headed down the hallway. Stopping in the middle of the shop, he pivoted on his heel and tucked his chin down to give Lucas a questioning smirk. "Yeah. You really need the extra space for your business. It's so crowded I can barely see the door." He squeezed his arms into his chest, pretending to dodge invisible patrons. "Excuse me, sir. Whoops, my apologies, ma'am. The goatee threw me off. Hey, watch your hands. I'm more than a hot body, you know." Snickering, he rolled his eyes and pushed the door open to head out onto the sidewalk.

As glad as Lucas was to get Law out of the way before Chrysta got there, his brother's joking had hit him in a sensitive spot. Sure, there was always a slight post-holiday dip in sales. Between people making New Year's resolutions to lay off the dairy and the local tendency to hunker down as winter roared into full gear, a lag was to be expected. But for the first time, his dad wasn't standing behind him, reminding him of the fact. His mom wasn't giving him a soothing pat on the back and quoting that Bible verse about there being a season for everything. He was alone. It was on him to keep the shop going, and if things took a turn for the worse, there was nobody there to back him up. Lucas swiped his hand through his hair and closed his eyes, breathing deeply. It was all going to be fine. This was what he had wanted, just him and his cheese.

Wasn't it?

Lucas's eyes flew open as the bell above the door dinged. Chrysta stood silhouetted by a burst of the sun's last brilliance for the day. With the light illuminating the honey-gold warmth of her hair and the beautiful fullness of her figure, she looked as if she had stepped straight out of a Renaissance painting. He found he had to remind himself to breathe before he could welcome her home. Her temporary, fake home, anyway.

He rushed forward to help her with her bags. "You shouldn't be carrying all this," he said, taking her rolling suitcase in one hand and a large messenger bag in another. The mesh bag over her right shoulder wriggled. Oh, no. He had completely forgotten about the Dark Knight.

Her eyes darted down to her right hip, then up to his face with a guilt-stricken flash. "Is this going to be all right? I promise he's very quiet."

With impeccable timing and operatic clarity, the bag's contents let out an impressive meow. Lucas personally didn't speak cat, but he was fairly sure that was the feline version of laughing hysterically at its mom's delusions.

Lucas cleared his throat. "It's fine. Uh, follow me upstairs. I'll show you to your room." He turned and headed for the entrance to the stairs behind his cheese lab, but stopped when he realized Chrysta wasn't following him. Setting the bags down, he swiveled his head around to see Chrysta surveying her surroundings with an unsettling gleam in her eyes. "What are you doing?"

She jumped a little, startled. "Nothing. Just… looking around." She smiled. "Your family has done a nice job with this place."

"Thank you." Lucas's chest inflated a little.

"We're a small shop, but we really work to produce the best quality product."

She nodded. "So what promotions are you going to be running next month?"

"Promotions?"

"Yeah," she said as if it was obvious. "Seasonal specials. Marketing gimmicks. With Valentine's Day three weeks away, there's so much fun stuff you could do. Pairing cheese with wines for romantic date nights with your special someone. Proposal ideas using the cheese."

"Proposal ideas using cheese?" Lucas's mouth fell open, but she kept on going.

"Or you could do a fun thing with the kids. Put balls of mozzarella in a jar and have them guess how many there are to win a prize. Like, 'How much do I love cheese? Let me count the wheys.'" She slapped her own knee and guffawed. "Get it? Like *W-H-E-Y-S*."

Normally that's the kind of joke he would have laughed at. Heck, it was the kind of joke he would have made. But his head was still spinning like a centrifuge. "I—I hadn't really planned on doing anything like that." He scratched his chin under his beard. "I mean, I guess I could do a swirl of chocolate in the strawberry yogurt."

"That's...something." She nodded half-heartedly.

He could feel his defenses rising. Was she saying the same thing his brother had before he left?

Were they thinking the shop was doomed to failure under his charge? And then another, smaller voice piping in that was entirely his own: Would he and his shop ever be good enough for her? He saw her biting her lip, a dimple trying desperately to emerge in one of her cheeks.

"What's so funny?" he asked.

"Your face," she replied with a giggle, then her eyes popped wider than should have been humanly possible. "Not that your face is funny looking. It's a very nice face, although if you cleaned up that beard of yours and trimmed your hair, you'd be able to see it better."

"Okay, this started out as an apology, but somehow it turned into an avalanche of criticism," Lucas retorted. "You really don't have a filter, do you?"

"Not even a little bit," she said promptly. "My point was, I could see your hackles go up the second I made some tiny suggestions. Just like mine did when you tried to give me business advice. I landed another party, by the way. One of the moms wants to host a cheese board building party for her ten-year-old's birthday. Georgia and I are cohosting."

"That's great," he said sincerely. Casting a look at the shop behind her, he sighed and picked up the bags again. "I guess adding a few seasonal touches here and there wouldn't hurt. As long as it's tasteful and not too—"

"Cheesy?" she finished for him with a wry twist of her lips.

Lucas snorted. "Well played, Chrystabell. Come on, I'll show you to your room."

He nodded to the staircase with his chin and she held on to the rail carefully with one hand, keeping the other protectively wrapped around the case on her right. As Lucas followed behind her, he chuckled softly to himself. "Let me count the wheys."

"What was that?" she asked over her shoulder at the top step.

"Nothing," he said quickly, an embarrassed flush heating the back of his neck. She already had the upper hand on him. No need to make it worse by letting her know he thought she was as funny as she was smart and beautiful.

The hallway upstairs was small, with two rooms and a single bathroom. Lucas had requisitioned the smaller room—formerly Law's bedroom—into a storage space for broken equipment he planned to fix himself but never got around to, spare aprons and hair coverings and bins full of old issues of *Cheese Club Monthly*. Even the thought of having to go through the flotsam and jetsam of his life was overwhelming and a little depressing, so he had decided to put her in his room and move himself to the construction site behind the shop. Anyway, it was a good excuse to get a closer look at some of the work Law had been doing…and to see what he would have to undo when the space was his.

He opened the door for her, cleared his throat and said, "I hope this will work. It's small, I know, but it's clean and there's a bathroom attached. You can put Bruce Wayne's litter box and food in there."

Lucas held his breath as she walked through the door and looked around. He had never lived with a woman before, excluding his mom. On top of that, she was a pregnant woman. Looking pregnancy needs up on the internet had been an eye-opening and thoroughly terrifying experience that he quickly regretted a few minutes into the search. There hadn't been time to do much of anything except give the room a good thorough cleaning and put on new sheets. Almost as an afterthought he had picked up an extra blanket to put on the foot of the bed. It was made of something called chenille and was a bright scarlet red. Since she had a touch of the color in basically everything she wore, he figured it would do.

She turned around and although Lucas braced himself for whatever obvious detail he should have thought of and missed, Chrysta's face beamed up at him as though he had offered her a palace. "Lucas, it's so cozy. I love it."

His chest dropped as the breath he had been holding finally escaped. "Really? If there's something missing, I can run out and get it later."

Her ponytail swung from side to side as she shook her head. "Given that I've been sleeping next to an army of haunted dolls for two weeks, anything would have been fine. But this—" she did a little twirl with her hands spread out "—is exactly what I need." She knelt down and set Bruce Wayne's carrier on the ground to unzip it. He stepped a hesitant paw out first, followed by a stretch of his round head out of the opening. Seeming to find the initial inspection satisfactory, he walked across the room and leaped onto the windowsill with a grace that Lucas's dancer cousin, Lindsey, would have envied. Turning once in a circle, he settled into the patch of waning sunlight and closed his eyes.

"Wow," Lucas said punctuating the statement with a low whistle. "It seems like Batman won't be taking on the villains of Gotham tonight. I've never seen anything look that instantly relaxed before." It was absurd how he suddenly felt envious of a cat. What must it be like, to feel so content and cared for that you could simply close your eyes and fall asleep instantly? A ridiculous part of him yearned to sit by the window and listen to the rumbling purrs emanating from the small black circle, hoping at least some of its secret magic might rub off on him, too.

"That's one of the things I like about cats," Chrysta said. "It takes so little for them to be happy. A patch of sunlight, a bowl of fresh milk and a warm body to snuggle when they're in the mood for some company."

"I can totally relate to that," Lucas said, before pressing his lips together and wrinkling his nose. "I didn't mean to say that out loud. I meant, that makes sense for a cat. Which I am not."

He turned and jogged back down the steps before she could hex him into further ramblings, but a small smile stayed on his face long after he left her. She had really seemed to like the way he set up the room. He, Lucas, had made her happy. The last time he'd felt this satisfied with himself had been when he had made a block of Roquefort so creamy and tart it belonged in a cheese museum. And tomorrow, every shop owner in town would see her leave in the morning and report back to his parents that he, Lucas, had a live-in girlfriend. This was all going to work out perfectly.

However, the next morning the first person to walk through the door was not Chrysta on her way out. It was Law, banging his way in with his toolbox in one hand and a large breakfast sandwich from Big Joe's diner in the other.

"'Sup, bro," he said, waving his sandwich in greeting.

Lucas shot to his feet behind the counter. "What are you doing here so early? Why didn't you call first? Is there seriously not any cheese on that sandwich at all?" He shook his head at the last question. "Never mind the last one, although I will be having a word with Joe about that abomination later. What are you doing here?" Lucas repeated the most pressing question before tossing a look over his shoulder at the staircase behind him. Chrysta would be coming down to leave for work at the inn any minute.

"I'm working in the kitchen today," he said with an expression on his face that implied Lucas should have already known this information. "I've got a guy coming who does locally sourced quartz slabs for the countertops. He's coming in half an hour to take some measurements."

"Well then, you'd better get back there." Lucas rushed around the corner and crossed the room in three steps to nudge Law toward the back hallway. Standing on his brother's right side, he could at least block his view of the stairway in case Chrysta was on her way.

"All right, all right, I'm going," he said with a

shake of his head. "You know, this kind of customer service might explain why business is so slow."

"Given that you haven't paid for your own cheese in years, I don't think you count as a customer," Lucas called after his brother's retreating shadow.

"Good morning." Chrysta's voice trilled from above him, and Lucas whipped around, throwing both his arms out to the side of the doorway where he stood. She stopped at the bottom of the steps and gave him a warm smile that soothed his panicked heartbeat back to a normal rhythm.

Coming around the corner, she leaned a hand on the counter in front of the cash register and tipped her head to one side. "I slept like a log. It's amazing how much better you sleep when you don't have to keep one eye open to make sure a porcelain Princess Aurora isn't going to steal your soul in the night."

"Uh-huh." Lucas gulped, refusing the temptation to check behind him to make sure Law was hidden away in the back. "I'm—I'm glad." He looked down at his watch. "Oh, it's almost eight o' clock. You know, that's when Georgia takes the first batch of cinnamon spice doughnuts out of the fryer. You don't want to miss that." Practically leaping across the room, he pushed the door open for her and nodded out toward the sidewalk. A blast of air hit him, threatening to turn the sweat beading at his temples into icicles.

Her eyebrows knitted together in confusion. "Um, okay. Well, that does sound good." She started toward the door, then paused and held her finger in the air. "I don't remember if I closed the door to my room." She squinted in concentration, then gave her head a shake. "Nope, definitely don't think I did. I'll just run back up and do that really quickly." She turned, but before Lucas could let out a sigh of relief, she pivoted around again. "And by run, I mean, waddle. And by quickly, I mean I'll probably have to stop to take a bathroom break because there is no ceiling for the number of times this baby does an Irish jig on my bladder."

Lucas laughed along with her, hoping that she wouldn't pick up on the fact that his laugh was about five decibels higher than usual and distinctly tinged with nerves. He dropped his arm and let the door close behind him, allowing his chin to drop to his chest.

"Why is it freezing in here?" Law asked.

Lucas's head jerked up again to see his brother standing in the doorway of the hall on the other side of the counter. "I thought you were working in the kitchen."

"I am," Law answered, then held up both his hands, a piece of tile in each one. "Which do you like better for the backsplash? I can't decide between the black-and-white subway or the mosaic design." He toggled his hands back and forth until Lucas sprinted across the room.

"I completely trust your ability to make this decision on your own," he huffed, placing his hands on his brother's shoulders and steering him around to face away from the shop.

Law swiveled his head around to stare back at Lucas. "Really? Because two seconds ago, you didn't trust my choice in breakfast sandwiches. Not that it makes a difference because I'll be the one using the space. Still—" he tucked the tiles into the back pocket of his jeans and gave Lucas a half smile "—I appreciate you saying that, man."

"Yeah, sure." Lucas nodded while continuing to nudge Law farther back into the corridor. "Anytime. Okay then, off you go. Lots of work to do, better get at it. You don't want to keep your granite guy waiting."

"Quartz," Law corrected him with a snort. "It really is a good thing I'm the one doing the work back there. You wouldn't know a sconce from a scone." He snorted as he headed back through the door. "I should write this stuff down."

Feeling more drained than a sliced-open burrata, Lucas walked back into the shop and plopped wearily down on the stool behind the counter, only to stumble back to his feet when Chrysta appeared at the bottom of the steps once again with her red coat draped over her arm.

"The room is secure, Captain," she said with a small salute of her gloved hand. "The door was actually closed, but then I left it open while I was going to the bathroom and wouldn't you know just as I was washing my hands, Bruce Wayne tried to make a run for it."

"You don't say," Lucas said, brushing his hand through his hair and gripping it to keep his anxiety from releasing out of his head in a yelp. "Well, good thing you caught him. Have a great day at the—"

"Would you mind if I go back and raid your storeroom?" she interrupted him, pointing at the refrigerated cabinet behind the counter. "I put everything I need for the party tonight on the email I sent you, but I wanted to see if you had any olives."

"I—" Lucas could have sworn he heard footsteps coming from the back space. "I think I have some in the pantry. I'll get them for you and bring them by the inn later with the rest of the supplies."

"Oh, it's no trouble," she said, as she put one arm through her coat with agonizing slowness. "I'll just pop in and get them."

"We'll go together," Lucas said, putting his

arm around her shoulders and walking behind the counter to push the pantry door open with his left hand. "It will be fun. Like a field trip."

"I mean, my class went to the Huntsville Zoo, but sure, the pantry could be educational," she said.

He flicked the light on and rummaged through the shelves. "Ah, here you go! Olives." Holding up the jar in triumph, Lucas winced at the ache in his jaw from his teeth grinding together.

"Do you have any pimentos?" she asked with a blink of those wide eyes. "Those are kalamatas."

He bit his lip to keep from sighing in exasperation, turned back to the shelf and scanned its contents. A sudden banging from the adjoining wall startled him and he clocked his head on the shelf in alarm.

"What was that?" Chrysta asked.

"Um, rodents?" Lucas pulled his head out, rubbing the tender spot that had made contact with the wooden shelf. "Large ones. Aggressive ones. Big enough to eat Batman. I mean, Cat Man. I mean, Bruce Wayne."

The banging sounded again and Chrysta folded her arms, lowering her chin as she waited for him to come up with a credible response.

"I'm having some work done on the space behind the shop," he answered, somewhat truthfully. "My parents used to live there, but since they're moving, we figured it was a good time to update it." Holding her eye contact, he reached an arm back into the shelf and pulled out a jar, hoping it was the right one. "Aha. Pimento olives. There you go."

"Hmmm," Chrysta murmured. She took the jar from his hand, but didn't appear convinced. "Who is we?"

"Me...myself, and I?" He shrugged. "Anyway, it won't bother you, since you'll be at the inn and they'll be gone long before you get home. I mean, back here. Not that this is your home. What kind of home for a family would this be? Maybe a family of mice. Because mice like cheese. Probably explains the rodents. Oh, my. Look at the time." He held up his wrist without actually looking at the watch. "You don't want to be late for work. Mrs. Van Ressler is a stickler for punctuality."

Chrysta narrowed her eyes, but walked out of the pantry. As she headed toward the door, she gestured at Lucas with the jar of olives. "Thanks for these. I'll see you later at the inn when you drop off the cooler with the cheese for the party."

"Yup." Lucas stayed close behind her, making sure that she didn't have the chance to turn around again. "I'll see you then. Not before that, though, right? You won't need to come back and change or anything."

"No, I'm just wearing this." She swept a hand down her black dress. When she stepped onto the sidewalk, she put her hand on Lucas's arm that held the door open for her. "Lucas, I want you to tell me if you're having second thoughts about me living here, okay? You can talk to me if anything is bothering you. I—I'd like to think that we're friends by now, right?"

By this point, Lucas couldn't tell if the pounding was coming from his brother's hammering or inside his own head. Yet there was something in Chrysta's voice, a sincere note of comfort that pierced through the chaos of the morning. He met her eyes and focused on her and only her. "I'm glad you're here. I like having you around." This wasn't close to the truth. It was the truth.

She flashed a smile that warmed him more than the sun rising over the pitched roofs of the storefronts on the other side of the street. "Good. I like being here with you."

As Chrysta headed down the sidewalk, Lucas closed the door, then leaned against it, his shoulders sagging with exhaustion.

He was going into his cheese cave and never coming out again.

LATER THAT EVENING he was cheddaring blocks of freshly salted curds when he heard a knock on the doorframe outside his workshop.

"It's Chrysta."

Lucas hadn't expected her back from the party so soon. For once, this was a surprise he liked. "Grab a head covering and come in," he called out.

She stuck her head through the middle of the joined curtains, the hair covering adorably askew. "I don't want to interrupt if you're busy."

He shook his head. "Nope. Just finished cheddaring."

"I was today years old when I learned that cheddaring is a verb." She grinned. The rest of her pushed through the curtain, her belly protruding first. Closing it behind her, she lifted her chin and peered at his table. "Ooh, that's a pretty color. What did you mix that with?"

"Bacon jam," he answered proudly. "Can't you just picture that melted onto a slice of crusty bread with hot tomato soup?"

"Oh, stop," she moaned, putting both hands on her stomach. "I'm starving. I had an early dinner before the party. Speaking of dinner…" She snapped her fingers in the air and walked over to stand next to the long metal table where he was flipping his curds. "Bill stopped by the inn to invite us over for dinner tomorrow night. Our ruse must be working. He said he and Bee-Bee are so excited to have another couple to go on double dates with. Their last one was with Joe Kim and his supplier and apparently it did not end well?" She grimaced. "Anyway, they think we're an item, so word's getting around."

She smiled at him, but there was something else in her eyes. Lucas had a hunch it was the same thing giving him indigestion at the moment.

"I don't like being dishonest either, but it's only for a little while," he said, giving the curds another toss and landing them on the table with a thud. "I really appreciate you doing this for me." He braced one hand on the corner of the table.

"It's not so bad." She shrugged. "We're not necessarily lying outright. People make assumptions and we're not correcting them. Besides, you're putting a roof over my head. The least I can do is let our friends think we're madly in love." She trailed one finger along the long end of the table as she took another step closer to him. "Have you ever been in love? I mean, I know you've had relationships before. But that's different than being in love."

Lucas huffed out a small breath and looked up at the ceiling. "I thought I was when I was with Sarah. My ex, whom we saw the other night," he added before looking back down into her gaze. "Looking back, though, I don't think it was love so much as wanting to be in love. My parents have been married for over thirty-five years. I wanted that—I want that," he corrected. "I want to find the person who accepts me just as I am. The person who will pick me first every time, even when there are plenty of other guys out there who are better looking or more charming or who get them chocolates on Valentine's Day instead of a box of assorted artisanal cheeses."

"I get it," she said. "It's hard putting yourself out there. Making the effort even though you don't think people will go for it."

"We're not just talking about relationships anymore, are we?"

"I could tell you were put off by what I said yesterday," she said. "I have a habit of saying everything that pops into my head, and sometimes it comes out wrong."

"I have the exact opposite condition," he said. "I second-guess everything in my head before I say it. Don't know which is worse."

"What I meant was that if you gave people a chance to see your passion for cheese, maybe even have a little fun with it, they might surprise you with how much they'd be into it."

"This isn't a party game for me, Chrystabell," he shot back with more intensity than he'd expected. "Cheese is…it's my work, my life, my—"

"Heart?" she finished for him. "I know that. I also know that hiding your true self away because you're afraid of rejection doesn't work, either. I spent months pretending to be someone

I wasn't to try to please Alastair, to justify my mistake of rushing into a marriage that was a mistake. But then I realized it was better to be on my own than to constantly walk around on eggshells, afraid to say what I really thought. Stop holding back, Lucas. Share your heart with the people around you." She took another small step forward, her hand gliding along the edge of the counter until it reached his. Then she swallowed and said in a lowered voice, "The people who care about you."

When her fingers found his, it was a touch so light, so small it was as much a whisper as the last words she said. Yet that small touch said so much more than words could. Because it wasn't for the show they were putting on for his parents' spies. It wasn't for anyone else but him. In that moment, she chose him for that intimate, trusting gesture. She chose him.

It ended almost as quickly as it happened. She pulled her hand away, put it back on its usual spot on her belly and walked back through the curtain, muttering something about needing to find food. But something had shifted between them.

Somehow, somewhere along the way, this relationship had stopped feeling fake.

At least it had for him.

CHAPTER TEN

CHRYSTA HAD KNOWN the Crystal Hill Dairy Farm wasn't your average farm.

After all, BeeBee had talked at length about her water buffalo pretty much every time Chrysta had met her. But there was talking about them and then there was actually experiencing them face to shaggy face.

"You know, I think there's a family resemblance with the facial hair," she teased Lucas, holding her hands up like a pretend camera lens going from the water buffalo to him and back again.

He grunted and smoothed a hand over his beard. "Hmph. Do you hear that, Fernando? I think we're being insulted." Reaching out to pat the creature's large nose through the wire fence, Lucas leaned in and whispered to it. "I know, buddy. People think big guys like us don't have feelings. You tell Uncle Lucas all about it."

Chrysta threw her head back and groaned, but not because Lucas was giving her snark right back. It was because every time she was around him, he did or said something that made him even more endearing. How was she supposed to maintain a professional relationship with a man who made cheese and whispered soothing words to a water buffalo? She had to put a stop to this crush before it ruined everything.

"You know," she said, touching Lucas on the arm, "I used to cut hair for the guys I worked with in yachting. I could give you a little trim if you want to look extra special for anything… or anyone. A real date with a woman you really like someday down the road."

She was desperately trying to give herself a hard dose of reality. A reminder that this was all pretend. But that went out the window as she touched the muscled forearm hidden under long flannel sleeves, crashed on the ground at the thought of him with anyone else and burst into flames when he leveled his piercing eyes directly on her.

"I can't think of anyone I need to get barbered up for," he said. "That's the whole reason we're doing this, remember? Cheese hermit for life?" He shook his head. "Maybe I should get a sign for my cheese cave that says Abandon All Romantic Hope Ye Who Enter Here."

"That sounds more like a cheese pirate," she quipped.

"I'll leave the piracy to that guy." He nodded

as Bill and BeeBee walked hand in hand out of the milking stand behind the barn. "I may hoard my cheese, but at least I do it honestly. Speaking of hair, yours looks really nice today."

Chrysta ran a hand through her long, straight hair. She had worn it down today, thanks to a slight, but persistent headache that had started that morning. Typically she liked wearing it up. It made her feel powerful, like a Norse warrior woman. But the way Lucas was looking at her now made her want to throw away her entire collection of hair ties, scrunchies and every bobby pin rattling around the bottom of her purse. Her cheeks warmed and she ducked her head behind the curtain of hair so he wouldn't see her blush.

"What are you two whispering about?" Bill asked, leaning on the fence post of the gate with one hand, still holding BeeBee's in the other.

Chrysta pointed at Lucas. "He called you a pirate."

"Wow," Lucas said, turning his head away from the water buffalo to look at her. "You're just gonna throw me under the bus like that." He gave her that full nose-crinkling smile that shot straight into her belly and warmed her from the inside out like a cup of hot chocolate. "I guess the honeymoon's over, huh."

"Honeymoon..." Chrysta tapped her chin with one finger thoughtfully. "Is that what the ride in your truck was? I thought it seemed strange that you spread out rose petals on the dashboard."

BeeBee snorted. "Oh my gosh, I love her. And also, I call Bill a pirate all the time, for the record. I even got him a toy parrot for his first dinner cruise."

"The only thing I ever stole was your heart." Bill winked at her.

BeeBee groaned. "You are such a dork." But her cheeks flushed bright pink, and she ducked her head briefly on Bill's shoulder before looking at Lucas. "Stop messing with my water buffalo and come in for dinner, Lucas. Bill's been slaving over a hot oven all day, and you know how cranky pirates get when their crème anglaise separates."

As BeeBee and Bill headed arm in arm back toward the house, Lucas smiled down at Chrysta. "Are you ready to do this?"

"Pretend to be a couple in front of our friends who are the poster children for madly in love?" She shrugged. "I do like a challenge."

Lucas held out his arm and lifted his chin in the air. "Then let's show them how it's done, Snoogie-Woogie Bean."

"Snoogie-Woogie Bean?"

Supporting her arm as they trudged through the half-frozen layers of mud and ice, he opened the gate with his other hand. "I figured if we're so in love that we already moved in together, we probably would have pet names for each other."

"And Snoogie-Woogie Bean is the choice?" Chrysta shivered and wrapped her arms around herself as he closed the gate. "You're standing by that?"

"Hmm," Lucas murmured under his breath. He draped one arm around her shoulders and pulled her close to him. The instant warmth was heaven. She couldn't stop herself from snuggling in against his chest. "Okay, so not Snoogie-Woogie Bean. How about Sugar Dumpling? You're from the South. That sounds like a Southern-style term of endearment."

She snorted. "The sad fact is you're not wrong. My mom used to call my dad 'Pudding Pie.'" The memory made her heart throb, so she shook her head. "Keep working, Cheese Hermit."

"Okay, I may not be great at this romance stuff, but I know Cheese Hermit isn't a term of endearment," he shot back indignantly.

"I don't know," she said. They reached the porch, and she hopped up the first two steps before turning to face him, for once at eye level. She put both hands behind his neck. "Cheese hermits need love too, you know. Plus, I already told you I think a cheese cave could be a perfect love nest. Just needs a woman's touch." She played with his hair that curled slightly just above the collar of his jacket. Their faces were so close, the visible cloud puffs of their breath in the cold merged together as one.

He gave a small grunt and swallowed hard.

Chrysta's heart pounded against her chest with an urgency she had never known before. Right here, right now, this feeling wasn't pretend. It was as clear as the glass creations in the inn's lobby.

She liked Lucas.

In every sense of the word, she liked him. In the champagne-bubbles-tingling-beneath-her-skin-at-his-touch sense, and also in the sense that she respected the man that he was and the way he treated the people around him. He was so different from Alastair's overwhelming charm and the grand romantic gestures that had seemed so sincere until she learned he had done the same things for all his women. The "spontaneous" trips to Paris on the private jet. The daily bouquets of flowers. The heart-shaped diamond necklace. Lucas didn't show affection effusively or easily. Yet when he did open up, it was personal and real. It was pregnancy-safe cheese made by his own hands. It was making sure she was always warm and taken care of. It was putting a blanket on the bed in her favorite color.

Lucas opened his mouth to say something,

and Chrysta held her breath just before the door behind them suddenly flew open with a creak. "Come inside, you loony lovebirds," BeeBee called out. "It's freezing out here."

Whatever he had been about to say vanished in the gust of wind that nearly knocked Chrysta off her feet.

After sitting down to a sumptuous dinner of coq au vin over creamy parsnip puree, Bill raised his glass of sparkling cider to Lucas and Chrysta.

"I know I already said this to Chrysta, but I'm so happy that two of my favorite people are now a couple," he said. His face beamed from the light of the candles standing in a neat row in the center of the table.

Lucas and Chrysta exchanged glances.

"Um, yeah," Lucas said, clearing his throat between syllables. "We are that. A couple…of people. People who enjoy spending their time together and, um, sharing things and, erm, doing…stuff."

Chrysta looked down at her hands clenched together in her lap and fought the urge to groan audibly. Lucas was clearly still uncomfortable over fake dating in front of their friends. It was painful to watch someone she cared about struggle, especially when it might not even be necessary anymore. Tonight she would do it. When they got back to the cheese shop, she was going to tell him that she had real feelings for him. There was something between them, she knew it. He couldn't fake the way he looked at her. Not a guy as genuine and sincere as Lucas.

BeeBee wrinkled her nose at him. "What is going on with you? Why are you being such a weirdo tonight?"

"I'm always a weirdo," Lucas shot back indignantly. "You used to call me your weirdo cheese maker cousin. This isn't any different than that."

"Your water buffalo are beautiful, BeeBee," Chrysta interjected. Lucas's ears were turning a startling shade of crimson. If someone didn't change the subject, she was afraid steam would come out of them. "What's the baby's name again?"

"Rodolfo," she replied, the expression on her face melting into one of maternal pride. "Oh, he did the cutest thing the other day. I took some pictures." BeeBee scrolled through her phone, then held it up to display several photos of a water buffalo calf in the barn doing absolutely nothing.

"So cute." Chrysta smiled indulgently. In less than two months, she would probably be holding up her phone to show pictures of her own baby blowing spit bubbles and finding it no less thrilling. "He should be the ring bearer at your wedding."

BeeBee gasped with delight at the same time that Bill threw his hands in the air.

"Why would you do that to me?" He pushed his chair back and stood to begin gathering the emptied plates. "I thought we were friends. I picked you up from the airport, and this is how you thank me?"

"We could put a little top hat on him," BeeBee said with a sparkle in her eyes that implied she knew she was pushing her fiancé's buttons and enjoying every second. "Have Jeremy Binkus walk him down the aisle on a lead."

Bill sighed as he leaned over BeeBee to pick up her plate. "You know I can't say no to you," he whispered and dropped a kiss on her cheek before standing up. "But I can say no to the buffalo in a top hat on my special day."

As he went into the kitchen, BeeBee leaned her elbow on the table and grinned wickedly at Chrysta. "I love to tease him about being such a groomzilla. He's even doing the food for our engagement party because he doesn't trust anyone else to make it. I told him he needs to be able to enjoy it too and not spend the whole time in the kitchen, but apparently neither Joe Kim's nor Renata's food is special enough."

"Well…" Chrysta sat back in her chair and

threaded her fingers together over her satisfied belly. The baby hadn't moved for a while, but that was pretty normal after a big meal. He or she was probably a foodie just like her. "If you're still interested, I could help. Georgia and I have been doing some light catering as part of my cheese board parties. We found that passing out appetizers before I do the demonstrations helps keep people from eating the supplies they need to build their boards."

Bill emerged from the kitchen with a dish towel over one shoulder. "That would work, actually," he said thoughtfully. "We were kind of going with a royal wedding theme for the party anyway to celebrate BeeBee as Queen of the Dairy. You know, tea sandwiches, small baskets of fish and chips. I just got a new deep fryer for next season's dinner cruises."

"BeeBee, does that work for you?" Chrysta nodded at the bride-to-be, who shrugged.

"It's his day, he can fry if he wants to," she said, turning her head to blow a kiss at Bill, who blushed happily. "Seriously, though, that would be awesome. My friends would love it and since I'm not exactly Betty Hostess, it would really take the pressure off from me having to entertain everybody." Her lips tugged down on one side. "It's at the rec center on Sunday, February

10. Would you be able to have everything ready in ten days?"

"Of course," Chrysta and Lucas answered at the same time. Her cheeks flooded with warmth as Lucas's hand rested on hers for a moment.

BeeBee chuckled. "Look at you guys. Such a great couple."

Bill stood behind her and placed his hands on BeeBee's shoulders. "They really are. Which makes it a shame that we're going to have to kick their butts in Heads Up!"

Lucas narrowed his eyes. Hunching forward, he muttered, "No one said anything about games."

"So?" Chrysta asked. "What's wrong with games? I love games."

"Yeah, probably because you're amazing at them and win all of them," Lucas said. "They're not so much fun if you lose every time."

"Aww, that's so nice of you to say," she said. "I am, in fact, amazing at them. And now that we're a couple, you will be too, my little grufflesmoosh."

He stood up first, then offered his hand to her. "Fine. I'll play." As she took his hand and scooted to the edge of her chair for more momentum—pregnancy really did add an extra layer of difficulty to everything—she smiled up at him and he shook his head, adding, "I think you'd better leave the nicknames to me, Chrystabell.

Grufflesmoosh sounds like a monster from a children's book."

"But a cute, furry monster," she said once she stood, stroking the side of his face with one hand.

The satisfied growl he gave as he followed her into the living room was enough to send her confidence soaring through the ceiling. The confidence in their strength as a couple in parlor games grew as they kept neck and neck with BeeBee and Bill, who were so like-minded it was as if they were the two-headed monster from *Sesame Street*. By the final round, they were tied. Chrysta had never seen Lucas so invested in anything that didn't originate from an udder.

"Okay, she's an actress, really pretty," Chrysta said to Lucas as he held the phone over his head with an increasingly bemused expression on his face. "She was in the Avengers movies."

"Lucas hasn't been out to see a movie since he was nine," BeeBee heckled.

Lucas narrowed his eyes, but didn't take his focus off Chrysta's face. "Ignore her. Keep going. We've got this."

"Ummm." Chrysta racked her brain, and then the lightbulb clicked. "Her first name is your favorite dessert cheese."

"Brie Larson," Lucas said instantly.

"Yes!" Lucas pumped one fist in the air, while holding the cell phone up on his forehead with the other, then pointed one finger at Bill. "Last one. When we win this, I'm going to do my victory dance for five straight minutes."

"Oh, no. Not the dance." Bill groaned. "I hoped never to see that again after our color war victory at Camp Herkimer. It changed my view of you, and not for the better."

"All right." Chrysta rubbed her palms together as the next word flashed on the screen. "Um, the Smithsonian Institute. The Rocky Mountains. It's the name of a Nicolas Cage movie where he overexaggerates every word."

"That's every Nicolas Cage movie."

"Fair point." Chrysta scrunched up her face in concentration.

"Twenty seconds," BeeBee warned.

"Michelle Kwan!" Chrysta burst out in desperation.

"*National Treasure!*" Lucas shouted as he jumped to his feet.

"Yes!" Chrysta pushed more slowly to standing, but once she was up, grabbed his hands and jumped up and down excitedly.

Lucas released Chrysta's hands only to wrap his arms around her and lift her up, spinning her around, then abruptly putting her down like he had just remembered there was a carton of eggs in the grocery bag he was carrying. "I'm so sorry. Are you all right?"

Chrysta shook her head, laughing. "I'm fine, silly. I'm pregnant, not made of glass."

Lucas grinned broadly and Chrysta's heart cracked open at a fault line she hadn't known existed. "Phew. Now that I know I didn't break you—" he whirled around and pointed one finger at BeeBee "—you know what's coming, cuz."

She backed away, holding up both hands. "No, don't dance. Please. I'll give you a discount on milk. I'll name my firstborn son after you."

Bill, who was sitting on the couch, jerked his head up sharply. "What now?"

"Oh, you know we only have girl babies in this town." BeeBee shushed him. "It'll be fine."

Chrysta couldn't stop giggling as Lucas performed what could only be described as a choreographed seizure, but with more gyrating. Once he had finished, he and Bill retreated to the kitchen to clean the dishes and discuss wedding details.

BeeBee and Chrysta adjourned to the porch where they had set up space heaters to combat the freezing temperatures. The moonlight lit the frost-tipped field, which sparkled like millions of tiny diamond chips sprinkled on the ground.

BeeBee handed Chrysta one of the thick wool

blankets she had carried out under her arm. They draped the soft knit fabric over their laps and sat in the rocking chairs with cups of warm tea.

"You and Lucas are really a great pair," Bee-Bee said, blowing steam off her mug. "Bill was surprised that you guys were already moving in together, but I always had a feeling that when Lucas met the right one, he would know immediately."

"Yeah," Chrysta said, looking down into her mug as if there were still tea leaves in there that could predict the future. "Except…"

BeeBee tipped her head to one side. "Except what?"

"Except…" Chrysta drew a deep breath, a small pang of indigestion hitting her side. She set her cup down on her lap and looked over at BeeBee. "I still feel like he's keeping me at a distance. Emotionally, even physically sometimes. Like the other day, he literally wouldn't let me into the space behind the shop even though there were strange noises coming from back there. Sometimes I can tell there's something he wants to say, but he stops himself." The truth came out of her in a rush. "I really care about him. He has to know it. So what's holding him back?"

BeeBee's forehead wrinkled as she furrowed her eyebrows. Sighing heavily, she looked out over the moonlit pastures as she spoke. "There's something very important you have to understand about Lucas. He is, without question, one of my favorite people in the world. He's kind, he's loyal, he'll literally do anything to help the people he cares about, and best of all, he truly appreciates and respects good quality dairy." She ticked off the list on her fingers before pausing and looking over at Chrysta with a grin. "But he's also a gigantic dummy."

"I'm sorry?" Chrysta said, covering her mouth after nearly spitting out her sip of tea. Wiping her lips with her sleeve, she closed her eyes and shook her head. "What do you mean?"

"Lucas Carl could feel an aged Fontina and tell you the current price of that particular wheel blindfolded, but he has no clue of his own worth," BeeBee said. "Somewhere along the way, he became convinced that no woman will ever want him because he doesn't ooze charm out of every pore or because his idea of a romantic evening is a night in his cheese lab experimenting with different flavor profiles and pairings."

Chrysta huffed. "Sounds romantic enough to me." Seriously. What woman wouldn't be fascinated by a man like that?

"And that's why you two are so great together." BeeBee set her mug down and leaned over the arm of her chair toward Chrysta to look at her intently. "I've never seen Lucas as happy as he looked with you tonight. It may not seem like it, but he really has opened himself up to you more than he has with anyone else."

"Even his ex, Sarah?"

BeeBee's eyes widened. "You know about Sarah?"

Chrysta nodded.

BeeBee leaned back in her chair and shrugged. "If you ask me, Lucas was too good for her. I went to high school with her, a few grades below. She was nice enough, but there was something about her that always reminded me of one of those animal predators from the nature channel. Like a lioness who goes after the weak gazelle in the herd. She pounced on Lucas immediately after his last girlfriend had broken up with him. Eventually she got bored and went on the prowl again. I just didn't think she was mean enough to go after Lucas's own brother."

Chrysta planted both feet on the wooden planks of the porch, stopping the chair mid rock. Surely she hadn't heard right. "His brother?"

"Yeah, Lawson. Well, Lucas is the only one who calls him that." BeeBee smiled to herself. "You probably noticed our town has a thing for nicknames. Everyone besides Lucas calls him Law. Law doesn't just ooze charm. He's, like, radioactive with it. You can practically see his charm glowing like a raccoon who wandered into Five Mile Island. Anyway, after Lucas and Sarah broke up, I took him out to Mama Renata's for a consolation pizza. That's where we saw the two of them—Law and Sarah—all cozied up in a corner booth together."

"That's…that's awful." Almost as awful as falling for a guy who she knew so little about that she hadn't even known he had a brother. "Did they date for a long time afterward?"

"They didn't really date at all, aside from that one time," BeeBee said. "That's typical of Law, though. Ever since high school, his relationship status has been one rotating girlfriend after another. Just last week, I saw him out with Ada Brunner, another woman Lucas put on a pedestal even though they never actually dated. It's typical for siblings to feel compared with each other. I've felt like the weak link in our chain more than once." She chuckled. "But Lucas takes everything so seriously. I swear he thinks that because Law is some epic ladies' man that he'll never be able to compete, so he stopped trying. When Aunt Rose—Lucas's mom—got sick, he took over the shop for his dad and basically became married to his work. No woman had a chance, at least not until you came along." Bee-Bee raised her mug in a toast.

Chrysta held her mug up to BeeBee's for a clink even though celebrating felt like the last thing she wanted to do at the moment. She had been fooling herself. Again. Lucas didn't want a relationship with her. People in real relationships introduced their significant others to their siblings who lived in the same town. People in real relationships didn't keep their homes and lives behind closed doors. He really was just sticking to the plan. Chrysta inhaled deeply through her nose, the cold air burning all the way in. Good. She deserved it for letting her guard down and opening herself up to being let down again. Her focus needed to be on hosting her cheese board parties and moving out before this baby arrived. That wasn't very long, but with the money from a gig as big as Bill and BeeBee's engagement party, she could make it happen. She would make it happen, all on her own.

No man required.

Chrysta put her hand on the arm of the rocking chair to lift herself to a stand, setting the mug on the rail of the porch. The blanket fell to the ground and she started to bend to get it, but a sharp pain in her side caught her midcrouch.

"Don't worry about that." BeeBee popped out of her chair and put her hand on Chrysta's arm, swooping down to retrieve the blanket. "Are you all right? You look pale."

"I'm fine," Chrysta lied, holding her side with

one hand. "Just tired. And gassy. In other words, eight months and change pregnant."

"Do you want some warm milk?" BeeBee asked, holding the door open with one hand, the blankets draped over the other arm she extended toward Chrysta. "I've got cow's milk, water buffalo milk, even almond milk since Lou was home from college for Christmas break and making these weird nondairy smoothies." She wrinkled her nose. "Nondairy. It's blasphemous, is what it is."

"We really should be going," Chrysta replied quickly. "I'll get Lucas out of the kitchen."

BeeBee snorted. "Good luck with that. You know how it is once they get going with their manly shop talk."

They both leaned into the doorway to overhear Bill say to Lucas, "So, for the reception appetizers I was thinking about an amuse-bouche of goat cheese panna cotta with an elderflower jelly on top, but I'm worried the floral notes of the elderflower will clash with the scent from the lilac centerpieces."

"Oh, I don't think so," Lucas said. "Those are complementary floral notes. I mean, it's not like you're pairing goat cheese with carnations. That reminds me, I have a goat-milk hand soap I got at a dairy convention last year. It really helps with the winter dryness."

"Aww, thanks, dude," Bill said.

BeeBee jerked her thumb over her shoulder in the direction of the men's voices. "See what I mean?"

Chrysta sighed. If Lucas could just stop being adorable for two seconds so she could end this whole pretend relationship before he pretended to get down on one knee and they pretended to live happily ever after.

As BeeBee predicted, it did seem to take an eternity to get Lucas out of the house and into the truck. Of course, it might only have seemed that way because Chrysta's gnawing unease grew with every passing second. She couldn't tell him she was starting to have real feelings for him because they were still living together and working together on her parties. She didn't want things to get weird between them. The situation was weird enough as it was already. Best to stick to an abbreviated version of the plan. BeeBee was without a doubt one of the key members of the spy ring. Since she and Bill had bought the ruse, that should be sufficient evidence for his mom to relax and get off his case. It wasn't quitting. It was declaring an early victory.

She turned to face Lucas as he flicked on the truck's headlights and started to slowly roll out of the driveway. "That went well tonight, didn't it?"

"It did." He nodded, then said softly, "I never

knew a couples' game night could actually be fun. Or any game night." His eyes caught her gaze and held it with an open tenderness that nearly broke her. "I guess it helps to have the right partner."

She swallowed hard. Those ocean-blue eyes of his were dangerous waters. "I wanted to talk to you about the next phase of the plan. The engagement."

"Me, too." He smiled at her. "What do you think about waiting until after BeeBee's party to announce it? I don't want to steal their thunder. Even if we need to extend the deadline past Valentine's Day—"

"No," Chrysta responded quickly. "Stick to the plan. Hard deadline of Valentine's Day." Her resolve was already weakening. Knowing Lucas, he would probably come up with some thoughtful, cheese-based Valentine's gift that would push her beyond the boundaries of her little crush and into full-on infatuation.

Or even worse, love.

"I'll stick to the plan," he replied, but she could tell from his eyes there was so much more he wanted to say. Before she could encourage him to let it out however, she gasped.

Lucas slammed on the brakes as she doubled over and clutched her belly where a tight stab of pain felt like an invisible vise had just tightened. "Chrysta, talk to me. What's wrong? Is it the baby?"

"I don't know, but oooh, this really hurts." She looked at him, hoping the feeling of safety and reassurance that she always found in him would quell the rising panic inside her heart.

His eyes doubled in size before he turned them back to the road, his jaw set in a determined grip. "We're going to the hospital. Hold on."

Chrysta braced herself against the dashboard with one hand, holding her belly with the other as he slammed on the gas, the sound of gravel spitting against the tires echoing in the snow-muffled air.

CHAPTER ELEVEN

IT WAS NEARLY sunrise by the time they returned to the dairy shop, but Lucas wasn't flipping the sign to Open anytime soon. At this moment, Lucas couldn't have cared less about supplying the town with milk or yogurt or even cheese. The only thing that mattered was the woman he supported with one arm around her waist and the other under her arm. He didn't even realize he was practically lifting her up the stairs until she said wearily, "I can walk up the small flight of stairs. The doctor just put me on modified bed rest for my elevated blood pressure. You squeezing me like a boa constrictor with abandonment issues isn't helping. It's worse than the Braxton-Hicks I was having."

He could tell she was exhausted because she allowed her Southern accent to take over from her usually controlled pronunciation. The honey-thick slowing of her voice combined with the smell of magnolias wafting from her soft loose hair only made him want to hold her closer. Instead, he loosened his grip, only slightly. "Sorry about that," Lucas said, his own voice gravelly from the strain of the long night. "I just want to make sure you don't fall."

The past eight hours had been a whirlwind of beeping monitors and various people in scrubs using words he didn't understand. Chrysta had taken it all in stride, staying calm and even cracking jokes with the nurses. If he hadn't already been dumbfounded by her strength, tonight would have done it. The doctors had given her a medication through an IV that had stopped the contractions almost immediately, and when the doctors showed her that the baby was all right on the ultrasound, Chrysta went back into her default planning mode, leaving a message for Mrs. Van Ressler that she wouldn't be in to work in the morning, rearranging her cheese board party schedule for the week and setting up her appointment with a high-risk pregnancy doctor for the next day. Contractions, even practice ones, had barely slowed her down.

Lucas, on the other hand, felt like his entire world had frozen the moment he saw that tiny shape appear on the ultrasound screen. It was real. He had known there was a baby in there, obviously. As clueless as his ex may have accused him of being, there were limits to his obtuseness. But since he wasn't really a visual guy, it was hard to picture an actual human being. The whole thing had seemed more theoretical than anything else. But now…now it was all so different and amazing and terrifying. A wolfish protectiveness had engulfed him when the little hand had seemed to wave right at him. He would have covered Chrysta with his body as a human shield for the next seven weeks if he needed to. She would have complained about his itchy beard after five seconds, but still.

Chrysta fell into bed fully clothed and after Lucas closed the door to her room, he stood in the hallway for a moment, just in case she called out for him. After several minutes, her even breaths lapsed into gentle snoring. He started to make his way down the stairs, but somehow he couldn't let himself be that far away from her and the baby. Lucas sat at the top of the steps and put his head in his hands. He wasn't cut out for this, clearly. One minor incident and he was completely unglued, unable to even think about work or anything else. How could he take care of them when he felt so helpless? How could he act like everything was fine when any second the people he loved could be hurt, or worse?

The thought made Lucas raise his head just in time to see the first sunrays beam through the front window of the shop below. No. It wasn't possible. He had only known Chrysta a few weeks and the baby wasn't ever going to be his to love, to hold, to raise. Chrysta had been very clear about this being a business arrangement from the very beginning. She had plenty to worry about without him developing some stupid crush. He would stick to her plan and put his feelings away, like he always did. The most important thing right now was making sure she and the baby had everything they needed. She didn't need a husband or a father for her baby, especially not one who fell apart at the first hint of trouble. What he could do—the only thing he could do—was make sure she didn't worry about her new business going under.

Putting a hand on each knee, he stood and jogged lightly down the steps so his normally heavy footfall didn't wake her. He had work to do.

A lot of work, it turned out. Chrysta had made her party-hosting business look so effortless and, well, fun, that he had blithely assumed that he could take over the planning so that all she had to do was log on and host her next party remotely from her bed. But as he quickly discovered, it was so much more than simply gathering the right cheeses. There were moving parts like props, plastic boards, knowing which flowers were edible and which would result in ridiculously bad stomach cramps (something he learned the hard way after saying he'd take over for her). He had to follow up on RSVPs so that he didn't risk the choice between wasting good cheese and—literally—eating her profits. Several of the guests at Mrs. Moffat's retirement cheese board party had arthritis, so they needed special adaptive equipment to pick up and arrange the small cubes, not to mention nearly all of them had dietary restrictions. Between running his shop and running Chrysta's errands, Lucas's head felt like it was going to explode with details, something he had never been very good at anyway.

Making matters worse, it seemed like every time he left the shop to pick something up for her, he returned to find it a little different than he had left it. Chrysta was allowed to go up and down the stairs on a limited basis. Apparently, she thought the best use of that time was to meddle in his shop. It had started with the decor, changes so subtle he hadn't even noticed for the first day or so. She had replaced the labels on the shelves that stated the ages of the cheese with heart-shaped stickers. That hadn't really bothered him. The next day he had been restocking the condiments when he realized that some of them had been moved to the cheese shelves with little cardboard cupids between each condiment and the cheeses that, admittedly, paired nicely with them. That was a little cutesy for his taste, but he had simply shrugged his shoulders and gone back down to his cave to turn his wheels so they aged evenly. On Wednesday, though, he was finally driven to say something. He had driven all the way out to Bath to pick up the edible flowers she needed for her party on Friday and returned to find a group of boys from the high school hockey team clustered around the front counter, where Chrysta was seated in the rolling desk chair Lucas had gotten her so she wouldn't be on her feet too much when she came down to the shop.

"So, after you've rolled the cheese slice— make sure you find out what kind is her favorite because Lucas can slice any kind you like— that's when you add the pepperoni petals," she said to a chorus of impressed "ooohs" from the gaggle of tall hoodie-clad teenagers.

"What is going on here?" Lucas asked, setting the bag of violets down on the floor.

"Ms. Ball is showing us how to make charcuterie bouquets," one of the kids said without turning around.

"That brings up more questions than it answers, the main one being why?" Lucas looked down at Chrysta from under raised eyebrows.

She used the breadstick in her right hand to point to the boy who had just spoken. "Kayden messaged me on Instagram asking if I could show him how because his girlfriend is obsessed with charcuterie boards and he thought it would be sweet to incorporate one into a Valentine's Day date. I told him to stop by the shop today and I would help him out."

Another one of the boys turned around and tipped his head back to shake his floppy hair out of his face. "When Kay told us about it after practice yesterday, we all decided to come, too. Most of our girlfriends' moms were at the last cheese board party and now all the girls are posting charcuterie board videos." He grinned. "I'm going to make a board that spells out my girlfriend's name in Gouda."

Lucas cleared his throat. "Um, Chrysta, can I speak to you for a moment in my cheese lab?"

"Sure." She put her breadstick and mozzarella flower down on the counter, then looked at the boys. "Can one of you nice young men drive this pregnant Zamboni out from behind the counter? I'll be back in just a moment to show you how to cut a heart into brie."

Kayden made his way around the corner and gently rolled Chrysta's chair out until she was facing Lucas directly. She looked up at him, her eyes sparkling with excitement. "Lucas, isn't this great?" she whispered, before turning her head over her shoulder to look back at the boys muttering together over the various types of charcuterie flowers on the counter. "They're so excited about cheese."

Lucas pushed her chair through the curtain and closed it behind them. "I wish you would have asked me about this first."

Her features crashed with disappointment. "I thought you would be happy about the new business. You're always complaining about how the town doesn't share your enthusiasm for gourmet cheeses. Now they are."

"I know, it's just—" Lucas ran a hand through his hair, then realized he wasn't wearing his hair covering. That's how distracted she'd gotten him. He reached through the curtain and grabbed two from the shelf, handing one to her before yanking down his own. "It's my shop. I should know what's going on, especially when you're using my cheese for the demonstrations. Plus, aren't you supposed to be resting?" His eyes fell on her belly and that new, protective surge of affection roared through him, chased by the ever-present fear of what he couldn't imagine losing.

"I took my blood pressure this morning with the cuff they gave me at the hospital and it was fine," she said, her voice tinged with defensiveness. "That's not the point. The point is, you don't like my ideas for your business."

That wasn't true, and suddenly, Lucas realized why he had been such a grumpy grufflesmoosh about all of Chrysta's additions. Every heart sticker, every pepperoni rose reminded him that Valentine's Day was coming. If they stuck to the plan, their fake romance would officially be over. Chrysta would be gone and everything would go back to the way it was before. Lucas might have been able to deceive everyone else so far, but he could no longer lie to himself about wanting time to stop on February 13.

When he saw her eyes take on the shine of tears, Lucas knelt beside her chair and covered her hand with his. "I like your ideas, Chrystabell. Really. What you've done to—to this town in a few weeks is nothing short of miraculous." Lucas had to stop himself from saying what she had done to him. His whole life felt different now, and even though he knew the romance was pretend, he knew he wanted her and her child in his life in any way she would allow "You're an incredible businesswoman. I guess I'm a little jealous that you've done what I couldn't."

"Thank you for saying that. I don't think I realized how much I needed to hear those words from someone I lo—someone I look up to professionally." She sniffed and wiped away a tear with the back of her sleeve. "You are amazing at what you do. Seriously. The only reason my parties are doing so well is because your cheese is so great."

"Good to know the hermit life is paying off," he joked, lightly stroking the top of her hand with his thumb. "Guess I'll have to actually start talking to people now that we have new customers coming in, but," he added, lifting his chin to stare at her in mock scolding, "I draw the line at charcuterie board bunnies for Easter. I see one mozzarella ball bunny tail and we're gonna have words, got it?"

She narrowly suppressed a grin. "We'll see about that."

On Thursday, he left with a cooler full of cheese and a list of instructions from Chrysta on how to get everything set up for the retirement party she was hosting via Zoom that night. After he arrived, Lucas arranged the plastic trays cut in the shape of surfboards, the ingredients for the cheese-straw-and-rosemary palm trees, and the red-pepper-jelly-striped cheese "beach" balls exactly the way she had showed him. Mrs. Moffatt was closing her craft store and moving to a condo in Kona, hence the theme. The errand took him longer than he had anticipated, mainly because Mrs. Moffatt and her friends insisted on plying him with multiple silk hibiscus leis. Under normal circumstances he would never have participated in their Polynesian shenanigans—he had been the only one at his "Tropical Paradise" senior prom wearing a traditional tuxedo instead of a flowered shirt—but this was for Chrysta's business. Sacrifices had to be made. However, when Mrs. Moffatt withdrew a grass skirt from her knitting bag, he made a hasty aloha and escaped out the door only to run straight into Joe Kim and Renata.

"Whoa there!" Joe held up his hands and took two steps back. "Or should I say, hang ten?"

Lucas rolled his eyes. "I'm just dropping off the supplies for the cheese board–making party. You know, Chrysta's business. I have some of her cards in my pocket if you're looking to book her for an upcoming event."

Joe and Renata both took one of the handful of cards Lucas dug out from his pocket.

Joe tucked the card into the brim of his frayed straw beach hat. "This whole cheese board–making thing is causing quite a sensation. My customers are asking for all kinds of special items now, like goat cheese on their chef salads or Fontina on their burgers."

"I'm sorry," Lucas offered. "I'm sure she didn't mean to cause any difficulty for you."

"Difficulty?" Renata chortled and waved away the concern with her hand. "Are you kidding? Special orders mean more money, Lucas, dear. We couldn't be more thrilled. By the way, I'll need my order of aged Parmesan Reggiano as soon as you can get it. People are requesting it with everything right now. And if you can throw in some more of the Fontina infused with basil oil. That's a hot one right now for take-home orders."

You could have knocked him over with a feather. Since when did people in this town try anything new? Since Chrysta arrived with her unique blend of magical charm and methodical type A planning. Lucas's chest expanded with pride and excitement for her. If it wasn't for the coating of ice shining beneath the streetlamps on the sidewalk, he would have sprinted all the way back to tell her.

Instead, Lucas bit his lower lip to suppress the goofy smile he could feel all the way down to his toes. "I'll get that for you right away, Renata." Jerking his thumb toward the house behind him, he said, "I think the party's about to start soon. Joe, I didn't know you and Mrs. Moffatt were friends."

"Oh, we're not," Joe said with a mischievous twinkle in his eyes. "But she's got a younger sister who owns a butchery in Bath."

Lucas shook his head. "Didn't you learn anything about mixing business with pleasure from your last relationship?"

"What can I say?" Joe shrugged. "I'm an incurable romantic."

"Well, good luck with your 'meat' cute," Lucas

quipped before clapping a hand to his forehead and groaning. "Oh, wow. I cannot believe I just said that out loud."

Joe and Renata exchanged wide-eyed stares.

"Lucas Carl making a joke," Renata said, her voice lowered with teasing awe. "This is a whole new side. You must really be in love with that woman."

Joe clapped him on the arm as they passed him on their way up the stairs. "Good for you, man. The whole town's been talking about how happy you've been since you kids got together. Don't screw this one up or you'll pay for it." He sighed. "Literally. My new ground chuck supplier charges twice what my ex did."

He wasted no time driving back to the shop, propelled by the thought of how Chrysta's face would light up when he told her how everyone was raving about her business. Her features were so expressive and he loved how she didn't even bother to try to hide any of her emotions. Tonight that twinkle of joy in her large brown eyes would be because of him. That thought made him step on the gas even harder.

When he got back to the shop, Lucas bounded out of the truck. He hit a patch of ice and almost lost his balance but was able to steady himself enough to whirl in a three-sixty spin. Just the anticipation of making her happy was enough to make him feel a little giddy. That exhilaration came to a screeching halt, however, when he made it to the door and caught a scene out of his worst fears.

Chrysta was in her chair behind the counter, her face beaming with happiness just as Lucas had imagined. But instead of that light being directed at him, it was looking up at Law.

Lucas sucked in a large draft of the cold night air to try and numb the disappointment cracking his heart in half before he pushed the door open. The jingle of the bell alerted Law and Chrysta to turn their heads sharply toward the sound.

"Lucas," she said. "You're back so soon. Did everything go okay with the drop-off?"

"Yeah," he replied, not trusting himself with more than one word.

She smiled even wider. "Oh, good. I was just coming down here to get my supplies before going back up to my 'office.'" Using air quotes with her fingers over the word, she rolled her eyes dramatically. "I wanted to make sure I gave myself plenty of time, since I'm both the size and speed of a glacier at the moment. Your brother was helping me reach some of the condiments on the higher shelf so I didn't have to stand on a stool."

Law bowed gallantly. "It was my pleasure." He shot Lucas a pointed stare. "Lucas, I don't know why you waited so long to introduce me to your live-in girlfriend."

"His girlfriend was wondering the same thing," Chrysta added.

Lucas scrubbed his hand over his beard, unable to find words. He certainly couldn't tell her the awful, embarrassing truth. *I wanted to keep you for myself.*

As usual, Law swooped in like Prince Charming to the rescue. "Chrysta and I were just talking about BeeBee's engagement party Sunday."

"Law offered to make custom wooden cheese boards for the event," Chrysta said. The excited flush of color returned to her cheeks, and the sigh curdled Lucas's insides with envy. She traced a delicate finger along the surface of the counter. "Having real boards to work with will make the event so much classier. I wish I could be there in person, but my doctor was very clear about sticking to household distances only."

Law patted her back sympathetically. They even looked like the perfect couple, close enough in height so that Chrysta didn't have to stand on her toes to hug him, and their stylish outfits coordinated so well together that they could have been on the cover of one of the pregnancy magazines Lucas had picked up for her at the market this week. This would normally have been the part where Lucas threw up his hands and conceded, once again pushing back his feelings before anyone could see his pain. This time, the words popped out before he had a chance to swallow them back.

"We could have the party here," he said. "In the space behind the shop."

For the first time Lucas could remember, Law's mouth fell open, yet remained speechless. It was immensely satisfying. Lucas lifted his chin and folded his arms over his chest. That's right. This time he wasn't giving up without a fight. He had made a silent vow to protect Chrysta and her baby from anything that could hurt them, including his reckless brother.

Chrysta clasped her hands together under her chin. "Are you serious? That would be amazing. But is there enough room? I wouldn't know since you've never showed me where you've been living this whole time."

There was a tinge of bitterness in her voice Lucas didn't understand. Maybe she was just impatient to get to her meeting. "It will be fine. Shouldn't you be signing on to the virtual party soon?"

She checked her watch and grimaced. "Yikes. I've got to start my long trudge up the stairs."

Lucas rushed to grab the basket of supplies off the counter before Law could and handed it to her.

Chrysta groaned as she pushed to a stand, then took the basket gratefully. "You're a lifesaver, Cheese Hermit. You know that?" As she disappeared up the stairs, he basked in the warmth of those words rising through him like the fragrant steam of a freshly baked brie in pastry.

Law put his hands on his hips and narrowed his eyes at Lucas. "What are you trying to pull here? There's not enough space to entertain a large party back there."

"There is if you knock out the wall between the kitchen and the living room to make it open concept," Lucas retorted.

"You hate open concept," Law countered, pointing a finger with a sizable cut on it at him. "When I suggested that very same idea before, you said—and I quote—'No one needs to see how the mozzarella gets made, Lawson.'"

"Yeah, well, people change," he huffed before quickly changing the subject. "Come on back, I'll get you a Band-Aid for that finger."

Law followed him down the hallway, apparently unfazed by Lucas's attempt to distract him. "You hate change. You always have. That flannel shirt you're wearing now is at least eight years old, and you've had the same beard since you started growing facial hair in ninth grade."

"Hey, I trim it when it starts to tickle my neck." He opened the door and gestured for Law to go through first. As his brother passed him, Lucas muttered, "Maybe if you had been around more over the last few years, you would know more of this stuff about me."

If Law had heard him, he didn't react. Instead, he stared at the wall between the kitchen and living room, knocking on it with a fist. "It's possible. One of my buddies from high school is a contractor. I can see if he can dig up a crew." He turned back to give Lucas a smug grin. "I can redo the cabinets in the kitchen as shelves to display my woodturning projects when I open my shop in here."

Lucas went through the master bedroom and into the bathroom to get a Band-Aid. When he came out, Law was standing in the middle of the bedroom with a pensive expression on his face.

"I was thinking—" he started, and Lucas interrupted him.

"Look at that, you've changed, too."

"Ha, ha, listen." Law snatched the Band-Aid out of Lucas's hands. "This is a really big bedroom."

"It used to be two rooms, remember?" Lucas said. "Their bedroom and Dad's office. They expanded it when Mom was diagnosed so there would be room for her to get around the bed with the walker." He swallowed hard. That office had been his dad's sanctuary, just like Lucas's cheese lab was to him. He had filled it with framed newspaper articles about the shop and a leather chair they had shipped back to the States from a trip to Italy to visit Rose's grandmother. Giving it up had to have been difficult, but Dad hadn't once complained. He had simply made some comment about finally getting the king-size bed they had always needed and Lucas had promptly left the room to wash out his ears with acid.

"Since I'll have a contractor coming in, what would you think about having them look into turning this back into the original design?" Law asked absentmindedly as he struggled attempting to wrap the Band-Aid with his right hand. Being a lefty had always made things harder for him, yet another reason why Lucas didn't see this woodworking passion sticking. "I can use the bedroom as a supply room and the smaller room as an office like Dad did. Don't worry, though. You can keep your room upstairs because I'm a nice guy like that."

Lucas frowned. "But where are you going to live?" He had assumed that if Law did win the space that he would need the bedroom. "You know what Mom said. The only way you get the land and the trailer is if you give her a daughter-in-law and a grandchild. What if you and your future bride don't have kids right away?"

"Don't you worry your furry head about that," Law said, trying once again to get the Band-Aid on securely and failing. "But you can have your old room back after your friend moves out."

"Oh, for crying out loud." Lucas threw his hands in the air and went to get another Band-Aid from the cabinet. Catching a glimpse of his reflection in the mirror, he lifted his chin and rotated his head from one side to the other. It had been a while since he had updated his look. He returned and took the mangled Band-Aid out of Law's hands. "Let me help you."

Law held out his injured finger as Lucas wrapped the Band-Aid around it. "Reminds me of when we were kids and I would dictate the answers of my homework for you to write down because my handwriting was so bad."

"Mom and Dad were so relieved when they realized it was just because you were left-handed." He chuckled. "They thought you would never be able to write legibly."

"I just mean it always felt like you were the one taking care of me," Law said, holding up his finger and inspecting Lucas's handiwork. "I'm the big brother. Isn't that my job?"

Lucas shrugged. "I didn't really mind. Taking care of family is just what you're supposed to do."

"Yeah, but—" Law's eyebrows crinkled together "—I feel like if you let other people take care of you, maybe you wouldn't have to take everything so seriously all the time. Maybe—" he slowed his words down and jutted his chin forward to look at Lucas "—you might even learn to have some fun again."

"I don't have time for fun," Lucas said. His voice sounded even more like a growl than usual, low and thick with emotions he didn't want to surface. "I have a family business to keep going and a sick parent who won't enjoy the time she has left until her sons start taking responsibility for their actions."

Law took a step back. His lips formed a thin, straight line as if Lucas's sharp words had slashed a visible wound across his face. "Fine. Stay grumpy and miserable and alone."

As Law brushed past him, Lucas's shoulders dropped. This constant battle between them wasn't helping anyone, not Mom, not Law, not himself. Pushing his brother away had never been the answer. If he wanted to win Chrysta— and by that, he meant the space, of course—then Lucas needed to be the best version of himself and hope that maybe this time, it would be enough.

"Law, wait."

Pausing in the bedroom doorway, Law pivoted on one heel and spun around. "What?"

"I need your help with something."

CHAPTER TWELVE

"BRUCE, WHERE ARE YOU?" Chrysta stage-whispered frantically as she rolled her chair around the shop. "Seriously. Bruce McFuzzyWhiskers Wayne, you have until the count of ten to get your furry butt out here, or so help me—"

"He's with me," Lucas said from the hallway behind the counter, his voice growing louder as he neared the front of the building.

Chrysta flopped back in her chair with relief. The last time Bruce had gotten out, she had found him pawing at the curtain of Lucas's cheese lab, mere moments away from breaking into the inner sanctum. She hadn't told Lucas about this, of course. He had been stressed out enough over the past week, between the renovations to the back space, which she still had yet to lay eyes on, and preparing for BeeBee and Bill's engagement party. Every time she saw him, the dark circles under his eyes seemed to have deepened. Spinning her chair around, the apology for her escapee disappeared from her lips, replaced with a gasp.

The surprise wasn't that Bruce Wayne, who Lucas typically approached with suspicion in his eyes and a lint roller in his hand, was perched on top of the cheese maker's broad left shoulder. It was that Lucas the Cheese Hermit of the Mohawk Valley looked like he had just walked off a *GQ* photo shoot. His typical cargo pants and stained overshirt had been replaced by a crisply tailored black suit over a white button-down loose at the neck. His untamed mane of wavy dark hair was shorter and swept off his forehead with gel. He had even trimmed his beard to a trendy shadowed stubble that accented the strong jawline beneath lips that tipped upward on one end in a half smile.

Picking her jaw off the floor, Chrysta swallowed and forced her eyes to blink. "There you are. I mean, there he is. That is to say, Bruce Wayne had just slipped out of my hands two seconds ago and definitely for the first time. Did you—did you do something different with your hair? It looks…different."

"Good different or bad different, as in go back to the bathroom and try to glue back some of the hair from the sink that Bruce Wayne was playing with for the last thirty minutes?" He arched one defined eyebrow—he had even trimmed his *eyebrows*—and lowered his chin to stare hard at her.

"Yeeeeaaaah, sorry about that." She bit her lip and scooted her chair toward him. Her blood pressure had remained only slightly elevated at her appointment earlier in the week, so the doctor had given her the okay to move around more freely as long as she didn't go too far. But the way Lucas was looking at her, she didn't trust her knees to hold up without buckling completely. "I may have lost track of him while I was getting dressed for the party."

"It's okay," Lucas said. He reached up to his left shoulder and stroked Bruce Wayne's nose with the tip of his index finger. "He's come in to visit me a few times this week, mostly when I was showering. I splashed him once to make him go away, but then he started playing with the water and it got to be kind of our thing." The cat pushed his round head into Lucas's hand, demanding more pets, and Lucas chuckled affectionately before shrugging his non-cat-bearing shoulder.

So not only had the man undergone a rom-com worthy makeover, but he had befriended her notoriously human-selective cat? This was wholly unacceptable. How was she supposed to stay professional, not to mention a little mad at him for not telling her he had a brother, when he was standing there, cooing at her cat out of his freshly shorn, ridiculously hot face?

"I should have mentioned he's the only cat in the world who loves taking baths," she said. Spreading her skirt over her knees with her hands, she avoided his eyes as she grudgingly added, "It's a good different, by the way. Not that you needed to change anything."

"That's good to know," he said. "You look even more beautiful than usual tonight, and that's saying something."

"Hmmph," she scoffed. "I know you're just returning the compliment to be nice. I've got bags under my eyes from not being able to sleep longer than half an hour without getting up to pee, I can't do anything to my hair because I keep getting headaches whenever it's up, and I can't bend over to see, but I'm quite sure my shoes don't match each other."

He lifted Bruce Wayne off his shoulder and set him down gently on the floor, checking Chrysta's feet before he rose. "Definitely not matching. But who can tell the difference between black and silver anyway?"

Chrysta closed her eyes and groaned. "Tell you what. You go host the cheese board party and I'll go down to the cave and drown my sorrows in Manchego."

He stilled her hands from picking black cat

hair off her red velvet dress by taking them in his. Finally, she allowed herself to look at him, and that was the biggest mistake of all.

"Chrysta," he said, somewhere between a growl and a murmur. "It wouldn't matter what you're wearing or how you do your hair. You will always be the most gorgeous woman in any room." He rose and gave her hands a squeeze as he guided her to her feet. "But if you mess with my cheese while it's still aging, you and your wonky-eared cat are bunking with Bee-Bee's water buffalo."

Now that she could see the full curve of his lips, she could tell he was kidding. Mostly.

"It's a deal," she said. As they turned to walk down the hallway where the party would be held, she noticed he kept hold of one of her hands even though there was no one there they needed to fool.

She didn't know what to expect from the space. Lucas had been so evasive about, well, almost everything in his life that didn't involve cheese that he could have had the entire cast of the Ringling Brothers Circus back there and she wouldn't have been any wiser. It had been his brother, Lawson, who had told her that's where their parents had lived and how the noises she had been hearing were of him renovating the space. There had been an undercurrent of tension between the brothers when Lucas had showed up late the other night. Not having any siblings of her own, it was hard to gauge whether it was due to normal Freudian rivalry or something new that Lucas was holding back. It felt like the closer she got to really knowing him, the more of himself he kept hidden away. But there was no time to worry about that today. One of the teens she had helped had agreed to livestream the party on all of Chrysta's official Cheese Party Girl social media pages. If the blast went viral, it could be the launching point to sponsorship deals, even franchising the concept. Everything had to be perfect.

When Lucas opened the door, she held her breath and closed her eyes before stepping through. She felt the warmth of Lucas's hand leave hers as he stepped away and said, "I know you don't like surprises, but hopefully this is a good one."

She opened her eyes and her shoulders fell as she exhaled with relief and delight. It was even better than she could have imagined. The space was open and surprisingly large with a slate stone fireplace that went all the way to the ceiling, flanked by gorgeous built-in shelves. The intricate carving work on the shelves reminded her of centuries-old estates she had seen in England, as did the brocade-patterned wallpaper above the rails on the wall to the right. Instead of living room furniture, small wooden card tables had been set up to face the sleek, efficient kitchen on the left. A portable island with carving similar to the built-ins separated the space from the kitchen area. Its quartz countertop sparkled beneath low-hanging copper light fixtures shaped like Moravian stars. It was old-world European charm mixed with updated modern stainless steel appliances tucked in the corners so as not to break the illusion of travelling back in time.

Chrysta walked slowly into the room, taking everything in. She picked up one of the four cheese boards that sat on each card table. It was a light wood that had been polished until it gleamed like gold, and carved into it were two cursive B's entwined with each other with a small crown above the letters and a heart below. She picked it up and held it up for Lucas to see. "Look at that," she exclaimed. "Lawson did such a great job."

Lucas took it from her, examined it and made a harrumphing noise. "Yeah," he said begrudgingly. "I'd thought the whole woodworking thing was a phase like all his other hobbies, but he really seems to be doing well with it." He shrugged, then tossed her a wink. "I've got something up my sleeve for you, too."

"Oh, really?" She folded her hands over her

belly and tapped it with her fingers. A foot kicked back. "Are you going to dazzle the party with some close-up magic? Has the Cheese Hermit become the Great Goudini?"

"First of all, that's a great name." He set the board back down on the table and pointed at her. "Second of all, you'll just have to wait and see."

"You won't have to wait too long." Lawson appeared in the doorway between the back space and the shop. "BeeBee and Bill were right behind me on the way over here." He walked in the doorway and spread his arms out. "What do you think? The space looks great, right? Even Grumpus—I mean, Lucas agreed," he said, jerking his thumb at his brother, who responded with a characteristic growl that would have validated the teasing nickname had Chrysta not been able to catch the small smile that twitched his lips upward.

"What's behind that door?" Chrysta asked, pointing to the wall to her right.

"It's my room," Lucas said. "There's a bathroom back there too, and a small space Dad used to use for an office."

"So that's where you've been staying," Chrysta said. Out of the corner of her eye, she noticed Lawson incline his head curiously at Lucas as if he was trying to figure out what was really going on.

"You guys have been dating for almost a month and moved in together, but you haven't seen his room?" BeeBee asked as she showed up in the doorway, hand in hand with Bill. "What's up with that? You afraid she'll see your collection of autographed Stars on Ice posters and run screaming for the hills?"

Lucas's startled eyes flickered at Chrysta and she jumped in, taking BeeBee by the hand and pulling her into the kitchen area. "I was joking," she said, quickly. "It's just that I need my own room for sleeping because—" she gestured to her belly "—I tend to take up a lot of room these days." She looked back over her shoulder at Lucas. "Also, what posters do you have? I've been hunting for a signed Tara Lipinski."

"Oh my gosh, there's two of them!" BeeBee groaned. Then her eyes lit up as she spotted the rows of cheese for the demonstration on the island. "Is that a wedding cake made out of Brie rounds? That is adorable, and also, I'm starving."

Chrysta laughed. "It is. I'm going to have everyone build a board centered around their own layered 'cheese cake,' then you and Bill can choose the winner. Don't worry," she added. "Georgia is bringing over cupcakes and other actual desserts."

"That's good," she said, mock brushing the sweat off her forehead with one hand. "Because my friends from the pageant love them some sweets." Her eyes shone as she looked over Chrysta's head at Bill. "This is perfect. Thank you both so much for this."

"It was our pleasure." Lawson swooped in and grabbed a cherry tomato shaped like a tulip from the display. "Just out of curiosity, are any of your beauty queen friends single?"

Lucas frowned at him and clapped a hand on his shoulder. "I thought things were getting serious with you and Ada."

Who was Ada? Chrysta wondered to herself. The way he said her name with such familiarity reminded her again that there was so much she didn't know about Lucas. How could she trust him when he held so much back? All the more reason this party had to go well. A sponsorship deal or a few more bookings and she would have enough money to put a down payment on a place of her own. Mrs. Van Ressler had been nice enough to let her start her maternity leave early and take short-term disability, but that only covered a small portion of her salary. Chrysta knew Lucas would extend the deadline past Valentine's Day. She also knew if she spent one Valentine's Day with this man, she wouldn't want to spend it with anyone else ever again. This time she would not let her stupid heart get in the way. After all, she wasn't her—

"Mama?" Chrysta said out loud, as a small woman with perfectly coiffed platinum-blond hair rushed toward her in a cloud of perfume. "What are you doing here?"

"I'm here to see you, Gingersnap," her mother said in her heavy Southern accent that was as much a part of her personality as her Chanel No. 5 perfume. She opened her arms and Chrysta accepted a dainty hug and double-cheek kiss before pulling away again.

"But—but how are you here?" This was the more significant question. Mama didn't travel farther than the local Kroger on her own. For years, Chrysta had offered to buy her mom plane tickets to meet her in various European ports, with stays at luxury hotels comped or heavily discounted because Chrysta was an employee. Every time her mother had politely—being Southern, there was no other way—but emphatically declined. "Last we spoke, you said just to come down after the baby was born."

"Well," her mom said with a flap of her manicured nails that always indicated a long story was about to ensue. "Mrs. Murray—you remember Mrs. Murray from church? She had four boys who went to your school, but several years after you? Anyways, she saw you doing your little cheese party thing on the internet. So Edward, my new gentleman friend, bought me a plane ticket here, made reservations at the bed-and-breakfast and drove me to the airport. Why, he even arranged the car to pick me up at the airport and drive me right to the hotel. Wasn't that so lovely of him?" She shook her head as if Edward the Great had arranged a solo flight to the moon and back just for her.

"Ah." Now it made sense. Of course, her mom had a man doing everything for her. "Well, um, I'm glad you're here." She looked over her shoulder at BeeBee, who had watched the entire exchange with amusement only restrained by Bill's firm grip on her shoulder. "BeeBee, I'll be right back. I just need to show my mom up to my room so she can get some rest after her trip." Chrysta swiveled her head back to her mom. "I'm hosting a party for BeeBee and Bill's engagement, and it's been planned for so long, I'm sure you understand they don't have enough room to add anyone extra at the last minute."

"Actually, we invited Marjorie to the party," said a woman from the doorway leaning on a walker. She was thin with dark hair and a warm smile. "We ran into her at the bed-and-breakfast, and once we realized who she was and more importantly how close our families have become—" she directed that comment with a significant stare over Chrysta's head at Lucas "—I texted BeeBee and asked if it was all right and she agreed."

BeeBee suddenly appeared very busy with the cheese party supplies.

"I can't tell you how relieved I was to hear that you had found yourself a new fellow," Chrysta's mom said, reaching out to place a hand on her belly before walking past her to stretch her hands out to Lucas. "Young man, you must be a saint to take on my daughter and her, um, addition."

Chrysta couldn't keep from rolling her eyes. "It's a baby, Mama, not a carport." The sky would fall before Marjorie would ever be able to discuss anything sensitive or awkward without veiled metaphors.

"And he's so handsome, too," Marjorie cooed. She yanked Lucas's shoulders when he went in for a hug, pulling him in with the strength Chrysta knew most people didn't expect from a woman who barely cleared five feet. Probably the only thing she and her mom still had in common. "Gingy, I can't imagine why you didn't tell me about your handsome new beau."

"I'm sorry. Gingy?" Lawson stepped up behind Lucas with one finger in the air. "I thought her name was Chrysta."

"Oh, it is," her mother replied flippantly. "But my daughter actually has strawberry blond— well, it's red hair, is what it is, but I called it strawberry blond until she was old enough to get her first highlights. You see, my grandmother was a Warwick," she concluded by way of explanation. "God couldn't make everyone a natural blonde, I suppose, or those of us that are wouldn't be quite so rare." She fluffed her curls with one hand and gave Lawson a wink.

"Great," Chrysta said flatly. "So you're staying for the party. Um, Lucas, can I see you back in the shop for a minute? I forgot some, um, cheese…stuff." She widened her eyes deliberately at him to get the message telepathically.

Lucas bit his lower lip and nodded before answering. "Cheese stuff is what I do best." He gave Chrysta's mom a courtly nod of his head. "It was really nice meeting you, Mrs.—"

"Oh, honey, Mrs. Cryschevsky was my mother-in-law. Bless her heart." Marjorie shuddered. "You can call me Marjorie. Or hopefully soon, Mama." She patted him on the arm as he strode past and started to walk with Chrysta through the door only to have their exit blocked by a small man with gray streaking his sandy hair.

"Lucas," the man said with a deep, booming voice that belied his height. "Finally, we get to meet the woman we've heard so much about." He held out a hand to Chrysta. "Gus Carl, dear. I'm Lucas's pop. Welcome to the family."

"I—thank you?" Chrysta said, putting her hand in his only to have him clasp the other hand over top and shake it so vigorously her teeth felt like they were chattering.

"Now, how did you hear about Chrysta when I've never said anything about her to you?" Lucas put his arm around her waist and gave a teasing squeeze. "Surely you didn't have people spying on me?"

"Such a suspicious mind this guy has!" Gus released Chrysta's hand to gesture at Lucas. "It's why he's such a good businessman, though. Very shrewd, always keeping an eye on the competition, always wanting to be the best cheese maker in the area. And will be just as devoted to his wife and child when the times comes, I have no doubt." He wiggled his eyebrows and grinned so infectiously, Chrysta couldn't help returning a small version of the smile.

"Chrysta, I'm Rose, Lucas's mom," the woman behind the walker said in a much softer voice than her husband's. "I honestly can't tell you how happy I am that you two found each other. Please feel free to let us know if you need anything. I can't knit baby booties the way I used to." She cast a wistful glance down at her hands which were covered in bruises from IV insertions.

"Oh, no, please don't worry about that," Chrysta

protested, reaching back to grab Lucas by the shirt and pull him down the hallway.

Once they were back in the shop, she cast a look behind them to make sure no one had followed before whipping back around to face Lucas. "We have a problem."

"You bet we do," said Lucas solemnly. "I've been calling you by the wrong nickname this whole time." His dark eyes twinkled with more mischief than she had ever seen in him before. "I'm the worst fake boyfriend ever. Gingy is so much better than Chrystabell. So much...zestier."

Chrysta clapped her hand to her forehead. "For the love of all that is holy, including Swiss cheese, do not ever call me Gingy again."

He cupped his chin in one hand and stroked it thoughtfully. "I mean, the real question is what to name the baby. Clove, obviously, if it's a boy. What if it's a girl, though? Cardamom Carl has a nice ring to it. Very alliterative. I like Nutmeg, but then people will just call her Meg and that's not nearly as exotic."

She slowly lowered her hand from her head and stared at him. For all the times she had told him not to take everything so seriously, he chose this moment to develop a funny bone? It was official. Lucas Carl was the most exasperatingly contrary and simultaneously adorable man on the planet. And also the way her heart sighed at the thought of her child sharing his name sent alarm bells pealing.

As she debated between throttling him and kissing him, he shook his head and held up one hand.

"Sorry, I'll stop now." His shoulders quaked with aftershock chuckles then settled. "Seriously. Tell me what the problem is and we'll fix it."

"Well, first of all, this whole fake romance thing just got real in a hurry," she said. Jutting her chin toward the sounds of their families talking and laughing back there, she raised her eyebrows as far as they could go, forehead wrinkles be darned. "It's one thing to insinuate to nosy nellies around town that we're dating. But when your mother starts talking about wishing she could knit me baby booties, it makes me feel a little uneasy."

"I know what you mean." Lucas crossed his arms and looked to the side, exhaling with puffed cheeks before looking right at her. "All of this started because I wanted my mom to be happy and able to relax in her new home without worrying about me. That was fine when she didn't know you. Now..." Lucas shrugged. "It's too late. She's met you, and for the rest of my life, I'll have to hear about why I couldn't make it work with that sweet Chrysta she loved so much."

Chrysta rolled her eyes and put up her hand to tuck her hair behind her right ear. "We only met five seconds ago. How do you know she's going to love me?"

Lucas unfolded his arms, reached out and took her hand as she lowered it from her hair, his thumb brushing against her jaw as briefly and softly as a whisper. "It's you, Chrystabell. Of course, she's going to love you. It's impossible not to meet you and instantly fall head over heels." The words trailed off on his lips before he gave his head a shake. The motion dislodged a strand of his hair perfectly over one eyebrow. "You said 'first of all.' What's the 'second' of all?"

He was still holding her hand, and for a moment, she couldn't think of anything but how warm and comforting it felt to have someone like Lucas there. Clearing her throat, Chrysta forced herself to let go and put her hand on her belly. This was what she needed to focus on right now. Getting used to taking care of her child without anyone there to reassure her that they could fix any problem together. "Second of all," she said, enunciating slowly to give herself more time to remember where she had been going with this list, "my mother."

Lucas cocked his head to one side. "What's the problem? She seemed nice enough." He frowned, tiny lines forming above his eyebrows that were, annoyingly, extremely attractive on him. "Will she think I can't provide for you and the baby? I mean, I know I'm not a tech billionaire like your ex. The numbers for this quarter are looking really promising, though, thanks to your parties and your social media posts."

"No, it's not about you at all," she said. "My mom and I have a difficult relationship. She's my mom and I love her, of course. She just has this way of making me feel anxious, like she's waiting for me to make a mistake, so then she can tell me how she was right all along about me needing a man by my side. The last thing I need right now is for my blood pressure to go up any higher than it is, or I'll have this baby tomorrow while both our parents are in town. If that happens, you can forget about a fake engagement because they'll guilt us into a real wedding."

His eyes darted down at her belly, wide with fear. She couldn't tell whether he was more concerned with the baby coming prematurely or the idea of being forced into marriage with someone other than the ex he still wasn't over.

"Whatever you need me to do, I'm here."

She sighed with relief. Men like Alastair made vague, sweeping promises all the time. *I would jump in front of a train for you. I would go to heavens and pull down every star in the sky to make you a diamond necklace.* The words were beautiful and ultimately as empty as the Waterford crystal vases he kept all over his flat but refused to put flowers in because they were "investment pieces, not decor items." When Lucas made promises, however, Chrysta knew he would keep them. Lucas was the only man she had ever felt she could trust never to let her down. When he said something, he meant it.

"It's going to sound contradictory," she said, her words faltering. "But, um, to prove to my mom that I can take care of myself and this baby on my own, I need you by my side."

CHAPTER THIRTEEN

THIS WAS NOT the first time Lucas had been confused by a woman. So often, they said they were fine when it later turned out they weren't, or they wanted gifts for Valentine's Day even though they said don't bother spending the money. So far, he hadn't encountered that kind of communication issue with Chrysta. She wore her feelings so openly that he had taken to carrying around small packets of tissues in the pockets of all of his pants because inevitably those emotions would take a tearful form. He liked that about her because for the first time in his life, he felt like here was a woman he could understand.

Oh, well. It had been fun while it had lasted.

"I don't understand," he said after a long pause. "You want to be alone, but with me there all the time?"

She nodded brusquely. "Exactly." Patting him on the shoulder, she started to head back toward the hallway. "Good. Glad we're on the same page."

He caught up with her, which was easy to do because she was moving more slowly by the day, and also, his legs were twice as long as hers. Blocking her path, he looked over his shoulder at the back room, then back at her. "No. Not on the same page. Not even sure we're reading the same book. It's like high school English all over again when they assigned *Catcher in the Rye* and I thought the book was going to be about baseball and sandwiches." He wrinkled his nose at the memory. "Greatest disappointment of my life."

She dropped her chin to her chest and snorted an annoyed exhale. "I liked Cheese Hermit better than Cheese Comic. Don't quit your day job," she quipped, lowering her voice before going on. "I need you to keep me calm. You know me. You can tell when my emotions are boiling over."

Lucas began to say that the process started when she woke up and didn't end until she went to sleep, but decided—wisely this time—to keep that particular thought to himself. "You need me to keep you calm? Usually I'd just feed you cheese, but it will be kind of hard for you to talk with a mouth full of Manchego."

"Honestly, there's not enough cheese in your shop to keep me calm around Mama," she muttered.

Fear caught Lucas by the chest again, the same

way it did when Chrysta had her scare two weeks ago. She was still almost six weeks away from her due date. That was way too early for the baby to come. The doctor had warned about all the risks of premature delivery: developmental delays, vision deficits and so much worse. This baby was not going to suffer a moment in his or her life if he had anything to do with it. He concentrated on the task at hand.

"Okay," he said, rubbing his hands together. "You need to stay calm. Happy. Distracted from your mom driving you crazy. I can do that."

She smiled gratefully, the expression waning as her mother called out. "Gingercakes, what is this that you're serving people to drink at your party? It says iced tea, but as far as I can tell, there isn't a bit of sugar in it. You must have forgotten to sweeten it. That baby brain's really kicking in, isn't it?"

Chrysta drew a sharp breath, her lips pressed together. When she didn't let it out after several seconds, Lucas put his hand on her lower back.

"Breathe, Chrystabell," he whispered, pushing her forward. "I'm right here with you. Just breathe and think of cheese."

The doorbell echoed behind them followed by the high-pitched sounds of female voices laughing and talking excitedly all at once. Lucas pressed his hand more firmly into Chrysta's back and quickened his steps. One woman at a time was confusing enough; an entire gaggle of them was downright terrifying.

For the first half hour or so, it seemed like his services might not be required after all. Chrysta turned on her magic hostess charm, weaving among the bevy of beauty queens BeeBee knew from winning the New York State Queen of the Dairy pageant almost two years ago. He hovered in the background, pouring drinks and setting out the cheese boards just in case she needed him to swoop in. But when they cooed over her belly and asked about the baby's father, Chrysta deftly switched the subject back to Bill and Bee-Bee's wedding plans. Her mother was occupied with his parents by the fireplace and Lucas felt the battling twinges of disappointment and relief that she had been right the whole time. She really didn't need him.

When the mingling wound down, Chrysta stood at the island and clinked a spoon against her glass of sparkling apple cider.

"Who's ready to get this cheese party started?" she said to a chorus of resounding cheers and squeals that had Lucas wincing and resisting the urge to cover his ears. "Everyone, take a seat. As you all know, we are here to celebrate the engagement of BeeBee Long and Bill Danzig."

BeeBee pulled at the legs of her navy blue pantsuit and sank into a curtsy.

"Many of you remember BeeBee as the Queen of the Dairy, and if any of you have spent longer than five minutes with Bill, you know that food is the great passion of his life, second only to Bee-Bee herself." She nodded at BeeBee and smiled. "So what better way to celebrate the incredible journey these two are about to begin than by creating our very own charcuterie boards inspired by their love for each other and, even more importantly, their love for really good cheese?"

That line got the biggest response from the crowd of female dairy farmers, and Lucas leaned against the refrigerator, trying not to spontaneously combust with pride. She was a natural, so charming and effervescent. The space worked perfectly for her too, with enough room for her to maneuver around the kitchen with everyone in the living room being able to see every fine motion of her small, nimble fingers. Lawson had replaced their woodburning stove with a gas fireplace that turned on and off with the click of a switch, and he had to admit it added the perfect touch of coziness and elegance to the party without the unsightly pile of wood taking up room.

"For today's party, we're going to be holding a little contest," Chrysta said. "Each of you is going to design a wedding 'cheese' cake that you think best represents our wonderful BeeBee and her devoted Bill. At the end of the party, our royal bride will pick which one she would actually want to see at the cheese table at her wedding." Chrysta leaned forward and gave BeeBee a playfully stern expression. "You will be having a cheese table at your wedding, right? If not, I'm afraid these dairy farmers might start calling for your abdication."

BeeBee threw her head back and laughed. "Oh, you better believe there is going to be a cheese table. Buffalo mozzarella for days."

"That's what I'm talking about." Chrysta stepped back from the island and spread her arms in front of her. "In the center of your table are the basic ingredients you'll be using to build your board. Here is your chance to get creative, ladies. The base of your 'cake' could be a circular round of brie or a square of Gruyère." She bit her lower lip and shook her head. "Apologies for the rhyming. I've been reading a lot of Dr. Seuss to get ready for my little one to pop. Now I can't stop. Last one, I promise."

Among the laughter, Lucas overheard Chrysta's mom say in a loud stage whisper from her seat in the back table, "Gingy, you said cheesecake, but I don't see any graham cracker crust. Betty Crocker would be rolling in her grave."

"Different kind of cheesecake, Mama," Chrysta said. Her smile stiffened and Lucas's heart rate shot up. She needed a distraction. He racked his brain and settled on the one thing that distracted him more than anything. Clearing his throat, he slid forward until he was standing next to Chrysta and pointed at the round of brie.

"Fun fact about cheesecake," Lucas said, and suddenly he felt multiple pairs of female eyes boring into him like the press he used to get the liquid whey out of his curds. Swallowing hard, he forced himself to do his best imitation of Law's smile. "Did you know that the first cheesecakes were served at the early Olympic Games in the Roman Empire?"

"What is it with men and the Roman Empire?" BeeBee rolled her eyes. "Bill mentions it at least once a day."

"Because it's awesome," Lucas shot back at his cousin before turning to Chrysta. Her large brown eyes were round with surprise, but she nodded as if to urge him on. "Anyway, it was thought that the hearty cheese sweetened with honey and baked on a wheat crust would give the athletes strength before competing in their events."

"That sounds way better than my pre-workout smoothies," one of the women said to her table.

Chrysta's smile softened as she held his gaze for a second longer than necessary before returning to her demonstration. "Ladies, my assistant for the day and the very talented cheese maker responsible for today's supplies, Lucas Carl."

Lucas bowed, then gestured to Chrysta. "As you were."

Without missing a beat, Chrysta picked the thread up once again. "Well, now we have the Romans to thank for two of my favorite foods—Caesar salad with fresh anchovies and a good cheesecake. I'll let you know we do have fresh honey to sweeten your cake made of cheese as well as a variety of fruits to add pops of color wherever you want it. BeeBee, you've chosen your wedding colors, right?"

"I tried, but Bill vetoed the dark brown bridesmaid dresses that matched my water buffalo," BeeBee said sulkily.

"Okay, so knowing that, whoever guesses Bee-Bee—or should I say, Groomzilla Bill's—color scheme gets a special prize at the end," Chrysta said. "So, as you choose your base cheese for the center of your board, think about what kind of flavor profile you want your cake to have. Are you going more savory? If so, you can use olives for a little splash of green or pickled pepperoncini for a bright red with some heat. Both of those would pair nicely with the garlic-infused mozzarella rounds as a base. Remember, true love means never having to apologize for garlic breath." She whipped her head around to stare Lucas down. "Right, Pookums?"

Lucas answered with a salute of his hand.

Girlish chatter and murmurs filled the air as the women got to work setting up their boards. Chrysta circled the living room, making small suggestions and joking with the women as they playfully bickered over basil leaves as decorations. When she got to her mother's table, Lucas lifted his chin to see if he could note any signs of tension from across the room. As her mother pulled at the hem of Chrysta's dress with a judgmental purse to her lips, he cupped his hands around his lips.

"Cheese fun fact number two," he called out over the background noise. "Did you know that in the sixteen hundreds, cheese makers across Europe began to tint their cheese yellow with natural flavors like saffron or marigold powder? It was thought that color meant better quality because the fine English cheeses had a golden hue from the cow's diet that was high in beta carotene. The word cheddar actually comes from the name of the town where that first orange cheese was produced."

Chrysta walked back to the island and whispered "Thank you," as she passed him. He gave her hand a quick squeeze, then retreated again to let her take over hosting.

"So, BeeBee, do you know what kind of flowers are going to go in your bouquet?" Chrysta asked.

"It's a mixture of roses and wildflowers from the grazing fields," BeeBee said after swallowing a mouthful of cheese. "Daisies are Fernando's favorite."

"There was a preacher from the Catholic church across town named Father Fernando," Chrysta's mom piped up from the back. "Lovely man, but I could never understand what he was saying because of his accent."

"It wasn't the accent, Mama, the Mass was in Latin," Chrysta said, her own accent becoming more pronounced with her restrained aggravation. "Moving on, I'm going to show y'all how to make roses out of our salami, but if you want to try making a daisy, you could use some of Lucas's beautiful golden cheddar for the center and sliced apple or pear for the petals. The sweetness of the fruit is a nice contrast to the richness of the cheese."

"You know what would be real good with this would be some pimento cheese," Chrysta's mom said to the woman next to her.

Chrysta's nostrils flared and Lucas leaped back to her side and touched her on the elbow. "Say, Chrystabell," he said loudly. "What kind of cheese would you use to disguise a horse?"

She blinked rapidly at him several times. Good. It was her turn to be confused by him for a change. "What…what kind of cheese?"

He held two small white rounds of soft cheese over his eyes. "Mascar-pony." The crowd half groaned, half laughed, but when he lowered the mascarpone from his face, he was relieved to see her face had dropped all signs of irritation as she picked up the salami and wove it into shockingly realistic looking petals. It was working. All he had to do was keep distracting her. Thankfully, he was basically a walking encyclopedia of cheese history, and while in general he took nothing in life more seriously than his craft, he would use every ridiculous cheese pun he knew to keep Chrysta and the baby calm and happy.

Lucas stepped back and watched the cakes take shape. The women chatted and laughed quietly as Chrysta showed them how to carve blueberries into little stars and arrange rosemary sprigs into a magical forest. The warmth filling the room came as much from the laughter and genial chatting as it did from the fireplace, and as Chrysta called out a five-minute warning for everyone to put on their finishing touches, Lucas was surprised to find himself disappointed that the party was coming to an end. Who was this person he was becoming? A man who had fun at parties and had taken to wearing hoodies with a pouch in front because a certain small cat would crawl in and fall asleep while he walked around the shop? He had used wax in his beard this morning, for Pete's sake. Maybe all this time he had only thought he hated change, when really he had simply been afraid of losing what he had. Well, if this feeling was what he had to gain, out with the old and in with the new might be his new slogan.

He locked eyes with Chrysta. Her cheeks were flushed, but with happiness rather than the irritation that had him worried about her blood pressure earlier. She opened her mouth to speak, and then her mother's voice piped up clearly over the murmurs from the back of the room.

"My goodness, what a mess we've made," she said to seemingly no one in particular. "My poor Chrysta's going to have a heck of a time cleaning all this up. Thank heavens she won't have to keep this little hobby up much longer once she gets married again."

Chrysta's knuckles turned white as she gripped the edge of the counter. She was practically vibrating with anger and as she started to walk around the island, Lucas clapped his hands.

"Hey there, everyone," he called out, and Chrysta froze. "I have one last surprise addition to today's demonstration. How would you all like to learn how to make your very own mozzarella?"

The crowd responded with hearty applause and Lucas held up both hands. "I'm basically robbing money from my business by showing you all the secrets of the cheese-making craft, but hey, who needs money anyway, right? Good cheese is meant to be shared and appreciated."

He reached into the refrigerator and grabbed a packet of mozzarella curds, then turned back to the island. "So, I've got some buffalo milk mozzarella curds here. Back in the lab, we add acid serum to the milk in a large vat and stir it to separate the solid material here from the liquid. Once it's packed, it needs a good salty bath." He nodded at Chrysta, whose breathing was still coming far too fast for his comfort. She nodded back and filled a large pot with water before putting it on the stove and adding salt. "While we wait for this to boil, I have a confession to make."

Chrysta turned around and crossed her arms over her chest, one eyebrow jolting up skeptically as if to say, "Where in the world are you going with this?"

He winked at her before turning back to the audience with a look of feigned humility. "I've been accused by women in the past of not being very attentive to details," he said as he chopped

the curds into large chunks. "Like not remembering anniversaries or not complimenting an
ex-girlfriend on that thing you women do with
your nails when you file them down to nubs and
then put some sort of shellac on them? That thing
that looks like a medieval form of torture?"

"It's called a manicure," the small blonde
woman in the front said with a giggle.

"Manicure, torture, potato, potahto," he said
with a shrug and the women laughed. "Anyway, oh good, our water is ready," Lucas added
as Chrysta stood next to him with the steaming
water she had poured into a container. He had
counted on her knowing what he needed to do
next, and he had also counted on the distraction
saving her from letting her emotions flare out
of control in front of the entire party. "So once
we've got our nice hot water, we put the curds
in and we stir gently until they've formed a nice,
shapeable consistency like this." He expertly ma-
nipulated the cheese, stretching and pulling it
until it was ready to mold. "Circling back to me
being a—" He stilled his hand to face Chrysta.
"What did you call me the other day?"

"Obtuse cheese hermit?"

"Such sweet talk," he said. She rewarded him
with a chuckle and put her own hands in the
water to finish working the cheese as he used
one hand to point at BeeBee. "Can anyone tell

this poor obtuse cheese hermit of a man what BeeBee's signature hairstyle is called?"

"It's a braid," one of the other women called out.

"A braid, you say?" Lucas nodded thoughtfully, then dunked his hands in the water with Chrysta's.

They faced each other, each with an end of the stretched cheese in their hands. Working in unison, they plaited the cheese slowly, gently. Lucas didn't dare breathe as the world around them fell away. He never wanted this feeling to end, and yet he knew that, sooner rather than later, it would. It always did. Feelings changed or people left. Relationships, even the success stories like his parents, always came with sacrifice, pain or loss. There was nothing he could do about that. But when his hands met Chrysta's in the middle of their completed braid, for just one moment his world was whole. His gaze moved from their handiwork to Chrysta's face, landing on the track of a single tear trailing down her cheek.

"Thank you," she whispered so quietly only he could hear.

That was enough. He had to be the one to break the spell now. Holding the cheese braid up in both his hands, he said with as much showmanship as a recovered hermit could muster, "Ta-da! Mozzarella braid à la BeeBee!"

A wave of cheers and whistles erupted and BeeBee acknowledged the love with a regal bow before raising her own applauding hands in Lucas and Chrysta's direction.

"You two are amazing," she said, walking over to stand between them and putting one arm around each of their shoulders. "Seriously. This was the best engagement party ever. Um, we get to eat all this cheese now, right?"

Georgia made her way out of the crowd and announced, "BeeBee is going to go around to each of your stations and judge your wedding cheesecakes in just a moment. In the meantime, I've got some bride and groom cake pops on the table in the back, along with champagne and ginger ale."

The ladies instantly made a beeline for the treats with BeeBee leading the charge.

Chrysta touched Lucas on the arm.

"Did I do all right?" He wrinkled his nose. "You make hosting look so easy, but I think I'm sweating worse than a Gorgonzola in the middle of August."

"Only you would make that reference." She laughed, then put her hand on top of her rounded belly.

"Is the baby okay?" Lucas asked, reaching into his back pocket for his cell phone just in case.

"No, it's fine," she replied. "He or she is just doing a happy dance. They like when I laugh."

"So do I," said Lucas softly. "It's much better than the tears." He reached out and gently placed a finger on her cheek to wipe away any trace of sadness.

She looked up at him and sighed. Her large eyes seemed to hold so much more than she was saying out loud. Then she blinked and nodded at the table in the back. "I'd better get in line before all the cake pops disappear. Nobody gets between a pregnant lady and cake."

She joined the crowd at the back and Lucas felt a hand on his back. His mom stood behind him, holding on to the counter for support with her other hand.

"Everything okay, Ma?" he asked, bending down so she could hear him over the noise.

"Yes," she said. "Do you have a minute? I'd like to speak to you about something in private."

Lucas glanced over at Chrysta in the center of the crowd, gesturing with a cake pop like it was a fairy godmother's wand. Holding out his arm for his mom to stabilize herself, he guided her across the room to the bedroom and closed the door behind them. As soon as Lucas turned back around, Lawson slipped out from Gus's office and surreptitiously locked the door behind him.

Lucas rolled his eyes. "Are you seriously locking me out of a room in my own place?"

"It's not yours yet," Law retorted. He wiped a smudge of paint off his cheek with one hand. It was a pale blue, which struck Lucas as an odd color choice for a woodworking supply room.

"That's what I wanted to talk to you boys about," said Rose as she lowered herself carefully down onto the bed. She patted the space next to her, and Lucas took it while Law leaned against the wall next to the small window and crossed his arms. She placed her hand on Lucas's knee, her fingers curling inward in a tremor that caused a lump to sting at the back of his throat. "Watching you with Chrysta today, Lucas, it's very clear that you've found your person."

Lucas's eyes shot over his mom's head to Lawson. He waited for his brother to spout protestations or at the very least insult Lucas's new look. Instead, Law simply waited in stony silence as Rose's faltering speech continued.

"I know this whole deal we made regarding the space seemed silly," she went on, turning her head to acknowledge Law, who shrugged. "But I promise we weren't trying to manipulate or rush you. As your parents, your dad and I know you both better than anyone, and we didn't want the space to become a source of contention in case anything happened to either of us. At least if you blamed us for the outcome, you would have a common enemy."

Lawson and Lucas snorted simultaneously, then Law shook his head and looked down at his feet. "Wow. You are the ultimate puppet master, aren't you, Ma?" He lifted his chin and nodded at Lucas. "Can you believe we both got played?"

"Like a couple of knucklehead fiddles," Lucas said with a small huff of laughter.

Rose reached into the small knit cross-body bag she kept her glasses in and pulled out a square box made of red leather. Lucas recognized it instantly. It was the box where she had kept her wedding rings ever since her medications and tremors put her at risk for skin tears and sores from the diamonds. She held it out to Lucas.

"Here," she said, a catch pulling at her voice. "This is for you. When you're ready, the ring—and the space—are yours. I've never seen you as relaxed and happy as you were with Chrysta today. I couldn't be more thrilled for you, and I know you are going to fill this space with all the love and laughter we've had as a family. Law even agreed that this is the right thing to do."

"He did?"

Rose nodded. "And as a gesture of appreciation for his maturity, your dad and I agreed that Law will get the trailer and an acre of our land to build a small woodshop on. We figured you would be okay with that since you won the best prize of all."

Lucas took the box and opened it, but a surprise rush of tears blurred the large diamond and the accompanying eternity band into a watercolor of sparkles. He blinked back the emotion and closed the box, slipping it into the front pocket of his pants. Swallowing hard, he placed his hand over his mother's.

"Ma, I really appreciate this," he said. He cleared his throat, emotion thickening his voice too much for his own comfort. "But I don't want the space anymore."

Law's mouth fell open.

"Hold on," he added. "I don't want Law to have it, either." Standing, Lucas walked over to his brother and clapped him on the shoulder before twisting his body to address the confused expression on Rose's face. "If Law agrees to it, I want the space back here to go to someone else."

Law narrowed his eyes, although one side of his lips twitched in a knowing smile. "Who did you have in mind, Cheesebro?"

After they finished talking, Lucas left the bedroom to find Chrysta in the kitchen, putting away her supplies. She beamed a radiant smile at him that was pure sunshine.

"Hey you," she said. "Wanna help me take

some of this stuff back to the storage fridge in your cheese lab?" She jutted a thumb behind her. "We'll need the fridge back there for the cakes to go in."

He nodded and held out his arms. Once she had filled them with the piles of unused cheese wheels and salami rounds nearly up to his eyes, Chrysta steered him back toward the shop.

"Don't be too long, lovebirds," BeeBee called out merrily from the center of the tables where she was presiding in the dual role of bride and cake judge. "I'll need your help picking a winner. They all look so amazing!"

Lucas chuckled as he and Chrysta made their way down the corridor. "Two years ago, I would have had to lasso BeeBee and drag her to an event filled with squealing beauty queens and demonstrations for making flowers out of charcuterie." He set the boxes down on the counter next to the cash register with a huff and wiped the condensation off his hands on his pants before facing Chrysta with a grin. "It's amazing what love can do to some—"

But before he could finish the word, she stood on the tips of her toes to grab his face in both hands and pressed her lips to his in a kiss that was so light he barely felt it, yet it might as well have been an eleven on the Richter scale for the way the earth seemed to shift beneath his feet.

She sank back onto her heels and lowered her hands to his chest. Biting her lower lip, Chrysta's eyes shone like mirrors. "I know, I know. That wasn't part of any phase of the plan. But I couldn't think of any other way to properly thank you for what you just did back there."

"Was it all right, the way I stepped in?" Lucas asked as he inclined his head to make sure she really knew how important her words were to him. "This is your business. I was just worried about you getting upset."

She made an incredulous face and shook her head, an errant wave of hair falling over one side of her face with the motion. "I kept thinking the whole time, 'I'm a grown woman. I'm not going to let her provoke me into unprofessional behavior,' and yet the second she opens her mouth, I can't fix my face, let alone control my words."

Lucas pulled the stool out from under the counter and motioned for her to sit. "I get it. No matter how well-intentioned they are, our parents can really mess with our heads, can't they?"

"Me and my cankles thank you." Chrysta sank onto the stool with a sigh that seemed to go all the way down to her toes. "She really doesn't mean anything by her little comments," she said, brushing her hair off her face and tucking it behind one ear. "I know she just wants me to be happy. It's just that she can't imagine how I would ever be happy on my own, without a man to take care of me." She looked back up at Lucas. "The way you helped me today was perfect. You supported me, kept me on balance like a—a—"

"Like my mom's walker," Lucas supplied.

Chrysta's expression softened. "How's she doing? Do you think our plan worked? Now that she's seen us together, surely she'll be convinced enough to go back to South Carolina and just relax the way you hoped she would?"

The hopeful lift in her voice plucked at some hidden string deep in Lucas's chest. Was she that eager to be done with their fake romance? Yes, she had just kissed him, but this was Chrysta. She couldn't restrain a single emotional impulse to save her life.

It was one of the things he loved most about her.

Pressing his lips into a smile he didn't feel, Lucas nodded. "I think so. My folks want to have dinner with you and your mom and Bee-Bee and Bill tonight after the party's over. Once that's done, I think our scheme will have worked out perfectly according to plan. Good thing, too. Valentine's Day is less than a week away."

Unfortunately, there had been nothing in the plan about what to do when he realized she and the baby were the only valentines he ever wanted.

CHAPTER FOURTEEN

CHRYSTA HAD ASSUMED that the most surprising part of the day would have been Lucas willfully and enthusiastically participating in a party where his beloved gourmet cheese was basically used as grown-up lady Play-Doh. However, what knocked her off balance most of all—besides her rapidly expanding center of gravity, of course—was that she was actually enjoying a dinner with her mother.

Having Lucas and his family there as a buffer made the biggest difference in the world. Lucas's mother, Rose, kept Marjorie occupied by asking her questions about acclimating to the warmer weather in the South and what kind of plants might grow best in her window box. Chrysta's mother loved nothing more than to share her wisdom as residing queen of the Huntsville Ladies Garden Club, so she chattered Rose's ear off. As soon as her mother accosted Lucas to show her where the bathroom was and also to explain to him the importance of having guest soaps available at all times, Chrysta leaned over her mother's empty chair to lightly touch Rose on the elbow.

"I'm so sorry," she said to Rose. "I know Mama's a lot. It's all right if you want to change seats. I can tell her there was a draft here or something."

They had pushed all the smaller tables together into one large table in the center of the living room and between all the people squashed into chairs next to one another, the crackling fireplace and the heat from the trays of lasagna bubbling in the oven, the room was far from chilly. Still, it wasn't fair for Rose to have to endure Mama's recitation of the entire gardening section of that month's *Southern Living* magazine.

Rose smiled, a gentler version of Lucas's broad grin. "It's fine, sweetheart." She glanced quickly down at Chrysta's belly before lifting her eyes back to Chrysta's face. "How are you feeling? I remember how exhausting those last few weeks were."

"Eh." Chrysta didn't want to complain, especially since Lucas had told her what Rose had to endure every day. "It's not so bad. I mean, I know my ankles are taking on more water than the *Titanic*, but since I can't really see my feet anymore, it's easier to pretend they're not enormous."

"You're funny," Rose said, patting her hand. "That's good. Lucas needs someone who can bring out his lighter side. He actually has a really great sense of humor on the rare occasions he's not worrying about me or the shop or if the new organic fertilizer on the grass is affecting the flavor of the milk in a way that only he can taste."

"Him and his cheese," Chrysta said, plucking a cube of cheddar off the tray on the table and popping it in her mouth. She swallowed and turned back as much as her torso would allow to see if he had emerged from Sherpa duty yet. "They're a match made in heaven, huh."

"The business suits him," she said. "Cheese making requires a lot of effort, time and attention. Lucas is a natural caretaker, always has been. When they were kids, you would have thought he was the older sibling, the way he looked out for Law."

Chrysta's mouth went suddenly dry. She reached for her glass of ginger ale and took a sip. No wonder it had been so hard for him when Lawson had pursued Lucas's ex. He had probably been too afraid of hurting his brother to fight for his own heart. That would be so typical of Lucas, the man who put everyone else first.

The thought sent her head reeling and the baby thankfully landed a kick to Chrysta's rib cage that jolted her priorities straight. They were almost to the final phase of the plan. A quick fake engagement followed by a Valentine's Day breakup. Then they would explain to everyone how they had simply gotten swept up in the romance of the season before coming back to their senses. It wasn't far from the truth. She had already gotten so carried away that she kissed him. The memory of his lips on hers, the rush of tenderness that had filled her heart, was anything but sensible.

Pushing that thought aside, she lifted her nose to the air. "Mmm. The lasagnas smell delicious. Do you mix basil oil into your ricotta, Mrs. Carl?"

"Yes, I do," Rose exclaimed. "That's amazing. I didn't realize the smell was so powerful."

"It's not," Lucas said, escorting Marjorie back to her seat with a polite pull of her chair. He dropped a hand on Chrysta's shoulder and looked down at her with the kind of devoted affection that Chrysta had only seen in paintings of Guinevere and Lancelot. "Chrysta's pregnancy nose is uncanny. She could outsniff a Malinois."

Chrysta playfully swatted him with one hand. "Very funny, Cheese Hermit."

Lucas tipped his head as if to say something, then frowned. "Did you know your shoes are on the wrong feet?"

"Oh, jeez," Chrysta groaned. "Do they at least match each other, or did I put a different pair on each foot again?"

"Oh, Gingerdoodle," Marjorie said with an exaggerated sigh and a hand on her heart. "Thank goodness you have Lucas here. I don't know what you would do without him."

"Survive a blister on my heel?" Chrysta muttered. She angled her chair and stuck her feet out. "This is only because if I bend down, the buttons on the back of my dress will pop off and hit someone in the eye. I'm allowing Lucas to help for safety reasons only."

"You keep telling yourself that, Chrystabell." He knelt down to switch her shoes.

The light touch of his hands on her ankles was so soothing. She hadn't even realized how sore and swollen they were until he took the shoes off and she couldn't stop an audible moan of relief.

Lucas looked up at her from under raised eyebrows. "Are you sure we shouldn't call the doctor about the swelling?"

"It's just normal pregnancy swelling," Chrysta said, pulling her foot back before her mom could make a comment about how her feet had never swelled above a petite size five even when she was pregnant. The sudden motion knocked Lucas off his heels, and as he put one hand to the floor on his right side for support, a small red box tumbled out of his pants pocket.

Chrysta gasped, but before she or Lucas could say anything, her mom shouted. "YES! She accepts. Oh, thank the Lord in heaven, now I don't have to find my daughter a husband on the internet."

Lucas grabbed the box and shoved it back in his pocket, shooting to his feet. "It's not what you think." He held up both hands.

"What's going on down there?" BeeBee yelled, peering across the table. "Lucas, what's wrong with your face?"

"I think Lucas is trying to propose," Bill said under his breath. "Why don't we let him finish asking her to marry him before you tease him mercilessly. We actually want this to work out."

"Oh, right, right, good point," she murmured back. She gave a queenly wave of her hand. "Go on. As you were."

Chrysta pushed uneasily to stand and grabbed Lucas by the elbows. "Lucas, what's going on?" Was this actually happening? Here? Now? This wasn't exactly her dream proposal, even if it was for a phony engagement that would last less than a week. And yet her heart had screamed YES louder than her mother the second she saw him down on one knee.

Lucas's eyes were wild, darting to the seven

faces around the table staring at him expectantly before settling back on Chrysta. His breathing came in fast bursts and he opened and closed his mouth several times like a fish forced out of water. "I'm—I'm not proposing, that's not what's happening." He closed his eyes and ran a hand through his hair as he finally exhaled deeply. When he opened his eyes, they were calm and also, strangely sad. "Not marriage anyway. I have something I think you'll like better than a ring."

"Let me guess—it's cheese?" She quirked a half smile even as disappointment battled confusion in alternating waves.

Lucas spread his arms wide and looked from one side of the room to the other. "It's this."

Confusion declared official victory. "What do you mean this?"

Lucas's eyebrows knit together over his nose, then he rubbed his forehead with one hand. "I guess I should have been more clear. This space behind the cheese shop. It's yours." He walked backward, his hands painting a picture as he spoke. "You can use this space for your parties just like you did today. Plus, you and the baby can live in the bedroom back there as long as you need to. I can go back to my room upstairs, but that way if you need anything, all you have to do is yell."

Chrysta jabbed her hands onto her hips. This was all so much to process and her head was starting to pound. "Is that it?" The anger and frustration rose in her voice before she realized it was even there. Something about all of this didn't feel right. "What's really going on here?"

The fall of his broad shoulders confirmed her suspicion. Lucas bit his lip and seemed to search for someone's face in their families behind them. She followed his gaze to Lawson, who half stood and raised his hand.

"I have a feeling I know what you're going to say, Lucas, and I really think you should not—"

"I have to tell her the truth, Law," Lucas said quietly before focusing back on Chrysta. "I was going to talk to you about all this later, in private. But now…" He shoved his hands in his pockets and fiddled with the box he had put back in one. "I have to be completely honest with you. It's the only way we can both move forward."

"Tell me." Chrysta put a hand on the back of her chair to steady herself. Something told her she was going to need it.

Lucas's words came out in a hurried tumble. "My brother and I both wanted this space behind the shop for our businesses. Our parents made a deal with us that whoever got engaged first would get the space."

It felt as though all the warmth and joy in the

room had been suddenly sucked back up into the fireplace. "Let me guess. That box in your pocket means you won." The hand not holding her upright curled into a fist at her side. "Why didn't you tell me? About the space? About Lawson? About anything that really mattered to you?"

Lawson spoke up again. "Lucas, I really have to talk to you."

"Not now, Law," Lucas snapped, whipping his head back and forth between his brother and Chrysta, the frustration tightening his features as they shifted to an expression of sober pleading. "I'm so sorry I didn't tell you the whole truth about the deal with my parents. I was afraid if you knew about Law, if you knew there was another option—" he winced before going on "—a better option, that you'd choose him over me. That's why I tried to keep the two of you apart for so long." Turning his body to face the table, he addressed the entire group. "While I'm coming clean, I might as well go all the way. Chrysta and I were never dating. I asked her to pretend to be my serious girlfriend so that Mom could stop worrying about me and focus on her health down in South Carolina."

"Oh, Lucas," Rose said, the words hushed almost imperceptibly.

The past four weeks all started to come together like a fractured vase being repaired. It all made sense now. It also made her even more angry that he didn't trust her to be smart enough to choose him in the first place. "So what happens now? I move into the space back here, host my parties and you go back to holing up in your cheese cave all alone? The math isn't mathing. Why would you go through all this trouble just to hand the space over to me? And why would your brother agree to this?"

Lucas didn't face her at first, then slowly pivoted just enough for Chrysta to see his profile, downturned and stony with regret. "The trailer and the land next to the dairy farm where Law's been staying were supposed to go to the first of us to give Ma and Pop grandchildren. I told Law he could have that even though, technically it would have been mine because we—I mean, you—your baby…" He couldn't even finish the sentence. He met her eyes so slowly as if it pained him to look at her. "I'm so sorry, Chrysta. All I wanted was for you to be happy. I thought giving you the space for your business was what you wanted."

She took a step close enough to him to smell the sandalwood in whatever oil he had used on his newly trimmed beard. The smell only added to her rage because the smell wasn't Lucas. Lucas smelled like fresh milk and herbs, like the cheese that he loved more than anything. She didn't know who this person in front of her was, and that made her feel stupid, which made her even angrier.

"Your ex was right," she whispered. The words came out almost in a hiss, and Lucas's chin jerked back like he had been slapped. "You don't have a clue what women want." She lifted her hand off the chair and waved it in the direction of the kitchen. "I don't want this space only because you won some family bet. I don't want you or any man to have that power over me ever again. My life, my choices, my mistakes." She pointed her finger at him, then stabbed it back at her chest. "They're mine to own."

"Exactly," he said, the volume of his voice rising to match hers. "I thought that's what you wanted. Your own space for your business so you can do everything the way you want."

"I don't want it like this," she shot back. "Not with you pushing down your own needs and thoughts and feelings like you always do. Tell me, Lucas." She placed her palms on his chest, needing to feel his heart pounding against them. "What do you really feel in here?" She pressed into his shirt with the last two words, then lowered her voice so only he could hear. "Please. For once in your life, say what it is you really want before it's too late."

He opened his mouth and for one hopeful second, she thought he might say the words she had been longing to hear him say ever since that night at the ice rink. Then he swallowed and Chrysta knew they were gone. She knew it the same way she could read his mind during their games, the same way from the moment they had met it seemed like he had been able to see right into her heart. What she still didn't know was why, but that no longer mattered. It was over. Pushing herself away from him, she shook her head.

"I'm done," she said, as she backed toward the corridor. "I know people just think I'm the cute girl who throws silly cheese parties. But this is my business and my baby and I don't appreciate anyone playing games with them. Or my heart," she added, immediately wishing she hadn't.

"Chrystabell," he started, but she swiped her hand in the air as if washing away everything that had happened between them.

"No," Chrysta said firmly, stopping at the doorway. "No nicknames. No more deals. No more plans. I'm taking my cat and going back to the inn. I'll stay in the room with Mama. I'll sleep on the floor if I have to."

Marjorie rose from her chair tentatively at the mention. "Ginger, are you sure about all of this?" Her hand fluttered between her heart and her hair as she whispered, "I mean, the man is offering you a place to stay and do your little party thing. Don't you think you ought to at least try to come to some sort of...understanding about all of this?"

"No," she repeated. "I'm going to the inn now. You can do whatever you want."

"Let me walk you both back," Lucas said, starting toward them. "You don't have to like me or talk to me, but please let me make sure you get there safely."

"I'm sure your brother wouldn't mind walking with us," Chrysta retorted icily. "Right, Law?"

Law rose, cringing as he shrugged his shoulders. "I don't mind," he said, hesitating as he walked behind the chairs and inched past Lucas. "Sorry, bro."

Lucas shook his head. "It's not your fault. Just make sure she gets there okay. I'll send her things and Bruce Wayne over with you later."

Law cocked an eyebrow at the cat's name, then nodded once and put his arm across Chrysta's shoulder. The gesture was kind and supportive, but she felt as numb as if she had spent the whole night out in the snow. She felt nothing except the throbbing in her heart and the ache in her heart as she, her mom and Law walked through the shop and out of the door. Even the frigid sting of the cold evening air didn't seem to penetrate the weight of sorrow blocking every other sensation from reaching her. Even her mom's nervous chatter about the last time it had snowed in Alabama faded into the background. She might as well have been alone. That had been the plan all along, hadn't it? To run her business, raise her child, all on her own?

She really wished whoever had made up that quote about best-laid plans was here right now.

It would be nice to have someone else to blame besides herself.

CHAPTER FIFTEEN

THE FEBRUARY ISSUE of *Cheese Club Monthly* had arrived right on time on the second Friday of the month. Usually Lucas would have dived right in, but this time it had been lying on the counter all morning with the plastic wrapping still untouched.

For one thing, it seemed like every time he reached for it, the doorbell sounded with another person coming in to "check on him." In their town, romantic gossip spread more easily than Breton cream cheese, and Chrysta staying in the hotel with her mom had been the biggest story since Bill and BeeBee's engagement was announced. Joe Kim and Ed Stevenson had already tried and failed to press-gang him into tomorrow's polar plunge, while Georgia had sent Caroline over with a box of sympathy orange buns. While he appreciated their intentions, all Lucas wanted to do was read his cheese magazine in peace and try to forget for just a few minutes that his heart was completely shattered.

Flipping the sign on the door to Closed for Lunch: Back at One, Lucas returned to the stool behind the counter and ripped the plastic covering off the magazine. Normally, this was a small pleasure that never failed to provide a satisfying rush of anticipation.

Today? Nothing. Not even a ripple.

But he opened the magazine anyway, only to close it at the sound of footsteps and the rumble of wheels along the hardwood floor behind him.

Rose, pushing her walker, was followed by Gus pulling their suitcase. She touched Lucas gently on the shoulder before pulling him into a brief, tight hug. When they let go, she reached back down for her walker and took him in with mournful eyes.

"I hate to leave you like this, sweetheart," she said. "We can reschedule our flight and stay longer if you want."

"I don't want you to do that," Lucas replied. It was the truth, something he was trying to get more familiar with these days. This whole mess was because he hadn't been completely honest with the important people in his life and now he was paying the price. Sure, he had been alone before. But now he was lonely, missing the one person—well, two people and one feline—who had made his life interesting. Even fun. "Ma, all

I want is for you to be healthy and happy. Don't worry about me."

Rose sighed and gave him a small smile. "Spoken like a true parent." She let go of the walker briefly to give him a pat on the hand. "Have you tried calling her? Even if she's not ready to forgive you yet, at least you'll have peace of mind that she and the baby are okay."

"That's not an issue," he replied grimly. He had taken a page out of his mom's book. Georgia saw Chrysta regularly to discuss the future of their party-hosting venture and had promised to update Lucas the second anything happened with the baby. He looked over his shoulder at his dad. "You sure you don't need a ride to the airport?"

"We're sharing an Uber with Marjorie," Gus answered. "She seemed a little anxious about navigating the airport on her own, and our flight isn't until this evening, so we offered to wait at the gate with her until they announce boarding." He shook his head and puffed out his cheeks. "She's high-maintenance, that one. Then again, not everyone is as independent as your mother," he added, gazing at Rose with a look that bordered on beatification.

On this, Lucas agreed wholeheartedly with his dad. "Well, that's true." He clapped his dad on the shoulder with one hand before taking the suitcase from him and carrying it out to the sidewalk, then jogging back inside to escape the wind flapping the awning over the door.

"You don't need to do that for us, Lucas," Gus said. "We're perfectly capable of taking care of ourselves. No need to go out of your way to carry our luggage or invent relationships to make us more comfortable."

"Although, we might share some of the blame for that last one," Rose said. "Again, I'm so sorry that you felt you needed to go through all of that. It was never my intention when I proposed that silly deal. All I wanted was for you and your brother to get along the way you did when you were little."

Right on cue, the other reason Lucas hadn't been able to concentrate long enough to read his magazine roared into action. Law had been working nonstop on their dad's former office ever since the disaster of a dinner and for some reason, the work had consisted of making as much ungodly noise as possible. At one point, it had sounded like the cast of both *Cats* and *Stomp: the Musical* had combined in the world's worst Broadway revival mash-up. It was all some sort of juvenile payback for Lucas trying to game the system with a fake engagement, he was sure.

Lucas rolled his eyes. "Not your best plan, Ma."

"Oh, I don't know about that," she said with

an enigmatic lift of her chin. "A mother always knows what's best for her children, even if she doesn't always get it exactly right. I'm not giving up on you boys anytime soon."

Gus held the door open for Rose and held the other hand up in a wave. "Bye, son. We'll call you when we land."

Lucas mirrored his gesture and watched to make sure they got into the car safely as it pulled up. The grating sound of some kind of saw in the back space whirred in the background and Lucas gritted his teeth until he couldn't take it anymore.

"That's it," he muttered, walking back down the hallway with long, angry strides. "I'm not letting him get away with this anymore." Once he crossed the room, Lucas flung open the bedroom door and pounded on the wall with his fist. "Lawson. Can you stop hammering for two seconds and get out here?"

The buzzing slowed to a stop before Law slipped out of the office door and closed it behind him. Crossing his arms and leaning his back on the doorframe, he regarded Lucas coolly. "What's got your cheesecloth in a bunch?"

"I'm not in the mood for puns, in case you couldn't tell."

"I'm not a mind reader, bro," Law retorted. "If you have something to say, come out and say it."

Lucas threw his hands up in the air. "Why do people keep telling me that? Is it so wrong that there are some thoughts and feelings I don't care to share with the entire world? Not all of us put our businesses and personal lives out on Instagram for everyone to see. I wish people would just accept that I'm a private person and leave me alone."

"Mmm-hmm, and by people, I'm guessing you have someone specific in mind," Law said. He pushed off the wall and started pacing in front of the window, stopping to pick up a hair tie off the nightstand before holding it up to Lucas like evidence in a courtroom drama. "Perhaps a certain blonde party girl with a weird-looking cat and an obsession with cheese that rivals yours?"

Lucas jabbed his finger at his brother. "Don't call Chrysta a party girl. She's more than that and you know it."

"I know she's more than that to you," Law said, dropping the hair tie back onto the nightstand and walking back to stand next to Lucas. "Look, man. You want to spend all your time alone with your cheese? Fine. You want your business to stay the same, small-town cheese shop it has been for decades, be my guest. But the reason 'people,'" he said with a dip of his chin and pointedly raised eyebrows, "keep telling you to say what's on your mind is because it doesn't seem like that's enough for you anymore. You're lonely and miserable, and I don't think it's just because Chrysta left. I think you've been lonely and miserable for a long time, but you're so focused on everyone else that you've gotten used to shoving all your feelings and wants deep into a cave. Newsflash, though—not everything ages as well as parmesan, Cheese Bro."

"Well, duh," Lucas said under his breath. "I mean, if you leave a semisoft cheese out even for half an hour it can grow fifteen different types of bacteria from the exposure alone, depending on the temperature and humidity—"

"Stop deflecting with cheese," Law burst out, burying his forehead in his hands. "Lucas, you're holding yourself back from everything in life because you're afraid. What I can't figure out is why."

"Because it's all terrifying," Lucas exploded. The volume of his words echoed in the small room, and he sank onto the bed in defeat. "Nothing good lasts. Even if you do get lucky enough to find the one person in the world who makes you feel at peace, they get mad and leave or get sick or—" He couldn't finish the sentence. All of the emotions he kept bottled up were fighting each other to rise to the surface, choking his throat.

"Like Mom?" Law sat carefully next to him and stared at his sawdust-covered hands in his lap.

Lucas shook his head and bit his lower lip, not willing to look at his brother. "You don't know what you're talking about." Finally, he turned his head and stared at Law until he met Lucas's eyes straight on. "It's not like you've been here for the past five years. You haven't watched Dad's face as she slowly freezes in front of us. He loves her so much and it's destroying him."

"Ah." Law's shoulders lifted and fell in a heavy release of breath. "Now it makes sense."

"What does?"

"Why you put distance between yourself and any chance of love," Law said quietly. "You did it with Sarah. Now you're doing it with Chrysta. There's no other explanation why a smart guy like you would make such a monumentally stupid decision like that one you did at dinner."

"Hold on." Lucas shot to his feet. "I'm not the one who pushed Sarah away. She broke up with me and you know this because it was your arms she ran into. She even told me she wished I could be more like you."

Law stood up as well. His face had dropped its usual mask of charm, and anger clouded the eyes that were normally a lighter shade of Lucas's own. "All right, we're doing this. For the last time, I didn't go out with Sarah. She and I were friends while you were together—that was it. After she tried to get you to fight for your relationship with her and you let her leave, she and I went to dinner, but it was to talk about you. About whether or not there was anything she could do to get you to snap out of your cheese coma."

Lucas went to rake his hand through his hair, but it was too short now. It simply brushed over the top of his head and went to the back of his neck. Rubbing the muscle there that was tight as a rope in the heat of a Camp Herkimer tug-of-war battle, he closed his eyes. Okay, so he had withdrawn from the relationship with Sarah. He could admit that. And other than that one night, he had never seen Law with her. The girl before that had been such a brief relationship that Lucas couldn't even remember her name at the moment. It hadn't been Law's fault that Ada Brunner had gone for him, either. All this time he had been mad at Law, but it had never been about girls.

He opened his eyes and sighed, his hand falling. "The coma had nothing to do with cheese," he said. "I was angry that you left me to take care of Ma and Pop all alone, angry that this was happening to us at all…and scared to death that someday I might have to go through this again with another person that I loved." It all seemed so pointless now, the anger and the fear, when on the other side of it all was Chrysta. The baby. Heck, even Bruce Wayne made him smile every day with his giant eyes and his adorable trilling meow. They were worth any amount of potential pain and loss life might one day hand them. "What do I do? You're the handyman. How do I fix this?"

Law's face relaxed into a grin. "Funny you should say that." He unhooked a key from the ring on his weathered tool belt and dangled it in front of his face. "I knew the first time I saw you and Chrysta together that you were wild for that girl and thus bound to screw it up somehow."

"I hate when you use the word *thus*," Lucas growled. "But I'm willing to put up with your insufferable smugness if you can help me get Chrysta back."

Law made a tsking sound between his teeth. "With charm like that, I can't imagine why she walked away. Now, if you'll let me finish, little brother, I was about to say that I've been working on something that will seal the deal. I had hoped that if I was loud enough about it, you would be motivated to ask me what I was doing or at the very least be inconvenienced enough to move back into your room with the girl of your dreams and we could have been spared your massive lapse in judgment the other night at dinner. But alas—"

"*Alas* is even more smug than *thus*."

Law rolled his eyes and turned away from Lucas. Placing the key in the door, he glanced over his shoulder as he jimmied with it. "Trust me. You'll put up with a lifetime supply of my *alases* once you see what's in here."

He opened the door and swung it wide enough for Lucas to see the interior.

Lucas's mouth dropped open and remained that way long enough to let in the smell of fresh paint and cause a severe coughing fit. Wiping his eyes, he stepped tentatively into the room, taking it all in before he looked back at his brother. For the first time in days—heck, maybe years—he felt something akin to hope.

"It's perfect."

CHAPTER SIXTEEN

CHRYSTA WATCHED HER mom's reflection from the suite's bathroom mirror as Marjorie gazed fondly at Queen Victoria and tapped her chin with her fingertip. "I just love the way Mrs. Van Ressler decorated this room," she said. Turning her head over her right shoulder to look at Chrysta, she pursed her lips in thought. "Didn't you used to have some of these dolls when you were little?"

"I had a figure skater doll, but I don't think she was one of these," Chrysta replied absently. The dull throbbing in her head hadn't gone away in days. What she wouldn't give to be able to take Ibuprofen again. "These are vintage and super expensive. I can't imagine that Daddy would have let you spend that much money on a doll."

Her mom smiled, her eyes cast downward. "Oh, you'd be surprised what I could talk your father into," she said in a dreamy lilt. "He may have been frugal, but he would do anything to take care of his girls."

Chrysta picked up one of her mom's nail polishes lined up on the bathroom sink. They were all various shades of pink, with names like Ballerina Blush and Peony Sunrise. She shook her head slightly. All her nail polishes were along the lines of Crimson Harlot or Lady of the Evening. At least they were different in that regard. She set it down before walking back into the bedroom and easing herself into the wicker rocking chair in the corner. Shifting slightly onto her left hip, Chrysta grimaced.

Her mom glanced over at her, then made a cooing noise. "I'm sorry, Gingy. I shouldn't have brought him up, not when your breakup with Lucas is still so fresh," she said.

"It's not that," Chrysta replied with an irritable huff. "I just can't get comfortable right now."

"If you say so," her mom said in a syrupy tone, indicating that Chrysta must be shattered over the loss of her man. Her low heels clicked on the floor as she walked briskly into the bathroom and began to toss her makeup into her pink Chanel travel case. "It's perfectly normal to grieve after a breakup. Especially with such a tall, handsome man." She put a hand on her heart and sighed, then zipped her bag before coming back into the room and gesturing at Chrysta with it. "Just don't let it get you down for too long. Once you get your figure back, I'm sure the men here will be falling in line for a chance to be with you."

Chrysta pressed her lips together. She didn't know which she cared less about at the moment, her figure or another man in her life. There was no one else like Lucas. If he didn't care enough about her to speak up once and for all, then she was better off alone. Just her and her baby. A sudden fear clenched her, the impending reality jarring her awake from the pleasant dream she had been living in for the past month. She was going to be raising this baby alone. If something went wrong, it was all up to her. Sure, the people in town were great, but the only apartment she could find available was ten miles away in Bingleyton. She couldn't ask Georgia or BeeBee to drive that far in a middle-of-the-night emergency. They had lives and families of their own. Even when it came to the good things—the baby's first steps, first words—there would be no one to share those moments with. Chrysta sat upright, catapulted by a single thought.

She couldn't do it alone.

Bruce Wayne brushed the length of his body against her legs as he strolled past, as if to remind her that he was there, too. But as sweet as her six-pound superhero was, he wasn't the hero she needed. There was only one option and it was the nuclear one.

"Why don't you stay a while longer?" she asked, hating how thin and sad her voice sounded. "I'm going to the next town over tomorrow to see about putting a deposit down on a place. You could even stay with the Longs while I'm getting situated. I heard BeeBee offer you one of their extra rooms if you want to stay for a bit."

Marjorie busied herself with smoothing the folded clothes in her suitcase. "Oh, Gingerpie, you know I would love that," she said, the words dripping out slow as molasses. "But, it's just that everything is so different here, and you know I don't do well in new places. Why, I got lost driving to the country club the other day because there was an accident and they had to redirect traffic." She looked up and smiled at Chrysta. "You understand, don't you?"

"Of course, Mama." Chrysta sat back in the chair. She should have known better than to even ask. When faced with something difficult or unexpected, her mother couldn't cope without someone else taking the lead. She wouldn't move any more than Lucas would spontaneously break through the wall around his heart to make room for her and her big feelings. "I understand completely. I'll be just fine."

For the first time, she put a lid on her emotions. Apparently, she had gained one helpful skill out of her time with Lucas, the master of repression.

"Of course, you will," Marjorie said, closing her suitcase with a snap. She made her way around the corner of the bed and leaned over the chair, placing one hand on each of Chrysta's cheeks. "You're my strong, capable girl. I'm so proud of you and everything you've done."

"Really?" Tears filled Chrysta's eyes and she couldn't tell anymore whether they were from the lingering panic or from the loving admiration beaming out of her mother's face. Even though she didn't feel the least bit strong or capable, it was still nice to hear her mom say it. "Thanks, Mama."

"You're welcome, Gingercup." Marjorie straightened and dabbed at the corners of her eyes with the tip of her pinkie. "Goodness, you've even got me blubbering. I don't want to ruin my makeup before I travel."

Chrysta wiped her own eyes, then chuckled a little bit. "Heaven forbid." She pushed to a stand, rubbing a hand underneath the mound of her belly. Every time she moved it felt like things shifted even more catawampus, one of her mother's favorite words. Chrysta wrinkled her nose. Perhaps it was time for Mama to go back to her home. Chrysta had found hers here, even if it wasn't working out the way she had planned. "Text me when you land, all right?"

"I sure will," Marjorie said. She picked up her

suitcase and unlocked the handle before rolling it out the door. Before she turned into the hallway, she called over her shoulder, "I want you to bring the baby down to visit as soon as you're able. By then, I'll bet you dollars to doughnuts you'll already have a new man."

Chrysta's chin dropped to her chest. Yup. There it was, proof that people truly didn't change. The only thing that could be counted on was that they would continue to disappoint you.

"Ahem." Mrs. Van Ressler's throat clearing was proceeded by a knock on the open doorframe. "Do you have a moment?"

"Of course." Chrysta's chin jerked up in surprise, and she spread her arms out to the small room. "Come on in. I was just saying goodbye to my mom. She's heading back to Alabama."

"Yes, I know," Mrs. Van Ressler replied as she leaned on her cane with one hand and pushed the door closed behind her with the other. "I ran into her on my way upstairs. I was rather surprised. She had booked the room for the whole week."

"Well, things didn't exactly go the way she had expected," Chrysta said, sitting back down on the edge of the bed. It seemed unprofessional to sit down while her boss was still standing, but the headache and the exhaustion and fear were teaming up to make remaining upright a Herculean task.

Fortunately, Mrs. Van Ressler sat down next to her. Facing the wall of porcelain pairs of historical lovers, they both remained silent long enough for Chrysta to count the grandfather clock in the corner ticking forty-two seconds. Then Mrs. Van Ressler inclined her head and gave Chrysta a scrutinizing side-eye. "And what was it she expected?"

"Oh, that I would have fallen madly in love with a handsome man and got engaged before the baby came," Chrysta said with a resigned shrug. "For some reason, she thinks that's what I need to be happy."

Mrs. Van Ressler narrowed her eyes. "Is it?"

"No," Chrysta exclaimed, twisting her body as much as was possible to face Mrs. Van Ressler. "I don't need anyone. Not Lucas, not my mother. I'm going to raise this baby on my own without anyone's help." She tried to keep the sobs down, tried to push them away like she had a few minutes ago with her mother, but her efforts were as effective as trying to hold back Niagara Falls with her thumb. "I don't know how I'm going to do this by myself. I feel like I'm already failing."

"Get used to that feeling," Mrs. Van Ressler said matter-of-factly before pulling a tissue out of her pocket and offering it to Chrysta. "It's called motherhood."

"What do you mean?" She accepted the tissue

and wiped her cheeks with it before balling it in her hand. "You think I'm already a bad mother?"

"That's not what I mean," Mrs. Van Ressler said, shaking her head. "But every mother feels like she's failing, all the time. You'll go to bed at the end of every day thinking about all the things you wished you had done differently with your child, and when you wake up, you'll start a new day full of failures and mistakes. Do you know why?"

Chrysta unfurled the tissue and blew her nose, then shook her head.

"Because," Mrs. Van Ressler continued, her sharp tone softening, "you're human. Just because you become a parent doesn't mean you magically become without fault. All parents make mistakes, just like your mother made a mistake by leaving when you clearly needed her to stay."

The truth stabbed at Chrysta's heart like a barb, yet her tears slowed. She knew her mother loved her; she had never questioned that, despite all her frustrations in their relationship. "I'm so scared," she said, standing to throw the tissue in the bathroom garbage can. It felt good to say it out loud, to acknowledge the feeling that had been chasing her for so long. "I'm so scared that I won't be enough on my own."

"Is it that you're scared of not being enough,

or are you more afraid that doing this alone isn't enough for you anymore?"

Chrysta's head whipped around so fast that her hair flew in her face. She brushed it aside defiantly. "You're talking about me and Lucas, aren't you?"

"Actually I was talking about myself." Mrs. Van Ressler stood and put one hand on her hip. "You see, when I was young I wanted to be an actress. I traveled with a theater company and was even in a few movies. While I was filming in Europe, I met someone and fell so madly in love I almost considered giving up my career in theater to be with him. That terrified me so much, the fact that I was even thinking about giving up something I had worked so hard for, that I left." She took a few steps over to the doll shelf, leaning more heavily on her cane than before. "Secretly, I had hoped he would follow me, but because I was young and foolish, I expected him to know what I wanted from him without actually ever asking him to come with me. When my acting career didn't take off the way I wanted, I got married to my late husband and that was that."

"Do you regret it?"

Mrs. Van Ressler stared at a particular pair of dolls dressed in what looked like clothes from an Italian festival. "I regret thinking that needing people was a weakness. Thinking that asking for what I wanted was a sign that I wasn't good enough on my own. But love…" She shook her head, then walked over to Chrysta and took her hand. "Loving someone else means trusting them enough to make mistakes and accepting that they're going to make mistakes, too. You can't expect someone to be perfect just because you love them."

Chrysta placed both hands on her belly, her palms splayed as if she could somehow protect her child from all of this worry, all of this hurt simply with her touch. "You're saying I should run blindly into this person's arms and not worry about the fact that they could leave me and my child completely helpless? Not a smart plan."

"Plan?" Mrs. Van Ressler rasped a dry laugh that sounded as if it hadn't been taken out and put to use in a very long time. "My dear, you can't plan for love, or life, for that matter. All we can do is take the lessons we've learned from our mistakes and use them to navigate the next challenge that comes our way. For example, if your ex-husband abandoned you—" she angled her chin down and stared over her elegantly long nose at Chrysta "—you would learn to seek out a very different man next time, yes? Say, the type who has proven himself to put your needs above his own at every turn? Someone you know to be good and kind even if he doesn't always say or do the things you want him to?"

The accuracy burned a hole through every argument Chrysta had tried to use as a shield. Mrs. Van Ressler was right. Lucas was a good man— she knew that, and she knew that he would never leave her or her child the way Alastair had. She had been the one to ask him from the beginning not to fall for her. To keep things businesslike, and that's exactly what he had done. It wasn't Lucas's fault that she had changed her heart without telling him and expected him to act accordingly. "I've got to go."

"Yes, I should think you do." Mrs. Van Ressler checked her watch. "The cheese shop closes in twenty minutes."

Chrysta grabbed her coat off the back of the rocking chair and her purse off the top of the bureau. Bruce Wayne let out a perturbed yowl as Chrysta yanked her scarf out from underneath his tail on the bench below the window. "Is it all right if I leave Bruce Wayne in the room? I promise I'll be out of here tomorrow."

"Your mother reserved the room for the whole week, so you have plenty of time," Mrs. Van Ressler said as she turned and slowly walked out of the door. She tapped her cane lightly on the floor, and Bruce Wayne leaped off the bed and trotted after her. "Also, your feline friend is welcome to explore. He's proven himself very respectful of my collections, and while I'm not usually an animal person like BeeBee," she said with equal parts disdain and affection, "I have to admit he's the type I don't mind having around."

As Mrs. Van Ressler and Bruce Wayne walked down the hallway, assumedly to do a perimeter search for maniacal villains—aka hotel guests who left wet towels on the bathroom floor— Chrysta clambered as quickly as she could down the stairs and out the door, winding her white scarf with the red polka dots around her neck as she closed the door behind her.

The snow was falling in light swirls kicked up by the breeze, and the sky was a light dove gray illuminated with a pearly sheen by the street-lights flickering on as she walked down the side-walk. The shop was thankfully still open by the time she finally got there. Out of breath and with a cramp in her right side that simply would not go away, Chrysta threw open the door.

"Lucas?" she called into the empty shop. "Where are you?" Peeking through the curtain into the cheese lab, she didn't see him at any of the stainless steel machinery or around the cor-ner at the sink. She closed the curtains and flew behind the register to knock on the door to his cheese cave, not daring to enter his sanctuary without his permission or his hand to stabilize her on those rickety steps. "Lucas? It's Chrysta. Are you there?"

Surely he wouldn't leave the shop completely unattended. Had she gone and broken the Cheese Man? Whether or not they ended up together, depriving the world of his cheese was an entirely unacceptable outcome. She spun around and pursed her lips. There was only one other place he could be and she really didn't want to go back there. He had probably already started dismantling the space, the perfect party hosting room that she had been too hurt and prideful to accept. A space that came with a room for her and her baby just a short, beautiful walk away from her day job at the inn. As much as she didn't want him to give it up for her, if she had only kept her stupid pride in check, they could have worked something out for both of them to share it. She exhaled a cross between a growl of frustration and an exasperated sigh as she forced herself to go down the hallway.

Surprisingly, the room was exactly the same as she had left it two days ago. Lucas hadn't yet turned it into a miniature history of cheese museum or whatever it was he had originally planned for the space. The tables from BeeBee's party had been neatly stacked along the side of the wall bordering the bedroom and from the open door, she could hear rustling and heavy footsteps. Chrysta crossed the living room to peer tentatively into the room.

"Lucas?" she said, knocking on the doorframe twice before entering. The room was empty but there were footsteps coming from behind the door to the small adjacent room that used to be an office. Lawson had said he had been doing a lot of work in that room in particular. The door was open a sliver, so she pressed gently on it. "Lawson, do you know where— Lucas?"

Lucas's tall frame stood out in the center of the sky blue–painted room and he whirled around as the door opened enough to display the entire space. "Chrysta, what are you doing here?" Nails fell out of his mouth as he spoke, and he lowered the hammer that was in his right hand.

She couldn't answer. Her heart was too full for words, too full even for tears this time.

Lucas had turned the room into a nursery— and not just any old nursery. The wall had been painted with a mural of Jane Street and Crystal Hill Lake, but instead of its usual denizens walking the streets, there were cats. Calicos sitting at tables outside Mama Renata's, a couple of white Persians snuggling in front of Stevenson's Antiques and Jewelry shop. A tuxedo cat held a half-eaten black-and-white cookie as he made his way out of Georgia's Bakery. Throughout the scene, little pops of red stood out, from the scarves around the cat's neck to a bunch of balloons a vendor sold to a group of kittens in front of the lake. There was a beautiful scarlet area rug covering the hardwood floor and the glider from the room upstairs had been reupholstered in the same color. Chrysta's eyes fell upon a beautiful crib that looked as if it had been carved by hand from a rich cherrywood. There was something inside the crib, and as she peered through the slats, she saw it was a large stuffed black cat with golden eyes and folded ears that looked exactly like Bruce Wayne.

Lucas ran one hand through his hair before setting the hammer down on the changing table next to the crib. "It's not quite finished yet," he said anxiously, scanning the walls with the same scrutiny she had seen him inspect his cave cheeses as they aged. "I haven't hung the curtains yet, and Mrs. Binkus is coming over later to drop off blankets she and other ladies crocheted for you."

Chrysta's mouth opened, then closed.

Lucas's eyes widened with dismay, and at once the words started pouring out of him. "I'm sorry. I know this is probably overstepping again. I know you want to do this on your own and if you want us to redo the whole thing, Law and I will get it done before the baby is born. It's just when Mrs. Van Ressler called and told me you were looking at a place in Bingleyton, I knew I had to do something big to get you to reconsider. You belong here in Crystal Hill. You picked this town to be your home and even if you don't pick me, I can't let you and your baby settle for anything less. It's yours—the town, this entire space and—" Lucas swallowed, taking a large step to stand in front of her and reach for her hand "—me."

Looking up into his eyes, love overcame every other sensation, every pain from her aching head to her wounded heart. She touched his cheek with her right hand as he took her left in his and placed it on his chest, pulling her close. As she tilted her head to meet his kiss, everything in her world felt as if it was finally balanced in perfect harmony.

Then, the pain in her head exploded into white fire and as if someone had removed the Jenga block holding it all in place, her world fell apart and faded to black.

CHAPTER SEVENTEEN

LUCAS WASN'T A fan of hospitals, having spent more than his share of time in them with his mom.

But after following Chrysta's ambulance to Mohawk Valley Memorial and spending the night gulping terrible-tasting coffee as he paced the creaky tile floor of the lobby, it was officially the happiest place on Earth for him when the doctors came in and said that Chrysta had made it through the emergency C-section with a full recovery expected.

"And the baby?" Lucas had croaked from behind his hand. His beard was growing back fast and in the uncomfortable in-between stage, yet he couldn't have cared less if it was down to the floor. Nothing mattered until he heard the answer to the question he had almost been too afraid to ask out loud.

"The baby looks fine," the doctor said with a nod. "We sent her up to the NICU for monitoring. It's standard procedure for any delivery prior to thirty-seven weeks. Her Apgar was within normal limits, however, and she didn't require supplemental oxygen. You can go to the nurses' station down the hall to get a badge, and then you can visit Chrysta in the maternity ward once she's out of recovery."

"Thank you," Lucas had breathed, exhaling fully for the first time in hours.

When he pulled back the curtain in Chrysta's room, he expected her to be emotional. After all, she burst into tears over cheese. But when he eased himself carefully around the IV pole connected to the tubes on her wrist and sat in the chair next to her hospital bed, the face she turned to him was a blank mask of resignation.

"Hey there," Lucas said, leaning over the guard rail to stroke her cheek. "You doing all right?"

She shook her head, her lips forming a thin line of disappointment before she said in a small, sad voice, "I messed it up."

"What are you talking about?" Lucas took her hand in both of his and interlaced his fingers with hers, squeezing as tightly as he could. "You're amazing. The doctor said you made it through like a rock star." He had also said that if Chrysta had gone one more day with the pre-eclampsia that caused her to pass out from the blood pressure headache that she could have had a stroke, seizure or even organ failure. Lucas would tell her that when she was a little more stable. He had learned never to hold anything back from her again.

"But she was still premature," Chrysta protested. Her eyes were puffy with fatigue and she frowned up at him from the semi-reclined bed. "We were barely at thirty-five weeks. All I had to do was keep her in for two more weeks and she would have been full-term. I'm failing her already."

Lucas didn't know if what he was saying was right or wrong in the moment, but he trusted Chrysta to know the words came from his heart. "Chrysta, you did everything right. You put your business on hold to keep her safe. Heck, you even gave up your favorite cheese this entire time and you lived in a cheese shop. If that isn't heroic, I don't know what is."

When she let out a quiet laugh, Lucas could have cheered with relief. Chrysta's sparkle was still there no matter what darkness came her way. "Don't make me laugh, Cheese Hermit," she said, moving her other hand to her belly. "I don't want to burst my stitches."

"Are you in pain?" he asked, half standing and looking out the door. "Should I get the nurse?"

"No, the incision is still pretty numb," she said, her eyes downcast. Inhaling deeply, she blinked several times before looking back up at Lucas. The tears he had expected appeared in the deep brown depths, yet she kept them at bay. "After the C-section, they put me back in the little recovery room next to the OR. It was just me in there for I don't even know how long, and Lucas—" she stopped and let out a ragged exhale "—I've never felt that alone in my life. It's like for months I've had this little companion with me and all of a sudden, she was ripped away. I was so scared and lonely for my baby and I couldn't feel or move my legs because of the anesthesia. I—I don't ever want to feel that way again."

"You won't," Lucas vowed, bending forward to place a kiss on the top of her knuckles, carefully avoiding the taped-over IV line. "The baby is going to be just fine and you're going to bring her back home to Crystal Hill where everyone loves you both so much."

"Everyone?" she asked with a meaningful lift of her eyebrows.

Before Lucas could respond, there was a knock at the door followed by the sound of wheels rolling in. One of the nurses pushed back the curtain to make room for the other, wheeling what looked like a small cart with high plastic walls. Inside lay a tiny bundle of blankets with a little red face poking out from under a pink-and-blue knit hat. "Did someone order a baby girl?" the nurse asked with a smile before leaning over Chrysta's bed to check the ID bracelet on her wrist. "Just making sure we have a match."

"Is she okay?" Chrysta asked anxiously. "Does she have to go back to the NICU?"

"Nope," the second nurse said cheerily as he locked the brakes on the cart's wheels. "She got the all-clear from the neonatologist to be down here. We're going to monitor her closely to make sure she can hold her body temperature, and the lactation consultant will be in shortly to get you started on feeding." He nodded at Lucas. "It's all right, Dad. You can pick her up. I promise she won't break."

Lucas started to correct him, but as he walked to the cart and stared down at the impossibly small being inside, there wasn't any need. Love unlike anything he had ever experienced crashed into him, breaking down every barrier and erasing every trace of fear or doubt. This beautiful, perfect baby girl was his. He held his breath as he reached in and ever-so carefully picked up the bundle. She was so small that both his hands more than covered the length of her and when he held her to his chest, she opened her small, dark eyes to look directly at him. He could feel a tear sliding down his cheek. Not bothering to wipe it away, he carried the baby to Chrysta and placed her gently into her waiting arms.

In the background, he could hear the nurses murmuring while they washed their hands in the sink and quietly slipped back out the door, yet everything faded away as he focused on Chrysta's face lighting up with sheer exhilaration.

She held the baby to her, crying and whispering softly into the little round cheeks. After a few minutes, Chrysta lifted a radiant smile to him. "Do you want to know her name?"

Lucas nodded. "Very much."

"Lucas—" she tilted her elbow to elevate the baby's face "—meet Rosabell."

"Rosabell," he repeated softly. "As in Rose, my mom?"

Chrysta nodded, lowering the baby to her chest. "This little one has already been through so much," she whispered quietly. "I wanted to name her after the strongest woman I could think of."

Lucas brushed his eyes with the side of his arm before lowering himself onto the edge of the bed. Leaning forward, he placed a kiss on Chrysta's lips that he hoped told her more about what he felt than any words could express. He reached into his back pocket.

"You know," he said carefully. "Yesterday was Valentine's Day and since I've been a little clueless about these things in the past, I got a little something for you."

Chrysta continued to murmur and nuzzle her daughter's nose with her own, only looking up when Lucas slipped his mother's ring over the baby's hand. She gasped as he held it up to her.

"Rosabell Carl," Lucas murmured. "I promise to love you and your mama for the rest of my life." Placing the ring on Chrysta's finger, he asked, "Marry me, Chrysta?"

She nodded as her tears traced tracks along her flushed cheeks. "Yes... Lucas, I love you so much."

He kissed her forehead, her eyes, her cheeks and at last her lips, before turning to place a kiss on his baby's tiny, perfect nose. "Our little baby Bell," he murmured, then the realization of what else bore the same moniker hit him. "Baby. Bell."

Chrysta's cries turned to laughter and she clutched her abdomen with her right hand. "Of course she's named after a cheese." She let out a small giggle. "Only you, Cheese Hermit."

He shook his head before bending to touch his forehead to Chrysta's. "Nope," he murmured, touching a finger lightly to his daughter's velvety soft cheek. "It's never going to be only me ever again. From now on, it's only us."

EPILOGUE

Eleven Months Later

"IT'S HERE!" Lucas said excitedly as he carried the mail into the living room and dropped it on top of the island. Mixed in with the usual assortment of bills was the December issue of *Cheese Club Monthly*. His and Chrysta's faces graced the cover thanks to their vlog, Two Guys, A Girl and Some Cheese, hitting one million subscribers in less than six months. The magazine, however, he tossed aside. It was the contents of the small box that he couldn't wait to show Chrysta.

"What's here?" she asked, settling Rosabell into her high chair and clicking the strap around the baby's waist. "The contract from that new grocery chain? I told them we can't bring them on as a sponsor until we get their offer in writing."

Lucas smiled. He loved that his charming and adorable fiancée was also a shark when it came to negotiations. They had several major companies offer to sponsor their business thanks to the Instagram post of BeeBee's party last year going viral, and even with a newborn to take care of, Chrysta had managed to get each one to up their offer significantly. He skirted the counter and wrapped his arms around her waist, planting a kiss on the side of her neck. She had chopped her long hair into a short style just below her chin once Baby Bell had started grabbing it. The style made her eyes look even bigger and brighter, so naturally he was obsessed. Then again, he could barely resist her in the white shower cap–like hair covering she wore when they worked in his cheese lab together. They were true partners in everything, and Lucas still couldn't believe his luck.

Baby Rosabell giggled as he rested his chin on top of Chrysta's head and made a silly face. "It might be, but that wasn't what I was talking about," he said, extending his arm and tickling his daughter under the little folds her chin made when she laughed. All babies were cute, sure, but there was something special about their Baby Bell. Complete strangers stopped them on the street to comment on the red-gold curls on her head and the enormous brown eyes ringed with dark lashes that were exactly like her mother's. Lucas tracked her every milestone with the wonder and awe that he had previously reserved for his very best aged cheeses. "Open the package on the island."

Chrysta turned and dropped a quick kiss on his lips before grabbing the brown cardboard box and pulling it open. Reaching in, she pulled out the tiniest pair of pink leather ice skates lined with soft white fur and held them up by the laces. "You're ridiculous. She just took her first steps last week. Why in the world did you get her ice skates?"

"I figured we might as well start her early." Lucas shrugged before shooting Chrysta a grin. "Besides, this wasn't all me—it was actually your mom's idea. I figured we could at least take some cute pictures in them to send to her."

After bringing the baby home, she had called her mom to ask for some advice about swaddling. Marjorie had been so pleased to be able to help Chrysta for once that the two had become closer than they had been in years. GrandMargie, as Marjorie had asked to be called, had flown up twice for visits, the last time even arranging her own ride to and from the airport. Just another confirmation that Bell was so much more than an ordinary baby; she was an honest-to-goodness miracle worker.

Chrysta rolled her eyes, then said thoughtfully, "I read somewhere that Tara Lipinski started when she was like three or something. Might as well start Bell early if we want her to get serious about it."

"Not too serious, though," Lucas interjected, leaning in to brush his forehead against Chrysta's. "It's important for her to have fun, too."

Dropping the skates back in the box, Chrysta cleared the mail off the island and started setting out the materials for that week's themed cheese board tutorial. They posted small reels daily, the content ranging from an explanation of the different types of cheese to highlight reels from the local parties Chrysta continued to host throughout the region. Once a week, however, they featured a newly themed cheese board demonstration that took viewers through all the steps, from the selection of the board with their resident woodworker, Lawson, to Final Fun Facts about Cheese with Lucas. They interspersed their content with the brothers' good-natured bantering and Chrysta's tips for how to balance entertaining with life as a new mom. The vlog had struck such a chord with their followers that they had been featured on several local news channels and Chrysta had even been offered a book deal with a large nonfiction publisher.

"Never fear, the cheese boards are here!" Law announced as he burst through the hallway with a stack of wooden boards in his arms. He set them down on the island, while Chrysta brought out the blocks of feta for today's board. He clapped Lucas on the arm before bending down to plant a raspberry on Bell's tummy. "There's my cheese baby."

"*My* cheese baby," Lucas corrected him. "You're just in time. We're about to start the shoot. Did you bring the Christmas tree–shaped boards?"

"Yup, made from authentic local pine," Law answered proudly. "I also brought one in the shape of a snowman. Figured we could do some playing around with rounds of the buffalo mozzarella with black peppercorns for the coal."

"Nice." Lucas nodded. "The kids at the birthday party Chrysta is hosting next week will love that." He crossed his arms and gave Law an appraising glance. "You know you'll make a great dad whenever you decide to settle down with one woman."

Law made a dismissive noise as he started assembling the boards, but Lucas and Chrysta exchanged knowing looks. That was exactly the same kind of noise Lucas made before he met the woman of his dreams.

Once they had all their ingredients lined up, Lucas manned the camera as Chrysta and Law introduced themselves and started their discussion with the different types of boards and ways to use them for winter holiday parties. Bell was off-screen, but out of the corner of Lucas's eye, he saw her eyes widen as they zeroed in on a round of brie that had been left precariously